Mary Fields
aka
'STAGECOACH MARY'

First Edition Design Publishing
Sarasota, Florida, USA

Mary Fields aka "Stagecoach Mary"
Copyright ©2016 Erich Martin Hicks

ISBN 978-1506-901-65-7 HC
ISBN 978-1506-901-01-5 PBK
ISBN 978-1506-901-02-2 EBOOK

LCCN 2015958627

March 2016

Published and Distributed by
First Edition Design Publishing, Inc.
P.O. Box 20217, Sarasota, FL 34276-3217
www.firsteditiondesignpublishing.com

ALL RIGHTS RESERVED. No part of this book publication may be reproduced, stored in a retrieval system, or transmitted in any form or by any means — electronic, mechanical, photo-copy, recording, or any other — except brief quotation in reviews, without the prior permission of the author or publisher.

All photos are courtesy of:
Ursuline Convent, Archives, Toledo, Ohio: Ursuline Convent, Archives, Great Falls, Montana: Wedsworth Memorial Library, Cascade, Montana: The History Museum, Great Falls, Montana: Charlie Russell sketch - Archives and Special Collections, The Town of Cascade, Montana: and myself.

Library of Congress Cataloging-in-Publication Data
Hicks, Erich Martin
   Mary Fields aka 'Stagecoach Mary' / written by Erich Martin Hicks.
   p. cm.
   ISBN 978-1506-901-01-5 pbk, 978-1506-901-02-2 digital

1. BIOGRAPHY & AUTOBIOGRAPHY / Cultural Heritage. 2. Personal Memoirs. 3. HISTORY / Women. 4. / Revolutionary

M3931

"A 'fantastic' novel, of a great American heroine's life."

Tariano (Tito) A. Jackson
The Jackson 5

To: The Almighty Creator, and all my friends

Through the long hours, days, weeks, months, and hardships over the years it took to make this epic story possible, this is dedicated to all that believed in me, that I could bring this story to the forefront.

I will always be grateful for your friendship, love, and understanding.

And to add to this process, my beloved animals.

Acknowledgements

- The All Mighty Creator

- To my editors - Donna West, Susan Muller-Robb

- To my very best friend - Tariano (Tito) Jackson

- To my very good friends - Norman and Susan Muller-Robb & family

- To my good friend - Donna West

- To my good friend - Dolores Albain & ANA Special Effects - Hayvenhurst Studios -Van Nuys, California

- To my good friend - Al Adams

- To my good friend - Maurice Kitchen and Street Corner Renaissance – Los Angeles, California

- To my good friend - Trooper Derrick Davis – Atlanta, Georgia

- To my good friend from down under / Eve Whelan - Australia

- To my old neighborhood friends - Ernest Ashford, Reginald Thomas, Myles Cranford, Dr. LaGrande Mason Jr., Dr. Sheila Newton – Los Angeles, California

- To my other good friends – Walter Manchuca, Kevin and Roxanne Mattox, Frank Lenard, John Russell, William Harris, Larry Shipp, Lance Yoshioka, Anthony Delzio, Robert Louis Carter, Furgus Wilson, Dilon Bernard, Rhonda R. Harper, Reggie Morgan - my barber, Walter Wendell Brady, Precious King, Jackie Dawson, Jodi Lea Stewart, Lennister K. Williams, and Prof. Art Burton

- Renowned Sculptor - Eddie Dixon - Lubbock, Texas

ERICH MARTIN HICKS

- ❖ Renowned Music Composer - Samm Brown – Los Angeles, California

- ❖ Colorization of black & white cover picture - Eric Bains - Los Angeles, California

- ❖ Re-enactors of the 10th Cavalry, H Troop - Buffalo Soldiers Mounted Cavalry Unit -Los Angeles, California

- ❖ Montana Guide - Frank Laliberity - Cascade, Montana

- ❖ Ursuline Convents - Archives, Toledo, Ohio: Sister Francis Xavier Porter, OSU - Great Falls, Montana

- ❖ The History Museum - Great Falls, Montana

- ❖ Wedsworth Memorial Library - Cascade, Montana

- ❖ Historian Office - United States Postal Service - Washington, D.C.

- ❖ Stockmens Bank - A Quiet Day In Cascade / Mayor Murry Moore - Cascade, Montana

- ❖ Best Western wear, west of the Mississippi - Country General Store - Van Nuys, Calif.

- ❖ The National Association of Buffalo Soldiers, 9th and 10th Horse Cavalry

- ❖ Phillips Bar-B-Que - The Greatest BBQ-Bar-B-Que west of the Mississippi River - Los Angeles, California

- ❖ Actors Fund - Los Angeles, California

- ❖ Combat Fire - Hollywood Motion Picture support – Van Nuys, California

- ❖ Stunt Pilot - Gene Soucy
  Stunt Wing Walker - Teresa Stokes

MARY FIELDS aka STAGECOACH MARY

- De La Mare Engineering - Motion Picture Industry – San Fernando, California

- Roger George Motion Picture Rentals - Van Nuys, California

- Weapons and Special Effects in the Motion Picture Industry - Mike Tristano

- Promotion Videos - Charles Shuford / Videographer - Jared Bentley

- Exposhows - David MacCormick - Associate

- ConSev Flag Company - Sidney, Nebraska

- Travel provided by: United Airlines; Delta Airlines; Hertz Rent A Car

In memory of good friends:

Gary Frank Bentley 1946 to 2014
Edward Mathew Tate 1949 to 2015

About the Author

Erich Hicks, founder of Alpha Wolf Productions Inc., is an acclaimed Special Effects Coordinator, producer and writer, with over 20 years of experience in the entertainment industry. The company is an independent production outlet that develops, writes, and produces feature film and television content.

Historically, Erich is the first African-American/Black to receive a Special Effects Pyrotechnic Operator's 1st class Master's License in the Motion Picture Industry. Thus, he is expertly qualified to produce and direct action sequences, stunts and explosions to achieve a realistic scene. As an apprentice to the late legendary Special Effects Coordinator Richard "Dick" Albain, whose credits include the original *The Three Stooges; Assault on Precinct 13; Bewitched* (TV series); and many more. Erich's work has included, the small and large screens including: *Scary Movie 2, Diagnosis Murder, Married with Children, Captivity,* and The Victoria Secret's Fashion Show. Currently, under Erich's belt, are two viral Music Videos, #1 featuring The Weeknd, entitled "The Hill" with over six hundred and fifty million hits, and climbing; and #2 featuring Justin Bieber and Chris Brown, entitled "Next 2 U" with over one hundred and eighty-two million hits. In addition, one of HOLLYWOOD'S most expensive produced Motion Picture Feature Films, *The Lone Ranger*.

As a writer, Erich's first novel, *Rescue at Pine Ridge*, was released in December 2008. The novel is a historical narrative, depicting the all-Black 9th Calvary. Known as the US military's famed "Buffalo Soldiers", which helped settle the American West in the late 1800's. Erich has completed an accompanying screenplay for a TV mini-series, Trilogy, and Epic Feature, and has garnered support from some of HOLLYWOOD'S acclaimed industry producers, directors and actors. Dedicated to exploring the history of African-American/Blacks and shattering stereotypes, his Alpha Wolf Productions, Inc. has also developed a feature film documentary, *Soul on a Wave* which exposes the life and times of surfers of color. Currently, Erich has produced this novel, *"Mary Fields aka Stagecoach Mary,"* from his motion picture screenplay, STAGECOACH MARY, based on the real life heroine, Mary Fields. Mary was the first African-American/Black woman to deliver mail for the United States Postal System in the late 1800's to early 1900's.

Erich obtains new ideas for his diverse projects from his many travels, acknowledging the direct correlation between nature and history. An avid outdoorsman, he has traveled near and far to climb the world's most celebrated mountains, including Mount Whitney (located in the Eastern Sierras of California), which is the highest mountain in the contiguous United States. Erich also descends from a family heritage that includes his grandfather's distinction as a Buffalo Soldier who served under General John Joseph (Black Jack) Pershing. Erich's grandfather was one of the highest-ranking African-American Military Officers in WW-1. As Captain in the 317th Ammunition/Supply Train Division, Captain Lee Jay Hicks was responsible for getting ammunition and supplies to the war front.

Erich is available for lecturing on the topics of, the Motion Picture Industry, and issues pertaining to African-American/Black culture and history, military, and politics, to schools, universities, libraries, clubs and organizations.

Please visit the webpage for more information at: alphawolfprods.com and for a comprehensive resume at imdb.com/name/nm0902436

Mary Fields aka 'STAGECOACH MARY'

Written By:
ERICH MARTIN HICKS

Table of Contents

Acknowledgements i
About the Author iv

Prologue 5
The Beginning 7
The Civil War 27
The Mississippi River and the Race 34
Toledo 67
St. Peter's Mission / United States Postal Service 76
The End of Mary's Story 136
Epilogue 156

Author's Opinion 158
Additional Historical and Validation Photos 161
Current News of Mary Fields 177

Prologue

This is the story of Mary Fields, "Stagecoach Mary", who got her nickname at the turn of the 20th Century. She earned this nickname by working for the, United States Postal System delivering the United States Mail through adverse conditions, that would have discouraged the most hardened frontiersmen of that period. All by herself, she never missed a day for eight years, carrying the U. S. Mail and other important documents that helped settle the wild open territory of central west Montana. Stagecoach Mary had no fear of man, nor beast, and this sometimes got her into trouble. She delivered the mail regardless of the heat of the day, cold of the night, wind, rain, sleet, snow, blizzards, Indians and Outlaws.

Stagecoach Mary was six feet tall, and weighed over 200 pounds, and even with those extraordinary presence, there were two more facts that made her history. She was the second woman in history to carry the U. S. Mail, however, even that was a matter of simplicity, for a fact, she was a Negro woman, and the only Negro, for hundreds and hundreds of miles when she first arrived in Montana.

This feature story will cover Stagecoach Mary's colorful life, from the plantation where she was born a slave in 1832, to the famous *steamboat race* between the Robert E. Lee and the Natchez on the Mississippi River, to her death in Cascade, Montana, in 1914.

Stagecoach Mary was a cigar smoking, shotgun and pistol toting Negro woman, who even frequented saloons drinking whiskey with the men, a privilege only given to 'her', as a woman. However, not even this fact sealed the credentials given to her, her credentials boasted that, 'she could knock out any man with one punch', who stepped upon her womanhood, a claim she proved true.

Despite the hardness of Stagecoach Mary, she had another side to her, a kindness so strong that even today in the beginning of the 21st Century, her name still runs the folklore extremes.

Her fame was so acclaimed that even actor, Gary Cooper, two time Academy Award Winner, told a story about her (somewhat exaggerated) in 1959 which appeared in *Ebony Magazine* that same year.

While, Annie Oakley and Martha Canary (Calamity Jane) were creating their history with Buffalo Bill, Stagecoach Mary was making her epic journey!

The first half of Mary Fields' life is speculative. Therefore, it is the writer's privilege to subject the most logical hypothesis to her story in this novel, which created this heroine, who conquered the Montana

Territory, which defeated General Custer, not more than 220 miles away, as a crow flies, nine years before her arrival, and the Missouri River that tested, York, Louis and Clark on their expedition, 80 years before she cross the Missouri River, into Cascade, Montana.

Mary Fields, in front of backdrop, posing with rifle and dog.

This story is unlike any other story you've read about Mary Fields. This fictionalized story you are about to read has been dramatically enhanced for your entertainment pleasures; however, most of the stories, and the outcomes within this novel, are historically genuine.

The Beginning

In a small simple two-room wood-plank cabin, on the outskirts of Cascade, Montana, the sound of wood, slowly creaking is heard. A smoky haze hangs in the air, permeated by sunlight, beaming through two windows, which are separated by the front door.

A coat rack stands on the left side of the door, with a coon cap laying on top of a wool coat, hanging on one peg, while on another peg, hangs a buckskin fringe coat.

A large animal skin rug lays in the middle of the floor. Hanging on the walls, is an assortment of baseball team pictures, nature and Indian type paintings, drying herbs that are becoming moldy, a few small animal skins, and a pair of snowshoes. On the right side of the room, a door leads to the bedroom, and several feet from the doorway, there's a potbelly stove, then a wood-plank table with one chair.

On top of the table, a newspaper lays partly open, with the date showing, 'December 1, 1914.' Next to the newspaper, a properly set eating area, with dinner plate, utensils, coffee cup, drinking glass, a Bible, and a side-by-side break-action double barrel shotgun, rests on the table, next to the setting.

In the other corner, a tall heavyset old Negro woman is rocking in her creaky rocking chair. She is somewhat ill looking, her eyes are drooping, as she coughs. She brings her personally rolled black cigar to her lips, taking a slight puff, and exhales, then says, "People call me, 'Stagecoach Mary' around here. I've been called many other names, Black Mary, Nigger Mary...Nigger." Then as she snuffs, she says, "My real name is Mary Fields. The reason they call me Stagecoach Mary is, because when I worked, I delivered the U. S. Mail and parcels for eight years without missing a schedule." She snuffs again, then says, "But my favorite past times are my garden, hennery, and baseball. Shoot, my team wins most the time, but I win all the arguments." She laughs, then says, "No one talks bad about my team." Then with seriousness, she says, "But I guess, it all started when I was a little girl on the plantation. My best friend, MaryJo Warner...well, I was her slave, but that was then though. Her family treated my mom and me good...I guess." Mary becomes sad, as she says, "But they sold my 'poppa'...they didn't want my momma to get pregnant again by...as they called him, that 'Big Nigger Buck'. My momma, she was their house slave, took care of them, she loved my 'poppa'. It broke her heart...she used to say, 'She could hear the Auctioneer, 'What do I get for this, big Nigger Buck''...then she would start cryin." With a resolved look, Mary then says, "...Anyways, when I was ten, I use to brin' things' back and forth for my momma in the Great House, anythin' she needed. Very few of us Negroes were allowed to enter the Great House. My friend MaryJo and I...we would play together after I finished my main chores..."

*****

In the spring of 1842, it is a hot day in Vicksburg, Mississippi, on the Warner Plantation. Sweaty African slaves, are chanting their, 'call in response', going about their arduous tasks, of transferring bales of cotton on their backs from plantation carts to transportation wagons, as several overseers watch with whips in their hands, near the Warner barn.

In the distance, slaves are going about repairing and painting the Great Warner plantation home, a mid-size two-story southern wood plank house, which is in need of work. In the back yard of the Great House, two young girls, of contrasting skin color, are jumping rope. One is Negro and the other girl is 'white'. Mary Fields, the slave girl, and MaryJo Warner, the daughter of the plantation owner, are both ten years old and virtually the same height and weight. Mary is very dark skinned, with her hair tied in short fat braids in the back of her head. She wears typical slave clothes, an old cotton shirt, drawstring pants, tattered boots, and is tomboyish. MaryJo has olive skin, brown hair, and bright blue eyes. She is wearing nice play clothes, shoes, pants and a blouse, and is a loving child.

The girls are having a jump-rope contest to see who can jump the fastest, as Mary shouts, "One hundred, one hundred-one, one-hundred two, one-hundred three..."

MaryJo shouts, "Eighty-five, eighty-six, eighty-seven..." She starts to tire, as she struggles, and shouts, "eighty-eight...eighty-nine," then barely completing another revolution, "...ninety." She stops, and looks at Mary, then says, "...You win...you win," as she puts her hands on her knees to catch her breath.

Mary continues jumping rope, and shouting, "One hundred-fifteen, one-hundred sixteen..." Then stopping, and looking at MaryJo, saying, "Okay." She also puts her hands on her knees catching her breath, then saying, "You're gettin' better MaryJo."

Still catching her breath, with her hands on her knees, MaryJo looks at Mary, and says, "Yeah, but you're getting much better too, Mary. Just like horseback riding. I've never seen animals take to anybody like they do to you."

Mary says, "Can't wait for tomorrow, MaryJo, to go horseback ridin' again, it sure is fun bein' on those animals."

Mary's mother Suzanna is thirty years old. She is dark skinned, wears typical house slave clothes, a cotton dress, apron, and a rag tied around her head. She is watching the girls play from the back door of the Great

House. She opens the door and looks at Mary, and says, "Mary, don't forget to wash MaryJo's clothes before supper."

"Yes momma, I'm comin' right now," says Mary. She looks at MaryJo, and says, "MaryJo, ya want those clothes washed you're wearin'?"

"No. You've got enough wash as it is Mary," says MaryJo.

"No worry, I can have those clothes washed in no time...okay? Leave your clothes outside your door," says Mary. She turns to leave, then, turns back, and says, "I'll see ya after I finish." Mary turns and leaves.

Both girls are walking away, when MaryJo stops, turns looking back at Mary, and shouts, "After I do my homework. Mary, and don't forget, you have math tonight."

Mary stops, and turns back, looking at MaryJo, saying, "Yeah, that math is gettin' pretty easy. It's kinda fun now." She thinks to herself, then, says, "...Twenty plus thirty is fifty. Fifty plus fifty is hundred. Hundred plus hundred is...two-hundred."

"You're getting pretty good Mary. You've only been in the house for a month now. Pretty soon you'll be doing multiplications. Jumping rope has helped you learn to count," says MaryJo.

"It sure has, and it's fun too. I better get goin', and get those clothes washed. See ya MaryJo," says Mary. Both girls run towards the Great House, MaryJo towards the front, and Mary towards the back.

Moments later on the back porch, Suzanna is walking up the steps from the root cellar, clutching her apron full of potatoes. When she reaches the floor level of the porch, she turns, and walks past her living quarters, where her bunk bed is situated. She walks pass the root-cellar door, holding her apron close with one hand. She stops, reaches up, and unties the cellar door rope with the other hand, lowering the door closed. She then pushes the swinging door open to the kitchen, and walks in. Mary opens the back door of the house, and follows her mother into the kitchen through the swinging door. As Suzanna reaches the preparation table in the middle of the kitchen, she dumps all the potatoes on top. She sits down on a wooden stool, and begins peeling the potatoes for her Master's supper.

When Mary approaches the preparation table, Suzanna, with a worried look on her face, looks at her. Mary sits on another stool across from Suzanna, as Suzanna says, "Mary ya don't be beatin' MaryJo that bad now. The Warner's may stop ya from playin' with her, and won't let ya come in the Great House anymore."

"Momma", says Mary, "MaryJo don't mind me beatin' her. We just playin'...it makes her better, and she likes teachin' me. I'm learnin' to count...and she is gonna teach me how to mul...ti...ply, that's the word, multiply."

"It's good ya learnin' to count Mary. Mrs. Warner said she wants ya to learn, so you'll be a good house Negro slave like your momma, not a field slave." Then with resolve, Suzanna says, "...Mary, I need help in the kitchen and the Great House. That's why Mrs. Warner is lettin' me teach ya about workin' in the Great House...instead of ya workin' in the fields."

"Momma," says Mary with a smile, as she then says, "I don't mind workin' in the fields. I have fun with the field slaves. They teach me things', like the 'Old Healer'."

Suzanna, somewhat upset, and looking at the potato, begins peeling faster, as she says, "I don't want ya hangin' around the field slaves anymore Mary! Ya can have a better life as a house Negro!"

"Momma, poppa was a field slave ya said, what's wrong with bein' a field slave?" asks Mary.

Suzanna, peeling the potato a little faster, and now looking at Mary, says, "Ya see how the overseers treats the field slaves, Mary? Yes your poppa was a field slave, and his life was hard. The overseer beat him...make him work all day without food, then beat him again. Your poppa fought against bein' a slave, Mary. He tried to get the other field slaves to fight with him." Suzanna then looks at the potato she's peeling, and notices, she's peeling in the same spot, peeling away almost half the potato. She stops peeling, and begins crying softly, looking out the kitchen window, saying, "The first time I saw your poppa, the Master got him from a plantation hundreds of miles from here, he'd been sold off. The overseer beat him...real bad the first evenin'...cause he was so big...so strong...they had to try to break him. Mrs. Warner was real mad at Master Warner. She had me take care of your poppa's wounds..." Suzanna then looks lovingly at Mary, and says, "That's when I fell in love with your poppa."

Mary says, "They sold poppa, huh momma?"

Suzanna stops crying, wiping the tears from her cheek with her apron, then, looking at Mary with a worried expression, she says, "How did ya find out?"

"The field slaves told me Master Warner sold poppa, he didn't die, that you're afraid to tell me...why ya like the Great House anyways momma? Some of the field slaves, say, ya think ya better cause..."

"Hush, child in what ya sayin'!" says Suzanna interrupting Mary, in a low angry apprehensive voice.

Suzanna gets up from the chair quickly, and looks at the open double doors that lead to the Great House. She hurries to the doors, looking in both directions, down the hallway that parallels the entry, and across to the dining area, to see if anybody heard Mary. Suzanna sees that no one is around, and walks back to the preparation table. She sits down, and begins peeling potatoes, as if Mary had not said a word. Mary looks at her mother. But then, Suzanna begins sniffling. A few tears begin to roll down her cheeks.

Mary seeing the tears, says, "I'm sorry 'Momma', I didn't mean to make ya cry." She gets up from the stool and walks over to her mother. Suzanna stops peeling potatoes, looking at her. Mary puts her arms around her mother, as Suzanna hugs Mary back, and says, "Ya didn't make me cry."

"I love ya 'momma'," says Mary.

Suzanna then holds Mary back, by both arms looking at her, saying, "I love ya too Mary…I wish ya could have known your poppa."

"Momma, why the Warners sell poppa?"

Suzanna quickly looks at the doors again, worried, and says, "…Quiet Mary. I don't want the Warners to know, ya know."

Mary looks around, then looks at Suzanna, saying, "Why not momma?"

"Because they may not allow ya in the Great House no more…they can sell ya Mary," says Suzanna. She begins to sniffle, then says, "I wouldn't see ya no more!" Suzanna looks at Mary with a tearful lost expression.

Mary looks at Suzanna with a curious hurt expression.

Suzanna sees Mary's expression, and tries to comfort her, by holding her close to her bosom, saying, "Mary…I've been holdin' the truth from ya because…I love ya and want good for ya." Suzanna looks towards the double doors, and lets go of Mary. She then quickly begins peeling potatoes again, taking a deep breath, and looking at her. Mary also looks towards the doors, as Suzanna exhales, and says, "Mary". She turns and looks at her mother with a solemn expression, as Suzanna says, "Mary…what I tell ya here…ya must 'forgive' the bad…'remember' the good…for ya, to have a good life."

Mary looks at Suzanna, and says, "What momma?"

"…Your poppa didn't die."

"I know momma," says Mary.

"Hush child," says Suzanna. She sighs, and then says, "Ya ten years old…I see the time has come…I don't have much time to tell ya this, ya got more chores to do Mary before night fall. I'm goin' to talk soft, cause someone might hear me. I want ya to listen 'real good'!"

"Yes momma," says Mary.

Suzanna, with a resolved look, stops peeling potatoes, and says, "Your poppa was sold."

Mary says, "Momma, why and when they sell poppa?"

"Before ya were born. I just became a kitchen Negro Mary. I cooked the Master's food, washed his clothes, and took care of the kitchen. They taught me to read and write...he let me eat the good food he left on the family's plate, and what was left in the pots. The field slaves don't get good food Mary. One night, after the overseer checked the slave quarters, your poppa came to the Great House...got me, and we ran away..."

They hear a noise approaching in the hallway outside the double doors, causing Suzanna to stop talking and to start peeling potatoes again. Mary looks at the doors. A Negro slave woman walks by pushing a broom, not paying any attention to the kitchen. The sound fades. Suzanna begins peeling slower, as she speaks softly, saying, "Later in the night, it was a half moon. Master Warner didn't want me to have a husband, or to have babies...cause there's no one to take care of the kitchen, nor cookin'." Suzanna with a cherished smile, then says, "That's the night we made ya." She sighs, and then says, "A couple of days later, the hounds found us near a swamp. They caught your poppa and almost ripped off all his clothes. I tried to fend off the hounds with a stick...but the overseer was not far behind. They caught us. The overseer beat your poppa with the hounds still tryin' to tear at him. They brought us back to the Great House. The next day, Master Warner received more slaves from another plantation. A slave company also came that day from a state called North Carolina. They tied your poppa between the posts holdin' the company's name, and they beat him again, to make an example...of him. The overseer made everyone watch, includin' the new slaves. I yelled, cried and begged Master Warner to not hurt your poppa." Suzanna begins crying, as she says, "...I can still hear the auctioneer, 'What do I get for this 'Big Nigger Buck'!' Master Warner sold your poppa for one-hundred dollars to a plantation somewhere in the north." Suzanna stops peeling potatoes, and gut wrenchingly, silently cries, saying, "...that was...the last time...I saw your ...poppa."

Mary has tears in her eyes. She walks over to her mother and hugs her. Suzanna then stops crying, and grabs Mary by the shoulders, holding Mary back with both hands at arm's length again, looking into her eyes, as she says, "When ya were born Mary, I gave ya the name of Mary Fields. Your last name comes from your poppa because he was a field slave."

"None of the field slaves' have last names, just nick-names momma," says Mary.

"That's because, slaves don't have last names Mary, like your poppa, his name is Buck...Anyways, I was pregnant with ya after your poppa was sold. Funny enough...Mrs. Warner was pregnant when I was. We gave birth around the same time." Suzanna now has a more resolved expression in her eyes, as she looks at Mary, saying, "Mary," then she sighs, and says, "...Some 'white' people believe negro women's breast milk is better than theirs. Mrs. Warner had me breast feed MaryJo before feeding ya...MaryJo sometimes would drink all my breast milk. If MaryJo drink all the milk, then I would have to feed ya, goat or cow milk. When Mrs. Warner wasn't near, sometimes...I would sneak and feed ya first." Again Suzanna looks at Mary with a resolved look, and says, "Mary...ya and MaryJo are like sisters. Ya must always look at her as your sister."

"Momma...don't ya hate 'em for sellin' poppa?"

"Yes Mary...but I can't show it. I try to forget. If I show it, Master Warner would put me back in the fields or sell me..." Then, with quiet empathy and panic, Suzanna says, "...and keep ya child, make ya have yellow babies...we never see each other again!" Then she becomes solemn, saying, "We lucky Mary. We have it good, we is together now, we is in the Great House, we is house Negroes." Suzanna and Mary look to the voice of Mrs. Warner, speaking with a proper southern dialect, talking to some house slaves in the hallway walking towards the kitchen, saying, "...U'all make sure u'all get all that dust now, ya hear," says Mrs. Warner.

"Yessum Mrs. Warner. Suzanna told us," says a house slave.

Suzanna quickly looks at Mary, and says, "Mary, go do laundry now, quick!" Mary hurries towards the double doors. Suzanna quickly begins peeling potatoes. Mrs. Warner walks through the doorway into the kitchen holding a medium sized package, stopping Mary in her tracks, saying, "Ah...how's my new house Negro?"

Mary semi-subservient, says, "...Fine Mrs. Warner. I'm gonna get MaryJo's clothes right now to do the wash."

"Good Mary. Ya talk quite well now since you've been in the house, keep up the good work, u'all be a good house Negro yet," says Mrs. Warner.

"Yessum, Mrs. Warner," says Mary.

Mrs. Warner smiles at her. Mary slowly walks past Mrs. Warner holding her head in a submissive posture, then, hurrying off to do her work. Suzanna is still peeling potatoes, as she says, "She's' learnin' real fast Mrs. Warner. I told ya she'll do real good in the house."

"Yes, Suzanna...MaryJo said Mary has taken to math quite well. I'm going to have Mary study more with MaryJo to prepare her for the house. It's good she learns while she is young."

"Yes, Mrs. Warner," says Suzanna.

Mrs. Warner sets the package she carried into the kitchen, on the other side of the preparation table. She pulls the string, opening the package, and brings out a pretty pink girl's dress, then white socks and pink shoes. She looks at Suzanna with pride, and says, "Suzanna, I ordered this dress and shoes for Mary to wear for our first Easter...I bought the same for MaryJo." Then, very proud, she says, "I thought they would look so sweet together, dressed alike."

Suzanna has stopped peeling potatoes and is looking at Mrs. Warner with an expression of joy. She is tearful and excited, saying, "...Oh...thank ya Mrs. Warner, thank ya. They is so pretty. I know Mary really will like the dress and shoes, it's her first dress...and she never had good shoes before, just 'em old hand me down boots."

Mrs. Warner walks to the kitchen window, and peers out, then says, "Suzanna...as ya see, the plantation is bein' worked on and painted. I'm havin' some trees and flowers brought to the plantation, to be planted before the Easter celebration next week, they should be here tomorrow. I won't be here Suzanna, I'll be goin' into town early. Make sure when they plant them, they'll look real nice."

"Yes Mrs. Warner. I'll make sure they gonna look real pretty." Mrs. Warner turns and looks at Suzanna, and says, "Suzanna...ya know, we Catholics believe in treatin' ya people real good. That's why u'all Negroes here, have it nice. Other plantations don't treat their slaves the way we treat ours." Then somewhat pointed she says, "As the two of them get older Suzanna, I know ya will make sure Mary will always keep MaryJo company, and take care of her since she has no other brothers and sisters."

"Oh yes', ma'am...yes, Mrs. Warner," says Suzanna.

About an hour later in the back yard, slaves are going about their difficult tasks. A wood fire burns under an iron pot of hot water near Mary, scrubbing a pair of MaryJo's pants on a washboard in an elevated tub, setting on wood crates many yards from the Great House. She finishes scrubbing the pants, throwing them into a barrel with other washed clothes.

Mary then grabs a handle of a wooden bucket. She picks it up and pours clean water into the barrel of clothes. She walks towards the water-well. When she reaches the well, she attaches the handle of the bucket to the well hook and lowers the bucket in, until it hits the water, letting it fill. Then she cranks the handle, and brings up the bucket full of water.

An elderly Negro woman, 'Old Healer', who is using her cane to walk, which she uses more for instructing, walks up behind Mary, with a hand rolled cigar in her mouth. Mary brings up the bucket, and puts the bucket on the rim of the well. 'Old Healer', takes a puff of the cigar, and with a rough raspy voice, she says, "Ya like the Great House Mary?"

Mary turns back somewhat startled. She looks at 'Old Healer', and says, "Oh...its' ya 'Old Healer', you're back from the plantation north of here. Ya been gone a long time."

"A lot of sick people, bad coughs'. They better now," says 'Old Healer'.

"Ya use warm-ash and vinegar on their chest like ya taught me?" says Mary.

'Old Healer' nods her head slightly. She then looks at the fields, and says, "The field slaves tell me they brin' ya in the Great House now." She looks at Mary and smiles, and then says, "Gonna to be a House Nigger. Doin' the house work." Then very serious, she says, "Master treatin' ya good child? Know your House-momma watchin' out after ya."

"Momma got Mrs. Warner to brin' me in the Great House last month." Master Warner been in the north, since last moon, some big city called…New York. Suppose to be back next week. Mrs. Warner, she treats me real good. She likes me to play with MaryJo, and MaryJo teaches me to read and do arith…metic," says Mary. She grabs the handle of the bucket and walks back to the washtub.

'Old Healer' follows Mary close behind, slowing her pace, saying, "They train ya good now to be a good House Nigger, wash clothes, take care of their babies, not field Nigger slave no more," says 'Old Healer'.

"We's Negroes, 'Old Healer'. Momma said only people think of field slaves, as Niggers. Momma is a house Negro. Momma eats good, sleeps in the Great House. Field slaves are cold and wet in winter, hot and wet in summer. Master lets field slaves keep little what they grow…gives 'em little to eat, if anythin'. I wanta' eat good, sleep in the Great House."

"Ya kinda' forgettin' were ya came from Mary. We slaves in the fields, and in the house," says 'Old Healer'. Grabbing Mary by the arm, 'Old Healer' stops her near the tub, turning her around, and looking straight into her eyes, saying, "Ya strong smart girl. Masters like smart Niggers in Great House…but not too smart Mary…know your place." 'Old Healer' motions for Mary to come to her, as she then says, "Ya watch, learn, like ya did since we raised ya from a baby. Cause one day, no more slaves Mary. We be free people. Ya go from here…"

Mary interrupts, saying, "Right now 'Old Healer', I'm gonna finish rinsin' these clothes so I can read and do…arith…matic with MaryJo this evenin'." Mary turns, walks a few steps, takes the bucket and pours the water into the barrel with the washed clothes, setting the bucket down. She then begins thrusting the clothes through the water, and brings several pairs of pants out of the barrel, ringing the water out with her hands. She takes the pants over to the clothesline with 'Old Healer' following.

Mary throws the legs of the pants over the horizontal clothesline, letting them hang. She then takes a pair of pants and wraps them around the wood vertical post, grabbing the legs, and begins twisting the last of the water out of the pants, as she looks at 'Old Healer', saying, "'Old Healer', why we slaves anyways?"

"Don't know why we slaves Mary. My momma told me, 'white' men bring us here, from our land, Africa, far away, over a lot of water. They take away our words, make us know their words...we sold like lost animals, beat like animals, given little food, what's left of the Master's meat we eat, and do the Master's work." Then, Old Healer' becomes sad, and says, "...Slaves fight the Masters to be free. Masters sell all boys, men or any slave from the plantation who make trouble...we never see 'em again, like your poppa."

Mary begins hanging the pants on the clothesline with split-wood clothespins, as she says, "Momma told me about Buck, my poppa. Why he was sold, cause Master Warner didn't want momma havin' any more babies."

'Old Healer' comes closer to Mary with a surprised expression on her face, saying, "Your momma told ya about..."

"Ya...she said it was time," says Mary interrupting. She grabs the other pair of pants to hang, as 'Old Healer', quizzically says, "She told ya everythin'?"

"I think so 'Old Healer'." Mary finishes hanging the pants then looks at 'Old Healer' with a hurt expression, and says, "Why didn't ya tell me the truth all this time?"

"Child", says 'Old Healer'. Then with a serious tone, she says, "If Master Warner knew ya knew, he think ya trouble...Master Warner sell ya, like all slaves, we never see ya again. That's why we don't tell ya child..." Mary is young, however she ponders what 'Old Healer' just said, and then says, "...I understand."

Mary then walks back to the washtub to retrieve the rest of the wash leaving 'Old Healer' behind. She gathers the wash out of the barrel, ringing them out, then walking back to the clothesline, with 'Old Healer', now sitting on a wooden crate holding her cane. 'Old Healer' looks at Mary, and says, "Mary...ya goin' to the Great House Feast next Sunday? We's gonna have a feast...ya gonna be there? Ya gonna be in the Great House?"

"Don't know what Master wants me to be doin' Sunday?" says Mary, as she hesitates, then says, "...guess I'll be there?"

"Child, 'em are your roots, not in the 'white' man's house!"

That Sunday, it's a bright beautiful Easter Day. A violinist is playing classical music, which fills the air in the front yard of the Great House. The newly repaired and painted plantation looks stunning with all the new flowers, trees, and decorations for Easter.

Everyone is in their best dress. Some children are Easter egg hunting around the Warner flagpole, with Old Glory flying twenty-six stars, waving in the breeze in the middle of the yard.

There are no slaves in sight, except for Mary. She and MaryJo are swinging on the front porch swing of the Great House. The girls are one hundred and eighty degrees apart in skin tone, however, they look identical in their pink dresses, white socks and pink shoes. One wouldn't know by looking at the girls, that slavery is thriving.

Mary is doing most of the work, pushing the swing with her legs against the wood porch, as MaryJo looks at Mary saying, "Mary, you sure look pretty."

"Ya do too MaryJo," says Mary.

They continue swinging, as the plantation owner, Francis Warner, opens the lower Dutch door for Mrs. Warner to exit. Mr. Warner is tall, a brown haired southern gentleman. He exits out the door with a newspaper under his arm, walking out with food plates and drinks. Mrs. Warner looks at the girls, as she says, "Girls, ya want somethin' to eat now?"

"Yes mom," says MaryJo.

"Yes ma'am," says Mary.

"Okay. Go inside and get u'all a plate," says Mrs. Warner.

Both girls excited, respond simultaneously, saying, "Okay."

The girls hurry towards the front door with Mary reaching the door first, then, opening the door for MaryJo to enter. Mary follows MaryJo inside, as Mr. and Mrs. Warner walk to the opposite side of the porch and sit down on chairs near a table. Mrs. Warner then looks at Mr. Warner, and says, "It's a shame the president's wife died so young."

Mr. Warner with a hardened southern dialect, says, "It was bad enough that President Harrison died, then Vice President John Tyler havin' to take his place, and his wife also dyin'." Mr. Warner unfolds the newspaper and begins reading, revealing the date of, 'Friday, March 25, 1842', with the headlines, 'PRESIDENT'S WIFE DIES.'

The head plantation overseer, Leroy Fogel, walks up on the porch, wearing overalls that show the muscular structure of his body, and a straw hat keeping the hot southern sun off his red burnt head. He walks over to Mr. Warner, and says, "Mr. Warner…gave 'em Niggers the rest of the hog like ya said. They finished most their work yesterday…they should be workin' today…not celebratin' Easter. They don't know nothin' about God and Jesus…they just a bunch of Mud Turtles."

"Now Leroy Fogel," says Mrs. Warner, giving him a look, as she then says, "Ya leave them Negroes alone…they work hard all the time."

Mr. Warner with food in his mouth looks at Leroy, and says, "...Tomorrow we start diggin' that drainage ditch, LeRoy, on the east ninety. How many of 'em do ya think we need to finish?"

"We'll need about...fifteen Niggers. That should be enough Nigger ditch diggers," says, LeRoy. He snickers, and then seriously says, "Mr. Warner...that so called Nigger medicine woman, she be trouble. Ya should stop her from goin' to the other plantations...maybe sell her. I hear she talks freedom to 'em Niggers."

"Mr. Fogel, that so called Nigger medicine woman takes care of all the slaves, on this farm, and the surrounding plantations, costin' us nothin'," says Mrs. Warner.

Mr. Warner says, "Mr. Fogel, what trouble can that old Nigger woman be? If she talks of freedom, it gives them Niggers hope...keeps their spirit alive, keepin' 'em workin'...ya just make sure they don't run away, ya hear?"

"Yes 'sir', Mr. Warner," says LeRoy walking away.

Suzanna opens the door for MaryJo, and Mary to exit. The girls walk out with plates full of food. Suzanna follows holding a pitcher full of lemonade. She walks over and looks at Mr. Warner, and says, "Master Warner, Mrs. Warner everythin' ok...more lemonade?"

"Lemonade," says Mr. Warner.

"Suzanna, everythin' is fine...lemonade please," says Mrs. Warner.

After Suzanna serves the Warner's their lemonade, she looks at the children Easter egg hunting, then looks at Mrs. Warner with a puzzled expression, saying, "Ma'am, ya don't mind me askin' somethin'?"

"Of course not Suzanna," says Mrs. Warner, looking at her, as she then says, "What's on your mind?"

"Ah...ah, ma'am, I just don't understand." Suzanna hesitates and looks at the children, then says, "Children tryin' to find eggs ya adults hide...pretendin' that a rabbit left 'em?" Then with more curiousness, she looks at Mrs. Warner, and says, "Rabbits don't lay eggs...do they ma'am?"

Mrs. Warner laughs, as she says, "No, no Suzanna...this is new to us too. Our German friends, the Venderveers, who ya see down there with that other couple." She points to them, then says, "They told us this is the way they celebrate Easter in Germany."

Suzanna's expression is puzzled. She looks at Mrs. Warner, then, looks back to the children Easter egg hunting.

The sound of drums begins to resonate from the Warner slave quarters, in the distance, in celebration of the Great Feast. Mary looks up from eating her food, listening to the sound of the drums emanating from the direction of the slave quarters.

MaryJo is too busy eating to notice Mary or the drums, however, Suzanna notices. She looks at Mary with a worried look, trying not to attract attention. Then like magic, faint drumbeats are heard coming from other distant plantations, as the Warner drums stop.

In the compound of the Warner slaves, smoke wafts through the air, from a fire burning in an open pit, under a large black iron pot. The pot is hanging by a homemade iron tripod, being stirred by a slave woman. Several clusters of pitched log shacks surround the compound. A sparse vegetable garden is growing in the middle, which is surrounded by an old wooden picket fence.

Slaves are dressed in their every day old ragged clothes; men are wearing stained drawstring cotton pants and shirts. The women are wearing stained cotton dresses, many, with head rags and aprons. Some of the slaves' feet are covered with old boots and tattered shoes, while others are bare footed.

The 'Old Healer' walks outside from one of the shacks with a woven basket in her hands, while some slaves are playing their homemade drums and musical instruments, singing slave-hymns in the background sitting on old wooden crates and barrels. Several slaves are dressed in colorful homemade tattered costumes dancing about.

The main enclave of slaves, are beating their drums, rhythmically, when they pause suddenly, as do the dancers and singers. They look and listen to the far distance, as other plantations begin beating their drums. Then, the distant drums stop. The Warner slaves begin playing their drums again, as if beating out some type of Morse code rhythm.

The 'Old Healer' walks up to the fire pit and pours her herbs from the basket into the black pot. She then looks at a man cutting meat on a large cut face log, as the 'Old Healer' says, "Hurry up with 'em hog guts George, got a while to cook." Then she looks at the Great House, and says, "That Mary sure gonna miss out." George walks up to the fire pit and drops the meat into the pot, as the 'Old Healer' stirs in more ingredients. She is stirring the brew, when she begins to sing in rhythm with the drumbeat, "Birds fly free...birds are free. Clouds fly free...clouds are free. Wind blows free...wind is free. One day...Negroes be like birds, clouds, wind...free..."

Five years later in the Warner slave compound, the slaves' drums beat a woeful sound. Many of the women slaves are crying and chanting. George and several male slaves are building a coffin out of scrap wood.

Several women walk in and walk out of the largest slave quarters, sobbing and crying.

Inside the slave quarters, a smoky haze hangs in the air. Homemade decorations adorn the walls. The room is full of bedding, lining the floor. Several women are sobbing while other women are happy, chanting, waving their hands in the air.

The 'Old Healer' has aged, and is on her knees blowing smoke over the legs of a body lying on the floor bedding. As she moves up the legs, she takes a puff from the cigar blowing more smoke from the legs to the torso.

Loud crying and sobbing can be heard outside approaching the quarters. All inside, look to the open door. Several women approach the doorway, holding a much taller, and larger sobbing teenage Mary by the arms. Mary is dressed in house slave attire, with a head rag, and as they enter, the 'Old Healer' continues blowing smoke along the body, moving upward to Suzanna's face.

The 'Old Healer' takes another puff and blows smoke into the eyes, nose, mouth and ears of Suzanna. After she finishes, two men help her to her feet.

Mary then rushes to her mother's side, dropping to her knees crying, then saying, "Momma, momma! Momma...Momma..." And then yells, "MOMMAAA!"

Later that day in the Warner slave cemetery, the 'Old Healer' is using her cane now more for walking. She is leading the procession of mourners walking on a path in the cemetery. She is carrying a homemade smoldering African spiritual container, suspended on a rope, swinging from side to side. Two male slaves, beating their woeful drumbeat, follow her. Others are chanting, while walking among the numerous graves.

George and five other slaves are carrying the homemade casket. They are followed by MaryJo supporting Mary by the arm on one side, as another slave woman supports Mary on the other side, followed by the other Warner slaves and Mrs. Warner.

As the procession reaches the prepared grave, the drums go from the woeful beat, to a very upbeat African rhythm. The mourners that were crying now begin singing, and join the dancers who have now also picked up their rhythm.

The celebration of Suzanna's transition, to move into the next life, has now caused Mary to be happy, sobbing and dancing, with her hands in the air, along with the other slaves in the celebration. MaryJo and Mrs. Warner are observing, standing along the fringes, gently moving with the addictive rhythm.

Later that day, in the slave quarters, Mary and MaryJo walk into the small room with the sound of the celebration of Suzanna's transition just outside the shack.

This is the first time MaryJo has ever been in the Slave Quarters. She sniffs the air. Her eyes are wide open scanning the room, when Mary says, "MaryJo, that sure nice your mom got my momma flowers."

"It was the best we could do Mary. Your mother was a good servant...she died so suddenly." Then MaryJo, with a resolved expression in her eyes, turns, and looks at Mary, saying, "Mary...I have something to tell you. I need you to be strong when I tell you this."

Mary looks at MaryJo with a quizzical look, and asks, "What MaryJo?"

MaryJo, somewhat hesitant, says, "...My family is sending...me to a Catholic boarding school next month when I turn sixteen."

"What's a boardin' school MaryJo...how long ya gonna be gone?"

"My father tells me...six years."

Mary can't believe what she is hearing. She rushes to MaryJo, and starts to sob, stopping in front of her, and then hugging her. Mary is now taller than MaryJo, and as Mary hugs MaryJo, the top of MaryJo's head comes to Mary's nose. Mary then pulls back and looks at MaryJo, and says, "No...no MaryJo, ya can't go. You're my friend. My momma's gone now." Mary drops her head, and then says, "I have no one else..." As she starts really sobbing, and says, "...Don't go MaryJo."

"I don't have a choice Mary, they're sending me to a school so I can study to be a Catholic nun."

Mary, holding back tears, releases her hold on MaryJo, and looks at her with hurt, and an inquisitive expression, saying, "...What's a nun, MaryJo?"

"It's a woman Mary...who teaches the Bible, educates, feeds and helps people in the Catholic religion."

Mary says, "MaryJo, can I go with ya and help people too?"

"I'm afraid not Mary. Your place is here, on the farm."

"I'll do anythin' ya want MaryJo, ya my only friend," says Mary.

"Mary you can't go with me, I'm very sorry. Your place is here."

There is a knock on the old wooden plank door causing Mary and MaryJo to stop talking. Mary looks at the door sobbing, and says, "...Yes."

George and the 'Old Healer' smoking her rolled cigar, walks into the room looking at Mary, saying, "Ya okay Mary?" Mary slightly nods her head.

George says, "Food's ready."

"'Old Healer', George...MaryJo leavin' the plantation for school," says Mary.

Later that night, on the back porch of the Great House, African slave hymns can be heard coming from the Warner slave quarters. A full moon is shining on Mary's face through the window, as she softly cries herself to sleep in her mother's bed.

Four years later, a coach travels down the long roadway towards the Warner plantation. As the coach approaches, it passes through a light smoke filled air, and Old Glory, flying thirty-one stars from the flagpole. A southern party atmosphere is in full swing. The plantation is looking more stunning, now that the trees have grown in, and new trees have been added, with flowers and plants adorning the property.

As the coach approaches the Great House, MaryJo looks out the window, and looks at a banner hanging across the front of the Great House with the words, 'WELCOME HOME MaryJo - HAPPY TWENTIETH BIRTHDAY'.

As the coach stops in front of the Great House, a male slave hurries to the coach, opening the door, and helping MaryJo step out of the coach, dressed in her Catholic school clothes.

A crowd of family and friends, along with Mrs. Warner holding the hand of a little girl, who is also holding Mary's hand, hurries to the coach. The well-wishers, surround MaryJo and the coach. Mrs. Warner, the little girl, and Mary work their way through the crowd. As Mrs. Warner reaches MaryJo, she lets go of the little girl's hand. Mary holds the other hand of the girl, allowing Mrs. Warner to hug MaryJo, saying, "'O' Darlin', I'm so glad to see ya. I can't believe it's a whole year since I went to see ya at the school."

MaryJo releases her hug around her mother, and says, "I'm so glad to see you too, mother, and my little sister, Josephine." MaryJo bends down and kisses Josephine on the cheek, and then rises, saying, "...It's good to be home on vacation. Only two more years to go, I can't wait." She then turns three hundred and sixty degrees, taking in the panoramic view of the plantation, saying, "The farm looks so beautiful Mother. Four years sure has changed things." She does another three-sixty, and says, "Where's father?"

"Your father had to go to Washington at the request of Senator Douglas of Illinois...to help get some bills signed into law. I don't think he'll be back before ya leave. He said to tell ya he loves ya and Happy Birthday."

"I had hoped to see father," says MaryJo.

MaryJo then, looks up at Mary, astounded, shaking hernhead. She can't believe her eyes, as she says, "...Mary...I can't believe how big you've gotten, you're taller than corn stalk in four years."

Mary hands Josephine's hand to Mrs. Warner to hold. Mary and MaryJo embrace, and as they embrace, the top of MaryJo's head comes to the bottom of Mary's jaw. Mary then pulls back from the embrace with jubilation, and looks at MaryJo, saying, "Your mom been tellin' me all about ya and how good ya doin' in school. She's been givin' me the books ya send for me to read."

MaryJo still can't get over how big Mary has gotten. She looks Mary up and down, saying, "...Mary...mother said you were getting big...I had no idea."

"Ah, I ain't that big MaryJo. It's sure good to see ya. Lot's happened since ya left, can't wait to tell ya." Mary then looks at the coach, and says, "Where's your things?"

MaryJo looks at Mary, and says, "Your English is much better Mary."

"Thanks to ya, and Mrs. Warner," says Mary.

The coach driver brings MaryJo's bags from around the coach, and drops them at Mary's feet, saying, "Here ya go Nigger!"

About an hour later, Mary and MaryJo still wearing her school clothes, are talking and walking along a road that leads away from the Great House, as Mary says, "...Everyone dressed alike...like we Negro slaves?"

"Well...they're not slaves Mary, all the nuns are dressed in robes and habits that cover their heads. All the girls are dressed the way you see me dressed."

With a curious eye, "Any boys?" says Mary.

MaryJo smiles and shakes her head, and says, "No boys."

"Your little sister, Josephine, has kinda taken your place." Mary smiles and then says, "...Not really."

"Mom got pregnant after I went to school, it was a surprise for everybody. My little sister, I hardly know," says MaryJo.

As they continue walking, the girls see a group of three young men approaching on the opposite side of the road. MaryJo looks long and hard at one of the men, as she says, "That looks like John...from the McKinney Farm. I went to school with him here before I left. He had such a crush on me. He's nothing but a bully and a jackass." She catches herself, and smiles at Mary, and then says, "I mean he wasn't a nice boy." As the young men approach, they cross the road to the side the girls are on. MaryJo looks at Mary, and says, "Mary let's move to the other side."

Mary and MaryJo walk quickly to the other side of the road, and as the girls cross the road, so do the young men, to their side, as MaryJo says to Mary, "You see what I mean."

"Yah...but don't think they gonna bother us none, do ya, MaryJo?" says Mary.

MaryJo looks at Mary with a concerned look, as the young men approach. MaryJo and Mary stop, as the men stop just in front of the girls, and begin looking up and down at MaryJo, totally ignoring Mary.

"Hello John, long time," says MaryJo.

Arrogantly, John says, "Ya been gone a long time MaryJo. Heard ya went to some Catholic school in the north...what'a ya dressed for now...Halloween."

John and his friends really have a laugh now, as Mary looks at MaryJo, saying, "What's...Hall...Halloween?"

"Irish celebration Mary," says MaryJo quickly.

John looks at Mary, and says, "What ya doin' hangin' with that Nigger?"

With concerned, MaryJo says, "Leave her alone John...she's my servant, she's not bothering you."

"Well tell your Nigger servant...get lost, or I'll get a rope!" He looks at MaryJo with an intended look, and then says, "Ya, me and the boys...we gonna have some fun. We just comin' to your party." John elbows his nearest friend, as they all become more aggressive, moving closer to MaryJo.

Mary then steps in between the young men, saying, "Ya leave Miss MaryJo alone!"

John is as tall as Mary, pushing her aside. Mary not expecting the push, falls to the ground, causing the young men to move in on MaryJo.

Before the young men get close to MaryJo who is backing up, Mary is on her feet and in John's face, nose to nose. His friends watching Mary, freeze in their thoughts, with surprised expressions on their faces. Mary looks at John, and angrily says, "I said...ya 'leave' Miss Warner alone...and don't 'push' me again!"

"'U'all' a big Nigger aren't 'ya'. Ya gonna hit the ground hard," says John. John's friends laugh. However, Mary doesn't react, still in his face. MaryJo believes this means trouble for Mary, and tries to come in between Mary and John, saying, "John stop this...you leave her alone!"

However, Mary steps back in front of MaryJo, in John's face, looking him straight in his eyes, saying, "No Miss Warner...ya let me handle this!"

MaryJo is shocked, and surprised by Mary's actions and words.

One of John's friends looks at John, and says, "John, ya can't hit a woman."

"Tom, this ain't no woman...this a Nigger slave!" says John, as he looks Mary dead in her eyes, and feels he has bagged a turkey, he smiles, then says, "I don't want to beat ya in front of the whole world, Nigger..." John then looks to an abandoned Warner barn in the near distance, pointing to it, and then saying, "Let's go yonder barn."

Mary looks at John, saying, "Ya the one lookin' for trouble."

"I'm gonna give ya trouble!" says John.

Moments later, at the front of the Warner barn, Tom and the other young men enter the dilapidated barn first, followed by Mary and MaryJo, then John. There's a lot of hay on the ground, and several piles of hay in the corner, with rusting tools laying against the walls, along with old slave chains and shackles hanging by hooks.

John and his friends look around curiously to make sure no one else is in earshot. After eyeing the barn, they turn their attention to Mary, with John saying, "Watcha' gonna do Nigger?!" John then walks up to Mary with his friends at his side and hits Mary, square on the jaw with his fist. Mary goes down on the hay floor, hard.

MaryJo rushes to Mary's side shouting, "Mary!" She then looks at John, saying, "You leave her alone John, you hurt her...you bastard, bastard!"

All of a sudden, a pile of hay in the corner of the barn begins moving. George pops his head up through the hay, saying, "What goin' on?"

MaryJo looks at George than back to Mary.

However, Mary has now risen up, slightly rubbing the left side of her face that is a little swollen. Her eyes are bulging with anger looking at John. She puts up her fist with determination, saying, "Ya hit me! Ya hit me! That's the last time 'anybody'...gonna hit me!!!"

John can't believe his eyes, nor can his friends.

George gets up from the hay and walks over to MaryJo's side. MaryJo has fear in her eyes, and goes to stop John, but George stops her, as she looks at George, saying, "George, please stop Mary. They're going to hurt her."

George smiles, and looks at MaryJo with confidence, saying, "Don't worry none Miss Warner...Mary take care of herself!"

John takes another swing at Mary. However, this time, she ducks his throw, causing him to spin around, almost falling. He is a little embarrassed in front of his friends, and especially when George laughs and MaryJo snickers. This causes John to be real angry. He looks at his friends, and says, "Who this Nigger think she is anyways? I'm goin' teach this Nigger dog some respect!" He throws two more fists at Mary, a left then a right.

Mary ducks both.

They continue going round and round till John throws another left, missing, as Mary throws a right hook, catching John with a hay maker. His head twists around from the hit, as he falls like a twisted wet rag. Tom and the other friend, begin to make a move towards Mary. She looks at both of them with her fist up, saying, "Come on! Ya want to sleep with your friend here?!" They both look at John, still out cold on the floor. They look at each other, then they look at Mary with her fists still up, ready for action, saying, "Come on!" They look at each other again, and begin backing away from Mary.

George then walks over to Mary, taking her by the arm, also backing her away with her fists up. He then looks at MaryJo, and says, "Miss Warner, ya go first." MaryJo hurries out the barn door, as George slowly escorts Mary backwards, backing her up towards the door with her fists still up. Tom and the other friend then rush to John's side.

Moments later, Mary, MaryJo and George are walking away from the barn on the road back to the Great House. As they walk, MaryJo looks at Mary with a surprised expression, saying, "Mary...I've never thought I'd see the day a Negro slave would defend themselves...how in the world did you learn to fight...and have courage to? You know what courage means Mary?"

"Yes Miss MaryJo...when I finished my chores, Mrs. Warner...I mean your mom...she don't mind me goin' to the slave quarters. The 'Old Healer', she kinda' gave me...courage, not to be afraid." Mary snickers, and then says, "She don't like 'white' man's books though..." Then saddened, she says, "...She died. I would take the books ya send me and I been teachin' the field slaves how to read. George here and the field slaves...they taught me how to take care of myself."

MaryJo smiles, and says, "Well...that you sure did today Mary."

"Miss MaryJo?" says George.

"Yes George?"

"Ah...ah Miss MaryJo, please don't tell that Mary beat up on 'em. Masters sell us slaves who trouble...we love Mary."

"Don't worry George, I'm not going to say anything, and I don't believe they are either. It would be kind of hard for John to explain, how, he got whipped by a Negro woman slave. I don't believe we will be hearing from John." MaryJo smiles, as they look at each other, and all begin to laugh, walking to the Great House.

The Civil War

Ten years later, Old Glory is flying thirty-four stars from the Warner flagpole in front of the Great House. The flag begins to fall. It's being pulled down by an older LeRoy, the head overseer. When the flag is within his reach, he quickly snatches and unfastens the flag from the rope. He throws the flag on the ground, stepping and spitting on the American flag. The other men that are with LeRoy, join him in stepping on the flag.

Under LeRoy's left arm is another flag. He quickly fastens the flag to the rope and hoists the flag aloft, proudly.

LeRoy, and all the men that are with him, look at the flag, and shout out, "Yay!" The Confederate Battle flag now whips in the breeze from the Warner plantation flagpole. LeRoy looks to older Mr. Warner sitting in his chair on the front porch, and says, "Mr. Warner, I've been waitin' for this day...those Northerners' are goin' to feel the wrath of the South."

"Are ya sure what ya heard LeRoy...Fort Sumter surrendered to General G. T. Beauregard?" says Mr. Warner.

"Yes sir...at about 2:30 in the afternoon, on the 13th, that northern Major...ah, ah, Anderson, that's it, Anderson, he surrendered Fort Sumter after Confederate batteries opened fire on the garrison," says LeRoy.

Proudly, Mr. Warner says, "Well, that means we Democrats are goin' to preserve our rights of the South under the Confederacy, the government of Jefferson Davis."

"Yes sir," says LeRoy. Excited, he then says, "Mr. Warner, the Confederacy is askin' for volunteers from all the plantations. That's why some of the other overseers are here with me now. They say it'll only take a couple of months to whip 'em Yankee Northerners."

"Gather the men LeRoy...we'll be all right until your return."

"Yes sir, Mr. Warner," says LeRoy. He then turns, and hurries off yelling, "YAHOO," with the other overseers.

Mary stands behind the partially open door, quietly, watching and listening.

Several years later, dark storm clouds churn in the sky. It's pouring down rain at the Great House. The wind blows, and a lightning bolt strikes a tree in the front yard splitting the tree in half, causing a loud crack of thunder that radiates out. Armed Confederate officers and soldiers, react to the lightning strike, and then continue carrying items out of the house, pots, pans, dishes, utensils, food, clothing, and any other provisions they can carry.

A much taller, stockier, matured Mary is respectfully yelling at one of the Confederate officers, saying, "We heard, Mrs. Warner died several years ago in the north...I'm the head Negro! Mr. Warner is very ill in his bed upstairs...this will kill him. Ya can't take the Master's..."

"By order of the Confederacy ma'am, we can take provisions leaving enough for your basic survival," says, the Confederate officer interrupting. He then turns to another officer, and says, "Make sure ya leave this great home an itemized list of items taken." The officer salutes, and both exit the front door of the Great House. The Confederate Officer looks at his soldiers, ransacking the beautiful plantation in the storm. Confederate soldiers are rushing through the mud, plundering the plantation, taking farm equipment, animals, and other items that aren't affixed, are being loaded on wagons, as mounted soldiers, ride away with their booty.

Moments later at the Warner main barn, several Confederate soldiers run by the barn door dragging farm equipment to their wagons. A lightning bolt strikes another tree nearby, and the clap of thunder cracks the air.

A Confederate soldier struggles, walking out of the barn, pulling on bedding that George is holding on to. He is trying to stop the soldier, as the soldier drags him through the mud. George is begging the soldier, saying, "Please sir, this my bed, please! Please!" Another Confederate officer rides up on his horse behind George, and shoots him at close range with his rifle. The musket round passes through George's body, hitting the muddy water in front of him. George falls in the mud.

Mary, looking out the back door of the Great House, rushes out of the door onto the porch in a panic state, stopping, fixated on George. She sees George lying in the mud, and hysterically, runs to him, yelling at the top of her lungs, "GEORGE! GEORGE! ...GEORGE!!!"

When Mary reaches George, she falls on her knees in the mud in front of him, and picks up his muddy head out of the water, caressing his head in her lap. She then looks at the soldiers with rain hitting her in the face, saying, "Why ya shoot him? Why...why..." Then she shouts, "WHY?!"

The Confederate officer that was in the Great House, walks up, and looks down at Mary, and then, to George bleeding in the mud, saying, "Sorry about this ma'am...this is war, anybody interferin' will be shot. This slave was interferin'."

The Confederate officer then turns and gives orders to another officer.

Mary begins to spring up, to attack the officer. However, dying George grabs Mary's dress, slowing and stopping her, in her movement. He softly says, "No Mary! No, ya mustn't! They'll kill ya." Mary looks at the Confederate officer shouting orders to his men, "Officers and men…assemble at the front gate of the plantation!" All the soldiers hurry away from the Great House and plantation, leaving very little. Mary looks out in dismay. The Confederate officer looks back at Mary, and at George bleeding to death in the mud, his blood turning the muddy rainwater red. The officer then turns without emotion and follows the rest of his soldiers off the plantation.

George's coughs capture Mary's attention. She looks back down at him with empathy, still crying, saying, "George…"

"Mary," says George, as he coughs blood out of his mouth, then saying, "…Mary…I want ya to have this." George reaches into his boot and brings out a knife, as he barely says, "…Mary…I don't think…you'll be needin' this…" George coughs up more blood, as he hands the knife to Mary, then saying, "…I want ya to have it. Just call it…good blessins'…if ya are ever in…serious trouble." George lets go of the knife in Mary's hand. His arm falls in the muddy water. Mary looks at the knife, then back at George, with sorrow, and with rain hitting him in the face, she says, "George, you're gonna be alright…don't die…don't die…"

A lightning bolt flashes high overhead, as thunder rumbles loudly. George looks at Mary for the last time, convulsing, and then closing his eyes.

One year later, late,1864. It's morning on the Warner plantation. The slave quarters, barn and plantation itself, have been destroyed. Confederate soldiers are in full retreat, running through the plantation, shooting over their shoulders. Cannonballs are exploding in front, and in back of the retreating soldiers, blowing some soldiers into the air that are filing past the plantation.

In the front yard of the Great House, portions of the two-story house have been shot up, burned and destroyed from previous battles. Some dead Confederate soldiers' bodies, lie about. Mary cautiously walks out past the partially burnt and broken front door, in tattered dirty clothes, with a determined expression in her eyes. She is carrying a black-powder bag around her shoulder, and a Springfield musket rifle in her hands, still smoking from the barrel.

Mary looks at the retreating soldiers, and hurries behind one of the pillars of the house to reload her rifle, with enemy rounds hitting the pillar. Mary finishes reloading, she stoops and peers around the pillar, picks a target, aims, and fires, hitting a Confederate soldier in the chest.

Mary retreats back around the pillar to reload, as she looks to several slaves, men and women peering out cautiously from the doorway in their dirty, shabby clothes. She winks at them, when a bugle charge call blares nearby, causing her to look towards the back of the Great House with a surprised expression.

Mary sees Union blue coat Negro soldiers on foot and mounted, carrying rifles, being led by 'white' Union officers, shooting and chasing after Confederate soldiers, as she says, "...Now, that don't beat all...'white' men leadin' Negroes...shootin'...killin' 'white' men." As she then shakes her head in trying to understand, she says, "...Huh?"

Several Union Negro soldiers on foot, and two officers mounted, are marching captured Confederate soldiers, at gunpoint, their hands in the air, back to the front yard, as the battle rages in the distance.

Mary looks at one of the mounted Union officers riding up quickly to the Warner flagpole. He pulls a knife from its sheath and cuts the flag rope, letting the war-torn, tattered Confederate Battle flag fall to the ground.

The Union officer then looks at the Great House and at Mary standing on the battered porch, smiling, looking at him, holding her rifle. He rides up to the porch, as Mary says, "Ya sure got 'em runnin' there, Master."

The Union officer looks at his Confederate prisoners being marched back towards the Great House by Union Negro soldiers, holding their rifles, at the ready, as the officer says, "Prisoners halt!" The Union soldiers come to a stop. The Confederate prisoners stop, haphazardly. The Union officer then looks at Mary and tips his hat, saying, "Good morning, ma'am."

"Good mornin', Master," says Mary.

"My name is Colonel Edward Hatch, Union Army. What's your name ma'am?"

"Mary...Mary Fields."

"Well Mary...you don't have to call me Master...matter of fact Mary, you don't have to call anybody Master, anymore." Then he says proudly, "Mary...Mississippi is free, and you are a free woman."

Mary, with a quizzical look, looks at Colonel Hatch with astonishment, as if she is hearing things. She squints her eyes, and then says, "Free? Free? Me...free?"

Colonel Hatch looks at the doorway of the Great House and points to the slaves. Some are cowardly crouching, as he says, "They are free too, Mary...you are no longer slaves."

Mary looks at the other slaves in the doorway, then back to Colonel Hatch, and partially smiling, she says, "Ya wouldn't be foolin' us now, would ya?"

Colonel Hatch smiles, chuckles a little, and says, "No, no Mary. By Proclamation of Abraham Lincoln, President of these United States...all slaves are 'free'."

Mary smiles, then she looks off in the distance in a trance, mumbling softly, saying, "The 'Old Healer'...she was right."

Colonel Hatch says, "Excuse me Mary...I didn't understand what you said."

Mary snaps out of her trance and looks at Colonel Hatch, saying, "Ah, Master, Colonel...I mean Colonel. Master Warner...I mean Mr. Warner...he died many months ago. Since the war, Mrs. Warner took their other daughter to a Catholic school in the north, where their older daughter is, then we heard she died." Then sadly, Mary says, "Don't know where they are now. There's no Masters here no more. Them gray coats took all 'em chickens...nothin' here hardly to eat."

Colonel Hatch says, "I'm sorry Mary...we need all provisions, and right now my unit has to make Greenville by next evening. You can take that musket," He points to Mary's rifle, and says, "Now that you are free...and it looks like you know how to use it...there's enough game to shoot for food around here. I'll have my men leave a little extra black powder."

Mary is puzzled. She looks at Colonel Hatch, and says, "Excuse me Colonel, what's game?"

Colonel Hatch chuckles, as he says, "...I'm sorry Mary. Game is animals, birds, deer, rabbits, those..."

"Oh...that we call huntin'," says Mary.

Colonel Hatch smiles, and says, "Yes Mary. Game is another word for hunting." Colonel Hatch looks at his men, then says, "I'm sorry Mary, my unit must prepare to march...good day." Colonel Hatch looks at Mary, and tips his hat, then looks at the Union officer next to him with urgency, and says, "Lieutenant, have the men leave about a pound of black-powder here for them to hunt with. Then have the prisoners taken to the rear and have the units form-up."

Colonel Hatch tips his hat again to Mary, and then rides off with the other officer. Mary looks back at the door, and the other slaves peering out, as she says, "Well...it looks like we's on our own now."

Two years later, the Great House and plantation is virtually destroyed, very little is left. Most of the trees have died, or have been broken and torn by the many years of war, with weeds now growing where flowers once bloomed.

Free slaves, men and women, tend to a sparse garden, as smoke wafts in the air from a cooking fire barely burning in a dugout pit, not far from what's left of the Great House, as a few chickens run about.

Mary is carrying her powder bag and rifle, and dragging a dead deer by the horns behind her, with a rope tied around her waist. She is walking towards the back of the Great House. As she reaches the back yard, she walks towards the fire, and shouts, "I'm back."

Before Mary reaches the pit, she sets her rifle down against a log, and unties the rope from around her waist. She then walks over to a tree, hangs the powder bag on a broken branch, and grabs an ax nearby. She walks to a medium size log pile and grasps a log with one hand, then moving over to a large old tree stump, she positions the log on the flat cut surface. She then steps back, eyes the log and swings the ax downward, splitting the log with one swing, as both halves fall away. She grabs one half, sits it back on the flat surface, she eyes the log, and she swings the ax downward, splitting the log. She reaches down and puts the other half on the flat surface, then swinging the ax, she splits the other one.

A very dark skinned young male, with wide brown almond shaped eyes, walks up to her, looking at the deer, and says, "Mary, that's a good deer. Be able to eat awhile. The animals are startin' to come back now." Then sadly, he says, "They sure killed a lot of animals in the war." He then looks at her, and says, "Mary, got the well-crank fixed again. Won't have to bring the water up by hand no more."

"Thanx Billyboy...hope it holds longer this time. I'm goin' to wash-up. Follow me." Mary puts the split logs into the fire as she and Billyboy walk towards the well. She then looks around to the war-torn dilapidated plantation, and says, "This place takin' a lot to keep after Billyboy...hardly not worth it for me." She stops and looks at Billyboy with compassion and seriousness, stopping him as he walks. He then turns and looks at her, as she says, "Billyboy...I be thinkin'...I want to see what's out there. Been here all my life...don't know what's out there."

"Aren't ya afraid Mary?" asks Billyboy. He then adds, "The 'white' man still actin' crazy...they put on 'em white sheets over their heads, run around at night on horses, burnin' houses, shootin', hangin' us." Then Billyboy gradually becomes real scared, as he says, "One night Joe and I, we's went over a hill about ten miles from here, we's see this bright light. We's look over the hill, there was a whole mess of 'em all with white sheets over their heads, lookin' like 'ghosts in a large circle, around a 'burnin' cross'. We's ran back like the dickens and didn't say nothin', not at all!"

"Shoot Billyboy...I ain't scared of 'nothin'." She then eyes Billyboy, as she then says, "I ain't worried about these 'white' people wearin' white sheets over their heads. They just actin' like fools. If someone shoots at me, I'm gonna shoot back!"

"Mary we sure goin'a miss ya if ya leave," says Billyboy.

Mary smiles, and then says, "I'm goin'a leave Billyboy. Goin'a miss ya too, and everybody else." Then with resolve, she says, "Ya make sure ya take good care of Martha now. She a good woman, treat ya real good."

"Don't think Martha and I be leavin' here Mary…nowhere to go."

"Billyboy, from what I hear, ya can homestead the plantation, if the girls, or Mrs. Warner don't come back to claim the property. Don't know what rightly happened to her, only heard she died after she took little Josephine to the Catholic school MaryJo is in. They say ya can…homestead…I think it means if ya take care of the land, grow food on it, it's yours. There is a future here Billyboy for ya and Martha."

"Where ya goin' Mary?" says Billyboy.

"To the big river, the Mississippi. They say there's good pay…do the same work on a boat I used to do here…everythin'." Mary then smiles, and Billyboy chuckles, as she then says, "Best to gettin' that meat cut"

"When ya goina' leave Mary," says Billyboy.

Mary smiles, and confidently says, "Tomorrow Billyboy. When I get there, I'll write ya. Ya know how to read and write now that I taught ya."

Billyboy smiles at Mary, as they walk to the well.

The Mississippi River and the Race

Six weeks later, in the late afternoon, shadows from the tall southern pines cross Mary's path, as she walks down a deserted road, headed for the Mississippi River, carrying two carpetbags. She is humming to herself and looking ahead, when she sees many elongated objects, hanging from a large tree limb off the side of the road. She continues walking, humming, and looking at the objects. She slows her pace, and stops humming, becoming mesmerized as she gets closer. She can't believe what she is seeing before her, bloated Negro bodies, displayed like trophies, seven women, and five men, hanging by their necks from ropes.

Mary has stop walking. She is frozen in place, and begins quickly looking around her, left, right, in back of her, in front of her, back to the left. Sweat begins to form on her forehead. She thinks she hears something in the woods, near the hanging bodies. She quickly looks to the noise. Still frozen in place, like something was holding on to her, she slowly turns back in the direction she was headed. She begins walking, then faster, walking faster, and faster, and faster, away from the noise, and the hanging Negroes, till she is running at full speed in a near panic, down the road with her two carpetbags in hand.

Two weeks later, it is a bright sunny afternoon, on the river docks, adjoining the Mississippi River in St. Louis, Missouri. Columns of black ebony smoke roll periodically through the air, high above the river and levee docks, coming from the many, stern, and side-wheel steamboats that are tied to the embankment, spewing smoke from their smokestacks.

The docks are organized chaos, as handcarts are rolled in straight lines with their sacks of rice, sugar and tobacco, going to and from their destinations, while other groups roll bales of cotton and barrels of liquids towards the boats.

Banjo, drumbeats, and organ music radiates out from the different steamboats.

Some boats are puffing and hissing steam from their twin steam vents. Other boats are blowing their whistles, while others clang their bells.

Hundreds of rich 'white' passengers, poor Negro and 'white', board and disembark the steamboats.

Some steamboats are barges, which are stacked up to the wheelhouse with lumber, while others, are passenger and freight-haulers, only stacked several feet high with cargo around the railings.

On the wood plank docks, hundreds of sacks of rice and sugar cane are piled four to five feet high, in neat forty to fifty foot rows, among the thousands of bales of cotton and tobacco in front of their designated boat-haulers.

Mule carts are driven up to their unloading stations with their cargo, as roustabouts, ex-negro slaves, go about their task of unloading goods from off the carts, sacks of rice, tobacco, sugar, and cotton bales weighing hundreds of pounds. Some roustabouts sing slave-hymns doing their work while others chant a, 'call in response', to their every move, orchestrated by their roustabout leader.

An older 'white' teenage newspaper boy is walking along the shipping dock near the steamboats selling his newspapers, shouting, "Read all about it! ...Read all about it! The U. S. Congress on April 9th, this year 1866, overrides President Johnson's Veto of the Civil Rights Bill. Read all about it!"

A passenger walks up, hands the newspaper boy a coin, and as the boy hands the paper to the passenger, he drops the coin on the ground. He stoops down to pick up the coin when a large pair of tattered boots steps up and stops in front of him. He slowly rises with the coin in hand, looking up at Mary dressed in her tattered house slave dress, rag tied around her head, carrying her two carpetbags, one in each hand, and is more muscular in appearance then most of the men around her.

The boy, astonished by what's before him, quickly stands upright, and puts the coin into his pocket, then, looking at Mary, he stutters, as he says, "...Where in the hell...did...they...make ya?" Mary is looking at the newspapers cradled in his arm. The boy looks at his papers, saying, "What ya lookin' at Nigger!?" He then takes a paper from his arm, and looks at Mary, saying, "Ain't no pictures here...ya Niggers can't read, much less talk right."

Mary drops one of her bags, quickly grabbing the newspaper out of the boy's hand. The boy tries to react, reaching for the paper, and shouts, "Hey!" The boy keeps reaching for the newspaper, but Mary keeps it away from him. She studies the newspaper, then looks back at the boy, saying, "It says...the United States Congress 'Passed' the Civil Rights Bill President Andrew Johnson Vetoed!" Then Mary, with a hard look, stares at the boy, and says, "This Bill allows us 'Negroes' to be free, like ya 'white' people...so ya see...we can read, and we do speak good!" Mary smiles sarcastically at the newspaper boy, as she hands him his newspaper. She then picks up her bag and walks away, leaving him with an astonished expression.

Mary strolls along the docks with her two bags in hand. She looks with amazement at the steamboats, becoming more fascinated with each step. As Mary gazes at the boats, some of the people walking by her, Negro and 'white', can't help but take a second glance at her. Some stop and stare.

Mary continues walking past the last boat when she looks at a large shining, side-paddle wheel steamboat with the name painted on the side, 'Robt. E. Lee', with its gala flags, strung from bow to stern. The boat is beginning its docking maneuvers, bow first, into the space near Mary.

She watches several very dark skinned deckhands standing on the Main Deck with their tie lines. The Captain, in the wheelhouse looks out the front window. He is talking into the speaking tube. Then, the Captain pulls a ring hanging on a rope-cord in front of him, twice, sounding the large bell outside.

The steamboat glides into the space, and as it nears the embankment, the Captain pulls back on a lever in the center of the wheelhouse, visible through the front window opening. The big boat's paddlewheels go from neutral to reverse, churning the water, slowing the boat. The Captain then pushes the lever upright. The paddlewheels slow to a stop as the boat's hull slices into the river mud, stopping the bow inches away from the embankment.

The Captain has salt and pepper hair, and beard. He wears a tuckapaw white shirt and Panama hat, and is soft spoken, as he shouts out the window, "Alright, deckhands, tie your lines, gangplanks out...roustabouts, get the special cargo on board."

The deckhands quickly scamper off the Main Deck of the boat to tie their bowlines, as the gangplanks are hoisted across the deck, sliding out onto the dock. One of the planks passes by Mary, nearly missing her. This causes her to jump backwards, dropping her bags.

One of the crewmembers on the Main Deck is not wearing a shirt. He is tall, dark skinned, muscular and handsome. With a slight Cajun dialect, he shouts at Mary, "Watch de plank lady!"

Mary looks back at the crewmember, and shouts, "Ya watch the plank...I be here first!"

The crewmember that shouted at Mary grabs a shirt off the rail, and then hurries behind the roustabouts onto the plank, as a 'white' gentleman with two packages under his arm, hurries past them onto the boat.

Roustabouts begin bringing aboard the cargo. The crewmember that shouted at Mary nears the dock, he jumps off the plank and onto the dock in front of Mary holding his shirt in his hand.

Not realizing Mary's size, the crewmember is surprised standing in front of her, at the same eye level. He looks at her, as he puts on his shirt with no buttons, saying, "...Ah...lady, sorry. We's in a hurry, gettin' ready for maiden-voyage, didn't see ya."

"That's okay," Mary says excitedly. Her eyes brighten, looking at the crewmember, then, saying, "Voyage! ...Where ya all goin'?"

"New Orleans," says the crewmember.

"Ain't that near the ocean?" says Mary.

"Yes, de mouth of this river, de Mississippi," says the crewmember.

"I'm from around the Mississippi area. That's where the plantation was I'm from," says Mary. She then, quizzically says, "I was told I have ta come north, to find fair work on the river, to St. Louis? Took me several months and some weeks, working my way to get here."

"Yes sir lady," says the crewmember. He wipes his forehead with a rag from his pocket, and then says, "Ya can find fair work on de river, the further north ya go, as long as ya can find a fair boss."

"Josh, Josh…Joshua," shouts the Captain now standing on the Main Deck, holding one of the packages the 'white' gentleman carried onto the boat. He rips open the package and looks at the crewmember, Joshua, who is talking with Mary.

Joshua bows his head to Mary, then turns and looks at the Captain, and says, "Yes, Captain Cannon?"

"Tell me what you think of this?" Captain Cannon walks over to the Jack-Staff on the Main Deck and fastens a blue pennant flag to the rope. He then hoists the flag aloft out of the package into the breeze, and as it unfurls, it shows the words written on the flag, 'Robert. E. Lee'. Captain Cannon looks proudly at the flag, and then looks at Joshua, saying, "What'a you think Joshua?"

"Fine Captain. De flag, she looks fine."

Passengers and sightseers begin flocking to the Robert E. Lee, looking at the Lee's flag, and steamboat. Captain Cannon looks at Joshua, and shouts, "Joshua, I wanta' get down river before night fall. Get what chambermaids signed on first, situated, the special cargo, then passengers."

"Yes Captain," says Joshua. He then turns and looks at Mary, saying, "Got to go now. Nice talkin' to ya…" Joshua looks at Mary quizzically for her name, however, Mary is mesmerized, looking at the Lee, and then looks at Joshua, saying, "…Ah…Mary."

"I'm Joshua…good bye."

Joshua smiles and starts to leave, as Mary says, "Wait Joshua…your Mas…I mean boss…he lookin' for servants…know how to take care of a house real good?" Mary then looks at the Lee, and says, "This mighty fancy 'house' on the water."

Joshua looks at the Lee, and says, "This here…this here is a brand new steamboat, de 'Robert E. Lee'…de fastest boat on de Mississippi…just got de name painted on her side wheel-housing'." Then, real proud, Joshua looks at Mary, and says, "I'm de First Mate. Ya speak good for bein' a slave."

"I ain't a slave no more!" says Mary with slight anger. Then pointedly she says, "...We free Negroes...I's just left the plantation...was a house Negro!"

Joshua looks Mary up and down, and with a slight smile, he says, "Ya sure ya didn't work in the fields...ya big enough."

"Did that too!" says Mary.

Joshua smiles again at Mary, as he says, "Ya good house Negro?"

"Head house Negro. Took care of the plantation after the Master died durin' the war. Shot at a few of 'em gray coat Confederates too!"

Intrigued, Joshua looks at Mary again, then smiles, and says, "...Ok...we see how ya do here. Maybe, ya head chambermaid...right now ya chambermaid, pay is twenty-five cents a day, plus ya meals, a place to sleep. Ya make sure all beds made in your area, water changed every mornin', noon, and night. Floors cleaned and mopped, and de payin' guests are 'well' taken care of."

Joshua turns, puts one hand on the plank and jumps up, in between roustabouts going about their tasks. Joshua walks up the plank towards the Lee, then, he looks back down at Mary still standing there in a daze. He shouts out at her over the noise, "What ya waitin' for? Grab your bags, and follow me. Get ya settled before I brin' de other chambermaids aboard."

Mary snaps out of the daze, and excitedly grabs her bags, hurrying up the plank, following Joshua. He steps onto the Lee's Main Deck, he looks back at Mary stepping onto the Lee, saying, "De first thin' I tell ya is about Captain Cannon. He's..."

Several hours later, in the wheelhouse of the Robert E. Lee, Captain Cannon is standing in front of the Lee's large helm, polishing the glass on the new compass with a cloth. He pivots over to the engine order telegraph, polishing the brass, then looks out the front opening, at the boat's pennant flying from the jack-staff. Then he looks at the elegantly dressed passengers and guests mingling on the Main Deck, as smoke radiates upward from the men smoking their cigars, conversing, while drinking their free flowing champagne, as waiters refill their glasses with the spirit.

The deckhands and roustabouts hurry, finishing their last minute tasks before the Lee's departure. Joshua walks up one of the gangplanks with nine chambermaids following him. Captain Cannon sees Joshua, and walks over to the speaking tube, blows into the tube, saying, "Alright Mr. McDermick...where is she?" Captain Cannon then looks over at the listening tube. Mr. McDermick, blowing in the tube, replies with a slight Irish accent, saying, "She building Captain...seventy-five pounds."

"Get her up and stand-by Mr. McDermick," says, Captain Cannon speaking into the tube.

"Aye, aye Captain," replies Mr. McDermick.

Captain Cannon turns around and looks at the 'white' gentleman standing behind him, saying, "Open the package, and let me see."

The 'white' gentleman opens the other package he carried on the Lee, and holds up Old Glory, a new American flag, with thirty-six stars. Captain Cannon has no expression on his face. He looks at the gentleman, and says, "Herman…when we back into the channel, hoist the colors."

"Yes Captain," says Herman.

"How many investors and guests are we entertaining with champaign, for the voyage Herman?" says Captain Cannon.

"Because we are not carryin' major cargo, only passengers, Captain…we have three-hundred and nine guests, with lots of room at three-hundred dollars a head."

"Not bad for our maiden-voyage, hey Herman?" says Captain Cannon.

A little meek, Herman says, "Yes Captain." He adjusts his bookworm eyeglasses, turns, and walks out the door. Captain Cannon reaches up, and pulls one of several rings hanging by rope-cords, sounding the steam whistles.

Moments later, the steam whistles sound again. Herman and Joshua are herding the last of the visitors onto the gangplanks, and off the Lee, as the whistles blow again and again.

Captain Cannon, looking out the window opening, looks at Joshua, and shouts, "Joshua, bring the head chambermaid to the wheelhouse, once you get the gangplanks secure before we depart!"

"Yes Captain," shouts Joshua looking up at him. Joshua then turns and looks at his crew, saying, "Secure de gangplanks, then stand-by with de axes."

The whistles sound again. Herman is escorting the last of the visitors off the gangplanks. He then turns and runs back towards the boat, jumping off the plank when he passes the boat's railing onto the Main Deck. The deckhands then slide the planks back onto the Lee's deck. Herman and Joshua make their way through the passengers towards the main stairwell.

Later, in the wheelhouse of the Lee, Captain Cannon is putting a log into his potbelly stove that's built into the wheelhouse. He then looks to the footsteps he hears coming from outside, walking up the steps to the door. He sees Joshua and Mary appearing above the lower wood panels walking up the steps. Joshua reaches the landing, knocks on the door. Captain Cannon closes the door to the stove, and says, "Enter."

Joshua opens the door, and Mary enters, with Joshua following, closing the door behind him. Her uniform is too small for her, with some buttons not quite able to be button, and the ones that are button, are about ready to burst. Captain Cannon, amazed by Mary's physical appearance, is looking at her, as she looks around the wheelhouse with awe. Captain Cannon then looks at Joshua, then back at Mary, and then looks back at Joshua, saying, "...Ah Joshua, I take it, this is the head chambermaid?"

"Yes Captain," says Joshua.

Mary quickly looks at Joshua, squinting her eyes, putting her hands on her hips, as Joshua says, "This is Mary Fields. She has already been acquainted with some of her duties, and where her quarters are."

Captain Cannon with a quizzical look, looks at Mary's uniform, as he says, "...and...what about her uniform?"

"That's the largest uniform we have," says Joshua.

Captain Cannon looks from Mary, to Joshua, saying, "She will mend her uniform to fit her?"

"Yes sir."

"Okay Josh," says Captain Cannon. He then looks back at Mary, and says, "Good afternoon Mary, I'm Captain Cannon, skipper and owner of the Robert E. Lee..." There's a whoosh sound on the listening tube near Mary. She jumps back, with a surprised expression on her face. She puts up her fists, saying, "What in tar-nations is that!?"

Captain Cannon chuckles, and says, "Sorry Mary...that there is a listening tube. It goes to the engineer in the engine room down below. That's how we talk to each other." There's another blow on the listening tube, as Mr. McDermick's voice radiates out from the tube, saying, "Captain."

Captain Cannon walks over to the speaking tube, with Mary watching in amazement. Captain Cannon blows into the tube, and says, "Yes, Mr. McDermick."

"She's there Captain...one-twenty."

"Very well Mr. McDermick. Keep her there, stand-by to get underway."

"Aye, aye Captain."

Captain Cannon then turns, and looks at Mary, saying, "Mary, I expect nothing but greatness from my crew, I'm sure Josh has told you?"

Mary looks at Joshua with a slight sarcastic expression, and says, "Yes Captain...Josh has told me all right!"

"Mary...like Josh, I believe it's now important that Negroes have opportunities to improve themselves, now that you are free." Quizzically,

Captain Cannon looks at Mary, and says, "You understand what I just said Mary?"

"Yes Captain. In the newspaper today, it said that Congress passed the Civil Rights Bill that President Johnson vetoed, that allows us Negroes to be free..."

Interrupting, Captain Cannon, a little astonished by Mary's response, says, "Very good Mary...where did you learn to read and speak so well?"

"When I was on the plantation, the lady of the house allowed me to read with her daughters. One of her daughters would send me books from where she went to school in the north."

"Good, very good," says Captain Cannon. He then walks to the front window and the speaking tube, and looks down at the Main Deck. He then turns and looks at Joshua, saying, "Joshua, are we prepared to shove off? Provisions for three weeks, special cargo and passengers aboard?"

"Yes Captain."

"Good. Tell Mr. Willis we'll stop for fuel at Woodland."

"Yes Captain," says Joshua. Joshua opens the door for Mary to exit, as Captain Cannon blows into the speaking tube, saying, "Mr. McDermick, stand-by."

Moments later, in the corridor of the Hurricane Deck of the Robert E. Lee, the interior of the Lee is much more elegant than a Victorian New York hotel. Scalloped beam ceilings, gothic ornaments, gold plated chandeliers, paintings, and elaborate dining room tables, setting on plush carpet. Waiters are preparing the tables for supper, as hundreds of guests mingle about, still drinking their free spirits.

Joshua is following Mary, who is walking very fast down the long corridor. She stops near the pianist playing the grand piano. Then she turns and looks at Joshua somewhat angry, but not enough to attract anyone's attention, saying, "Head chambermaid...and still clean the rooms!?"

"Thirty-five," says Joshua.

"Fifty!" says Mary.

"Forty-five...!" says Joshua.

"Fifty-five!"

Joshua looks at Mary, and chuckles knowing he's met his match, saying, "...Okay, fifty-five cents a day...but ya better be good, as ya say, ya are..."

"I am," says Mary confidently, cutting Joshua off!

"Alright head chambermaid...follow me." Joshua and Mary hurry down the stairs of the Hurricane Deck, to the Boiler Deck, and then out on the Main Deck, with Mary following, as both stop in view of the wheelhouse.

Well-wishers are waving good-bye, from all points surrounding the Lee. Joshua looks at Captain Cannon in the wheelhouse, who's looking towards the stern of the boat. Captain Cannon then turns, looks back at Joshua, holding his fists in the air. Captain Cannon talks in the speaking tube. He then reaches up and pulls a ring attached to one of several rope-cords, causing the boat's large bell to ring.

Black columns of smoke and red embers begin pouring out of the Lee's black shining smokestacks, as steam hisses from the escape pipes.

Captain Cannon then pulls another ring blowing the Lee's whistles, then he pulls the lever on the 'engine order telegraph', backwards, and as he does that, the Lee comes alive. The paddle wheels churn the water, backing the Lee out of the mud, straightening itself against the tension on the bow tie-lines, then becoming perpendicular to the embankment.

Captain Cannon then pulls the ring causing the Lee's whistles to blow, and at the same time, Joshua's fist comes down, and the deckhands follow with their axes, cutting the bow tie lines.

The Lee begins backing into the Mississippi River, as several roustabouts and crew begin singing, *Amazing Grace*.

Moments later, on the Robert E. Lee, forward of the Texas Patio, the sun is low in the sky. Joshua is pointing out parts of the boat to Mary from the patio area. The Lee backs into the middle of the river with the roustabouts and crew still singing, *Amazing Grace*, below them, as Joshua says, "As I told ya, normally we sleep de top guests on de Hurricane Deck below us, de Boiler Deck is de Crew Deck where your quarters are, forward of ya is where the livestock and the poor people stay when they come on board in New Orleans. Come, follow me."

Mary is taking all this in, as she follows Joshua. When they arrive on the deck, Joshua points, and says, "Here is the Texas Deck, officers and the Captain sleep here in cabins, then where ya were, up there, de wheelhouse where de Captain steers de boat."

Crewmembers, and officers stare at Mary walking past them. As they continue walking towards the stern, Mary looks at Joshua, and says, "Joshua, can I send a letter?"

"Ya, at Cairo, tomorrow, our second stop."

When they reach the stern, they watch Herman hoisting the American flag on the flagstaff, with Mr. Willis saluting.

The Lee's whistles sound. The paddlewheels slow to a stop, then the whistles sound again, and the wheels begin turning and propelling the boat forward. The Robert E. Lee is now steaming down the Mississippi River. Mary walks to the railing with the sun at her back, and looks out at the massive river and at the far riverbank in the direction she came from.

THE ROBERT E. LEE
Drawing by Samuel Ward Stanton (1870 - 1912)

Later that night on the Robert E. Lee, in Mary's small quarters, the sounds of the Lee echo inside. A lit lantern hangs above Mary's head, slightly swaying from side to side, highlighting a calendar on the wall with the passed days, marked with an X. The swaying lantern also cast a shadowy light on her letter, as she is reading it to herself.

9 April, 1866
Dear Billyboy,
Got work on a steamboat in Saint Louis, the Robert E. Lee on the Mississippi River. I'm head chambermaid. Look at the geography book I left you to see where I am. Going to New Orleans, will write then.

Then Mary begins speaking softly, as she writes the last part of her letter,

Tell all and Martha I'm fine, I said hello. Miss ya.

Mary then signs and folds the letter, and puts it in an envelope. She then marks an X on the ninth on the calendar. She turns, and picks up the mended uniform off her bed, looking at it with approval. She then lays it on the back of a chair, raises the glass of the lantern, and blows out the flame.

The next day on the Lee, in Captain Cannon's cabin, Mary, wearing her mended uniform, is finishing the Captain's bed when the Lee's whistles sound. She hurries, tucking in the corners, and then rushes out the cabin doorway. She closes the door and runs down the stairs. As she passes a chambermaid in the stairwell, she looks back at her, and says, "Elisabeth, make sure ya clean the brass real good in the Captain's cabin."

Elisabeth acknowledges Mary with a nod of her head. Mary hurries down the stairwell, past the Hurricane Deck. She passes the crew and guests. When she reaches the Boiler Deck, she sees Joshua walking from around stacks of firewood, which are neatly stacked alongside the boiler-room. Joshua, not wearing his shirt, is very sweaty, causing his dark muscular skin to glisten in the sun. He walks towards a man, standing on the portside of the boat chewing tobacco.

As the Lee nears Cairo, Mary hurries towards Joshua pulling the envelope from her apron, and shouts out, "Joshua".

Joshua is speaking with the man, when Mary approaches and stops near them, Mary hears Joshua saying, "...Ten cords pine knot wood we got last night Mr. Willis."

Looking at the woodpile, Mr. Willis says, "Good class two wood Joshua...should get us a third of the way. Soon as the guests board, prepare to depart right away."

"Yes Mr. Willis," says Joshua. He then turns and looks at Mary, and says, "Good mornin' Mary. Please come here." Mary walks over to Joshua, as Joshua says, "Mr. Willis this is Mary, de head chambermaid. Mary, this is Mr. Willis, de Pilot of de Lee."

Mr. Willis is also taken aback by Mary's size. Looking her up and down, he says, "Head chambermaid...Big chambermaid!"

Mary takes in the humor, and smiles a little, when something in the water catches her attention, causing her to look over the side of the boat. She points at the object with concern, saying, "Look, Joshua, tis a big log in the water?" Then a little panicked, she says, "We gonna hit it!" All of a sudden, the big log splashes away quickly, splashing water on everyone, and causing Mary to step back, her eyes wide open, saying, "Jumping Jehoshaphat...what was that?!"

Joshua grabs his knees, and starts laughing, saying, "That there Mary...was a nine foot gator."

"No it wasn't, ten foot," says Mr. Willis.

"Is that what that was? Seen pictures of 'em, never seen a live one before," says Mary.

The Lee's whistles sound. Everyone looks at the wheelhouse, at Captain Cannon, sounding the whistles again. They then look at the Hamlet of Cairo, situated between thick river foliage, and to the several guests, standing on the riverbank. Mr. Willis looks at Mary, and says, "Welcome aboard the Lee, Mary...ya make sure thin's are right, and the other chambermaids do their work."

"Mr. Willis, I can tell ya, the Lee will be well taken care of," says Mary.

A couple of hours later, The Robert E. Lee, in its maiden voyage, is steaming towards New Orleans, on its nearly three week trip. It stops in many ports, as Mary is kept busy, every day by her duties, cleaning the Captain's cabin, changing the water, making the bed, as well as sweeping the corridor outside the cabin, and supervising the other chambermaids.

On some nights, Mary stands near the stern of the Lee mostly by herself, smoking her own rolled cigars. She looks at the stars and the natural scenes before her, from partial moonlit nights, to total non-moon nights, causing total blackness, with a blanket of stars before her.

Several days later, Mary is watching a chambermaid making an officer's bed. An hour later, she enters the Game Room, watching other chambermaids doing their work. Mary shows one chambermaid where to dust around a craps table.

That night, Mary is in her quarters, reading a book by candlelight, and smoking her cigar.

A week later, Mary is watching Joshua work on the Roulette-Wheel, then, when he finishes, she begins cleaning the brass.

One day out from New Orleans, Mary is walking around the Lee, inspecting her chambermaids' work. That night, on the Lee, in her quarters, a smoky haze hangs in the air. She sits on her bed, taking a swallow from a whiskey bottle, corking it, and then, putting it on the floor. She picks up a hand rolled cigar, taking a puff, and blowing the smoke out her window. She looks out the window for a moment, and then begins singing softly to herself, *"Swing low, sweet chariot; Comin' for to carry me home; Swing low, sweet chariot; Comin' for to carry me home."* She stops singing, and picks up a letter, holding it under the lantern, its light, illuminating the letter, and also the calendar on the wall with an X marked through the 1st of May, 1866.

Mary then begins to speak the last part of her letter she wrote,

> *"...and the boat stops in different places, picking up rich guests. The Captain and crew treat me real good. Will be in New Orleans tomorrow..."*

There's a knock on the door, Mary says, "Yes, who is it?"

"Mary, it's Joshua, a tray of food spilled in the game room."

"Okay, be right there." Mary quickly puts out the cigar, then lays the letter down, ties her boots, stands, and opens the door. Finally, she blows the flame out in her lantern, then closing the door behind her. She walks to the door next to her quarters with the word, 'Chambermaids', carved in the wood-placard, hanging on the door. She stops, and knocks on the door, and shouts softly, "Elisabeth...come to the game-room...food spilled."

Moments later, in the Lee's game room, Mary and several chambermaids walk into the cigar smoke filled room. They look at the hundred or so high-stakes, top hat gamblers pushing their luck on a roulette wheel, playing Monte Carlo, craps and many poker games, while riverboat showgirls mingle about entertaining the gamblers.

Joshua waves his hand at Mary in the middle of the room. She sees him and begins working her way through the crowded room towards him, with the chambermaids following, carrying a broom, mop and bucket.

When Mary reaches Joshua, he points to the food mess in front of him. The chambermaids begin picking up the dropped food immediately, and cleaning the carpet. Mary looks around the room, at the excitement, then she looks at Joshua, saying, "This my first time in here when the room is open. These people look happy, Joshua...but, they seem to be losin' their money."

"Mary, these people have lots of money to lose...that's why they here," says Joshua.

Mary looks at the chambermaids cleaning the carpet, but then still astonished by the excitement before her, she looks up, and surveys the room more thoroughly. The shouting at the craps table attracts her attention, causing her to look over at the table, to people shouting their numbers. She then looks at the poker tables and the crowds that surround them. She notices a man who seems to be sneaking his hand into a gentleman's pocket close to him. The man pulls a wallet out of the man's pocket and begins to put it in his, when a large Negro hand comes out of nowhere, and grabs his forearm, stopping him.

The pickpocket turns, and is surprised. He looks at Mary standing to the side of him, tightly holding onto his arm, with his hand holding the wallet. The pickpocket is as tall as Mary, and believes he has an advantage and try's to jerk his arm away. However, Mary has a firm grip, and this causes the man to yell, "NIGGER! Let me go...NIGGER!"

The loud outburst causes the room to go quiet, instantly. So quiet you could hear a pin drop, except for the sounds of the Lee.

Joshua looks at Mary, and then to the pickpocket, shouting, "Leave de lady alone!"

Joshua starts towards Mary when four well-dressed men grab him by the arms, stopping him in his tracks. One of the well-dressed men, looks at Joshua, saying, "Where ya goin'...NIGGER BOY!" Joshua struggles, saying, "Let...me go...let me go, let me go!" As the gamblers take hold of

Joshua, the chambermaids that came with Mary, are now cowering in the corner.

The man who's wallet the pickpocket took, looks at Mary, then at the pickpocket holding his wallet saying, "Hey, that's my wallet."

The pickpocket looks at the man, saying, "The Nigger was tryin' to take your wallet."

"Then why do 'you' have my wallet in your hand...and she has your arm, 'sir'?"

The pickpocket looks at Mary, and shouts, "Let me go ya...DAMN FILTHY NIGGER!" The pickpocket struggles against her strength.

Mary looks at the man the wallet belongs to, saying, "He's lyin' to ya." Indicating with her head to the pickpocket, she then says, "He took ya wallet."

All of a sudden, the pickpocket drops the wallet, and throws a left hook at Mary. She turns right and ducks it, letting go of his other arm, and standing back upright. She then looks him straight in his eyes, and says, "Only one man hit me, and he was the last!" The gamblers begin quickly backing up to the walls of the game room, giving room to the pickpocket, and Mary. The pickpocket swings again. She moves out of the way, angrily, saying, "Oh...ya want'a play, huh'. Come on!!!" She backs up with a slight smile, and puts up her fists.

"Stop this...she's a woman!" shouts Joshua.

Not taking her eyes off the pickpocket, Mary says, "I'm alright Joshua...few lessons gonna be taught here!"

Mary and the pickpocket begin to circle, eyeing each other. The room begins to hum with talk. Then the murmur builds in excitement. The room begins taking bets. One of the well-dressed man holding Joshua, shouts, "I put two-hundred on the gentleman against the house."

A riverboat gambler shouts, "Five-hundred on the gentleman against the house!"

Joshua is still struggling against the other gamblers to rescue Mary.

Another gentleman gambler takes off his top hat and uses it as a collection pot, taking the feverish bets.

Mary and the pickpocket maneuver in a circle. She quickly looks at the betting in the room, then looks back to the pickpocket, saying, "Looks like they gonna lose their money mister."

"'NIGGER'," says the pickpocket. He takes two swings, a left and right. Both miss, as Mary ducks each one. The entire room now encircles them cheering on the pickpocket, including the man who had his wallet stolen. The pickpocket looks at Mary, and says, "Who ya 'NIGGERS' think ya are anyways! Ya think cause of the war, ya free!" He takes another swing at her.

Mary leans backwards, he misses her, as she says, "We Negro people are 'free', I'm 'free', that's 'who' I think I am!"

"The 'hell' ya are, ya 'NIGGER' bitch!" shouts the pickpocket. He swings again at Mary, and misses, just as she throws an uppercut, catching the pickpocket squarely on the jaw, causing the whole room to go silent. He falls back like a giant pine tree, cut at the base.

Just then, Captain Cannon opens the door and walks in with four security crewmembers, with clubs in hand. He looks at the crowd that's gathered into a large circle, and then he looks at the gamblers holding Joshua. When the gamblers see the Captain looking at them, they immediately let Joshua go, he then rushes to Mary's side. The man with the top hat full of money, walks over to Captain Cannon, handing him the hat.

Captain Cannon looks at the hat in his hand, nods his head, then, walks towards the large circle that parts open for him with the security crewmembers following. He stops and looks down at the pickpocket out on the floor. He then looks at Mary, who is beginning to relax her fists at her side, looking for more challengers around her, as the Captain says, "Well...what do we have here?"

The crowd slowly begins to dissipate, going back to their business of gambling. Joshua standing next to Mary, points to the pickpocket, then looks at Captain Cannon, saying, "Ah Captain...de man is a thief, Mary caught him, he assaulted her...she defended herself. The room took bets on the pickpocket, but Mary won."

Captain Cannon looks at the top hat in his hands, then back at the pickpocket being helped to his feet by a gambler, and crewmember. He then says, "Take him to the Brig."

Two of the security crewmembers take the pickpocket away by his arms.

Captain Cannon looks at the pickpocket, and says, "By the looks of it..." He then turns and looks at her, saying, "Mary, ya defended yourself, 'quite well'!"

Mary smiles a little at Captain Cannon.

Still smiling at Mary, Captain Cannon, says, "Mary, you have a job with the Lee, as long as you want."

Mary very elated, quickly goes and hugs the Captain, picking him up off his feet, saying, "Thank ya Captain Cannon."

Smiling, and barely holding on to the hat, Captain Cannon, says, "Mary, please put me down." Mary lowers the Captain back on his feet. Some of the gamblers are still looking at them. Captain Cannon looks at the room of gamblers, and says, "Everyone, please go back to your business." He then walks towards the exit with the top hat in hand, looking around the game room, with the other security crewmembers following him out the door.

Mary turns, and looks at the other chambermaids walking towards them, as she and Joshua walk towards the exit door. The chambermaids are excited, and smiling at each other. They hurriedly walk towards Mary. As they catch up to her, they discreetly congratulate her, walking through the exit door of the game room.

Moments later, Joshua and Mary are standing at the port rail, with the wind in their faces. Joshua turns to Mary, and says, "I guess ya cleaned up pretty good." Both have a good laugh. He then smiles at Mary, taking his forefinger under her chin, he moves closer, kissing her on the cheek.

Mary smiles, and looks at Joshua, and says, "Ah, ya shouldn't of done that...but thank ya Joshua."

"I just felt like it Mary. Where ya learn to fight like that, Mary?" says Joshua.

"After my mom died, the field Negroes took care of me, even though I was in the Great House. At night, I would leave the Great House, and visit the slaves in their quarters. There, they taught me everythin' I know...the Civil War taught me more."

The next day on the Main Deck of the Robert E. Lee, docked in New Orleans. The taste of New Orleans is in the air, from the numerous open-air food venders. Banjos, singing, and cries of chants of 'call in response' are also heard, while the sounds of whistles and bells, are echoing along the docks, which come from the numerous steamboats.

Dozens of roustabouts are leading goats, cows and horses onto the gangplanks, leading to the Lee, while others carry crates of chickens and cargo on their backs. Mary is standing near the side of a gangplank, holding a letter between her fingers, and reading another.

Joshua runs up the plank giving orders to roustabouts rolling barrels off the plank onto the deck, saying, "...load those five on de starboard-side, just forward of de boiler room." He then walks over to Mary saying, "I see ya got some letters..."

"Oh, hi Joshua. Yes, was hopin' to get one, but I got two letters. One from the plantation...they say they have to leave cause the family has to sell for taxes." Then, Mary becomes very happy, as she looks at the other letter she was reading, and says, "This one is from my old friend MaryJo, well, her name isn't MaryJo anymore, it's Sister Annunciation. She's a Catholic nun, and her sister is going to be one too..."

"Joshua," shouts Captain Cannon from the wheelhouse. Both Joshua and Mary look up to the wheelhouse, and see the Captain and Mr. Willis looking at them, as the Captain, shouts, "Joshua as soon as the cargo and live stock is loaded and secured, passengers are aboard, have Mr. McDermick holler on the tube so we can prepare to shove off."

"Yes, Captain, aye, aye," says Joshua. He then looks at Mary, and says, "That man ya knocked out in de game room...he wasn't a passenger, he was a stowaway, came on at Cairo." He then looks at New Orleans, and says, "He's in jail now. He still don't know what hit him." They both laugh.

Roustabouts are hurrying, finishing their tasks, as Mary looks out at the docks, to a train stopping in front of one of the warehouses in the distance. She then looks at the wagons coming and going, then to New Orleans, it's buildings and tall church steeples, as she says, "Jesus, Joshua, this is bigger than Saint Louis."

"This is my home now...gets bigger every year."

"Joshua, ya never told me about ya."

"Not much to tell. Escape de plantation in Tennessee, went to St. Louis, heard it's free, like New Orleans...came here, been here ever since, workin' on de river."

Mary then looks at the cargo on the docks and points, saying, "Joshua, that be cotton and tobacco tied up there...what's all those barrels and sacks?"

"Molasses, cider and whiskey are in de barrels...beans, sugar, rice and flour are in de sacks. All this is goin' to all parts of de world." Then he looks at the Lee, and says, "De cargo ya see on de boat, we take de supplies, drop it off at towns along de way back to Saint Louis. That's how de Lee makes money, gettin' de cargo, supplies and passengers, up and down de river fast. De Lee is de fastest boat on de river."

A roustabout shouts to Joshua, "De las' sack', de las' sack Joshua."

Joshua looks at the roustabout foreman, and a roustabout carrying the last cargo sack onto the Lee. He then, looks around the boat, and shouts, "Launch stage! Launch stage! Get de passengers aboard, and guests off. Launch stage!"

The deckhands begin bringing rich passengers aboard, carrying their luggage, while the poor passengers have to carry their own. Joshua smiles and bows his head to Mary, and then walks towards the boiler room.

In New Orleans, four years later, 1870, late spring. New buildings add to the river front skyline. The Robert E. Lee is tied to the dock, where there are twice as many steamboats blowing their whistles, and clanging their bells, as there was before. Banjos and organs are playing their tunes, with people singing along the expanded docks. It's a sea of organized chaos, as hawkers sale their goods.

Herman is running along the docks carrying a piece of paper in his hand. As he nears the Lee, he begins shouting, "Captain...Captain, Captain!" When he reaches the Lee's gangplank, he runs up the plank to the Main Deck still shouting, "Captain, Captain Cannon, Captain Cannon!"

Most crewmembers begin to appear, looking out the Lee's windows, and hurrying out of the doors, Mr. Willis, deckhands, Joshua, roustabouts, engineers, Mr. McDermick, cooks, cabin boys, chambermaids and Mary. Some stick their heads out of windows, while others alert their mates, then rush to the railings above, looking at Herman below, still shouting, "Captain Cannon...Cap..."

"What's so urgent, Herman?" shouts Captain Cannon from above.

Herman looks up, slightly out of breath and sees Captain Cannon standing on top of the Hurricane roof with several officers. Herman announces, "Captain...Captain Leathers of the Natchez...just beat the river record, from Orleans to Louis...three days...twenty-one hours, fifty-eight minutes." Herman holds up the message. The crew look at one another, and begin to talk among themselves.

Captain Cannon ponders a few moments then looks at Herman, and shouts, "...Herman, telegraph Captain Leathers in Saint Louis. Tell him...the Robert E. Lee challenges him to a race."

As more crewmembers join the gathering, Mary, Joshua and now all members begin cheering, and some, throwing their hats into the air.

Later in Saint Louis, at the Harbor docks, in the steamboat Natchez' wheelhouse, Captain Leathers, wearing a black suit, lace-frilled, puff-blossom shirt, is looking out the side window and down at the Natchez clerk. The clerk is standing among mostly 'white' Natchez crew, with the Negro fire-stokers looking like they just came out of a coalmine, as Captain Leathers says, "Send the message...the Natchez accepts."

The entire crew erupts into cheer, including the stokers, as the Natchez clerk runs off with the message.

A month later, in New Orleans, it's race day. There are numerous gala flags and banners announcing the race, waving in the smoke filled air, strung from numerous buildings. The food smells of New Orleans, and the music, radiates out from all points.

Ten thousand people have come to New Orleans, lining the docks, sitting or standing on boats, barges, riverbanks, porches, rooftops of houses and buildings, trying to get the best sight of the extravaganza.

Men are playing banjos walking along the docks, as hawkers sell their wares, wood-pit cooked meat, cakes, pies, gumbo, everything of the southern delight of New Orleans, are being sold.

All types of bets are being made. Two bettors go round and round, as the Wager says, "I wage ya nine to seven, the Lee makes Vicksburg run in twenty-four hours sir."

The Bettor says, "I'll bet ya ten to seven the Natchez makes Baton Rouge in nine hours..."

A Negro newspaper boy walks through the chaos, shouting the front headlines, "Read all about it! Today, thirtieth, June, eighteen-seventy, de Robert E. Lee races de Natchez on de Mississippi River! Bets are being made in Europe! Read all about..."

"Newspaper! Newspaper!" shouts Mary interrupting the boy.

The newspaper boy looks at Mary holding a hand-rolled cigar standing on the Main Deck of the Lee, as he says, "Ya a big lady." And with even more surprise, he looks at the cigar between her fingers, and says, "...Ya smoke cigars?"

"Never mind, been smokin' cigars long time, before ya born, give me a paper." Mary tosses a coin to the boy. He catches the coin, he walks up to the Lee and hands Mary the paper.

"Sorry lady, didn't mean disrespect," says the newspaper boy.

Mary smiles and winks at the boy, as she says, "That's ok...you're not the first, and won't be the last."

Mary turns, and looks to the shirtless, sweaty roustabouts, Joshua and the deckhands, feverishly working, chanting, their 'call in response', stripping the Lee of most the outside wood panels, and building a 'V' shape structure at the bow.

Other deckhands are bringing aboard cords and cords of fire wood, stacking them neatly in uniform columns around the front, while shirt wearing crew members bring aboard sides of beef, bacon, crates of chickens and boxes marked champagne.

Moments later, on the Robert E. Lee, in the boiler room, Captain Cannon, Herman, Mr. Willis, and Mr. McDermick, are talking in front of the eight boilers, as Mr. Willis says, "We almost finished strippin' her Captain, and the wind screen built."

"Good, less wind resistance and weight. We goin' to need it," says Mr. McDermick, as he looks at Captain Cannon, and says, "That Natchez is barely a year old..." Then he looks at the Lee with passion, and says, "We four years old Captain...we've had a lot of hard fast runs over the years."

"Don't worry Mr. McDermick, you just stay on those valves, she'll hold together." says Captain Cannon.

"Aye, aye Captain."

Joshua walks in the boiler room and looks at everyone, then looks at Captain Cannon, and says, "Captain, she about ready. Fuel and food stores about loaded, our special guests are waitin' on de dock." Then he looks at Captain Cannon with a puzzled look, and says, "Captain...I don't understand...the Natchez is down de way...they not gettin' ready for de race."

"Captain Leathers must believe the Natchez is much faster than the Lee, Joshua." Captain Cannon then brings a piece of paper out from his jacket, then looks at Herman with urgency, saying, "Herman, I want you to take this to the telegraph office, get it off right away."

Herman takes the message and leaves. Mr. Willis looks at Captain Cannon, and says, "Captain, according to my calculations, we'll have to make several stops to re-fuel, first at Vicksburg, then Greenville..."

"I just made arrangements for all that Mr. Willis." Then he looks to everyone and says, "Prepare to launch."

Moments later, in the Natchez wheelhouse, Captain Leathers looks down at the last passenger and cargo being brought aboard. He looks at his clerk, and says, "Jared, let's get the cargo and passengers on fast." He then looks at the Lee, and says, "Looks like the Lee is almost ready."

"Captain, the Lee lightenin' their load, not takin' on a manifest of cargo or many passengers."

"Don't worry Jared, the Lee is a wood burner, she's old. We are new technology...coal, we won't have to stop for fuel as..." Captain Leathers hears a whistle, causing him to look up, and sees Captain Cannon in the wheelhouse pulling the Lee's rope whistles.

On the Main Deck of the Robert E. Lee, the Lee's whistles blow again. Mary and the Lee's crew who are not working, assemble at the railings along with the passengers. Joshua is standing on the bow, looking at Captain Cannon in the wheelhouse behind the helm.

Black columns of smoke and red embers pour out of the Lee's smoke stacks, as steam pours from the escape pipes. Steamboats' bells and whistles begin to sound along the river, as church bells begin to ring around New Orleans.

Captain Cannon pulls the rope-cord, again, ringing the bell, and then pulls the lever back on the engine order telegraph. The Lee's paddlewheels begin to turn slowly, straightening the Lee against the bow tie lines, as Captain Cannon shouts, "Stand-by."

"Launch stage, prepare to launch," shouts Joshua. He raises his arms in the air, with his fists clenched. Captain Cannon reaches for the whistle rope-cord, pulling the cord, blowing the whistles. Joshua's arms come down, and the bow tie lines are cut. The Lee begins backing into the

Mississippi River. All crew and passengers begin to cheer, as hats and handkerchiefs wave in the air.

Mary watches a deckhand roll a small cannon towards the bow. She follows the cannon with a curious excited expression till it reaches Joshua. She stops with the cannon, and looks at Joshua, saying, "What's that for?" Then more excited, "Who we gettin' ready to shoot?"

Joshua laughs, and says, "…We are not gonna shoot anybody Mary. It's to signal de Lee's start of de race at Saint Mary's Market over there…" Joshua points, and then says, "The Natchez has to do de same."

"That's funny…Mary like my name."

Joshua smiles, and says, "Ya can say that."

Mary smiles at Joshua. She and Joshua then look out at the thousands and thousands of well-wishers, standing on everything and anything possible trying to get the best vantage point along the docks, as New Orleans cheers them on.

Captain Cannon pulls the whistle's ring, then pushes the engine order telegraph handle back upright, stopping the Lee's paddlewheels in mid river. Then he pushes the handle forward and the paddlewheels dig into the current, thrusting the Lee forward. He then pulls the ring blowing the Lee's whistles.

On the docks of New Orleans, and the Mississippi River, the sea of humanity is exuberant. The Lee proceeds up river, blowing its whistles. Then the Natchez's whistles begin to blow. This causes the crowd to cheer with more jubilation, as a brass band plays, *Hail Columbia*.

Black columns of smoke and red embers pour out of the Natchez's red smoke stacks, as its bow tie-lines are cut. The Natchez begins backing into the Mississippi River, and as it reaches the middle of the river, the Natchez's whistles blow again, and the paddlewheels stop. Several moments pass, as the Natchez now begins to drift backwards, with the current towards the sea.

The Natchez spectators quiet their cheers. They look on with anxiety on their faces, towards the bets they have made. Then, steam bursts from the Natchez escape pipes. The paddlewheels begin propelling the Natchez forward, as the Robert E. Lee's cannon fires.

At Saint Mary's Market, the Lee spectators cheer. Black smoke now replaces where the Lee was. The Bettor and Wager look at their pocket time pieces, with the Bettor, saying, "Five oh three." They both then look to the Natchez steaming its way up river after the Lee, and when the Natchez passes the start line, it fires its cannon, as the Wager looks to his time piece, and says, "Five oh six."

Crowds line the Mississippi River banks on both sides, as far as the eye can see, cheering on the Lee, and now the Natchez.

Moments later, on the Lee's Main Deck, the wind blows in Mary's and Joshua's faces from the Lee's momentum. They look at the hundreds and hundreds of spectators on both sides of the river, on horseback, wagons, horse driven buggies, and on foot, chasing after the Lee along both sides of the levees.

Mary looks at the spectacle. She then looks at the boiler room where Mr. McDermick is heard shouting, "...Aye, aye Captain, one-twenty she is...keep her stoked laddies!"

Mary then looks at Joshua, pushing the cannon back towards the boiler room. She begins walking with him, saying, "I never seen the such, Joshua, ya told me there be a lot of people, I didn't think this many, all the yellin' and excitement."

"This a big race Mary...de winner get de 'horns'."

Mary with a look, says, "Horns...no money?!" Then she puts her hands on her hips, and with a comical, quizzical expression, she says, "...What kind of 'horns' they get?"

"Deer...it tells that ya are de fastest on de river. De Captains put them under de wheelhouse so people see 'em," says Joshua. He then points to the wheelhouse, then says, "There...when people see 'em, they want to pay ya to ship their cargo and to get 'em from here to there, fast. De Captain has had them since de Lee was new."

Mary excited, looks at Joshua, saying, "Speakin' of from here to there, let's see where the Natchez is. Hurry up, put that thin' away." She rushes to the side railing, looking back down river. Joshua pushes the cannon into a hollow, securing it, as hot sweaty stokers rush by him with wood logs, cradled in their arms, rushing into the boiler room. Joshua finishes securing the cannon, and then walks towards Mary. She looks back at him excited, saying, "Josh look, they way back there."

Joshua looks, then says, "Ya...this is Carrollton Bend, the Captain opens her up here." The Lee's whistles blow, and the steamboat picks up speed, as Mary and Joshua look back to the Natchez.

Later that night. The Lee paddles its way north at half speed to St. Louis, with red embers coming out of the Lee's smoke stacks. Bonfires light up part of the levees in the half-moonlit night, as sporadic cheers echo from the human ghostlike figures on the riverbanks.

Guests and crew walk by torch lit baskets, lining the decks, hanging on the outside bulkhead of the Lee. Mary is walking down the front staircase, wiping her hands on her apron. She looks at Joshua on the port side, and says, "Do ya see 'em?!"

Joshua looks at Mary, and says, "No...not even their embers."

Mary walks over to Joshua, standing in front of him, and looks back to the stern looking for the Natchez, saying, "This is not a race Joshua…we beatin' the hell out of 'em."

They both chuckle. Joshua then looks at Mary with a 'passionate expression', and says, "Mary…ya ever thought of gettin' married?"

Surprised, Mary says, "…Are ya crazy Joshua…'naw'…haven't given it any thought, ever…like bein' single, free like a bird. Been a 'slave' all my young life, I want to be free Joshua…if I didn't…" She looks at Joshua with a passionate smile, and says, "Ya be the 'first' Joshua." Mary smiles and walks up to Joshua, and kisses him on the cheek.

A loud hissing sound echoes from the boiler room, followed by a painful scream. The Lee begins to slow down.

Joshua and Mary rush to the boiler room.

In the Lee's boiler room, the temperature is two times hotter than outside, as steam escapes from a pipe above Mr. McDermick. He is rolling around on the deck, in pain, being attended to by a stoker, as other sweaty dark bodies look at them. Several engineers work feverishly turning valves and pulling levers, as Mr. McDermick cries out in pain, saying, "…shut down…the boiler…shut it down…" Joshua and Mary come running in, and stopping. Joshua looks at the situation, as Mary looks at Mr. McDermick, and goes to give him aid. At the same time, Joshua knowing what to do, has gone to work on a valve, turning it, venting the steam, stopping the steam from turning the paddlewheels.

The listening tube vibrates from Captain Cannon's voice, saying, "What's going on down there, why we stopping?!"

Joshua hurries to the speaking tube with urgency, saying, "Captain, steam-pipe burst!"

"Where's Mr. McDermick!" shouts Captain Cannon.

"He got burnt' Captain…he's in a bad way," says Joshua.

The engine order telegraph goes from full, to stop, in front of Mary, ringing. She stands-up, stepping back, a little shocked, looking at the unit, saying, "What the blazes. I'll never get used to seein' thins' move, without seein' someone movin' 'em."

"How's Mr. McDermick?" says Joshua.

Captain Cannon rushes in and looks at Mary standing above Mr. McDermick, laying on the deck, moaning, as he says, "How bad is he?"

"Badly scalded Captain…his skin is comin' off," says Mary.

"Mary, do you think he'll be okay until we reach St. Louis?" says Captain Cannon.

Mr. McDermick moans in pain, as Mary looks outside at the approaching riverbank, and says, "I'll need river mud Captain, it'll soothe his flesh till we make St. Louis. Not much out here anyways."

A deckhand outside the boiler room, shouts, "Stand by, we're going to hit!" The Lee softly hits the mud bank, causing everyone to lean forward. Captain Cannon then looks at the crowd of passengers and crew gathered at the boiler room door. He looks at an officer, and says, "Clear the people back...get a deckhand, get some mud from the bank...there are 'gators' out there, tell 'em to be careful!"

The officer acknowledges the Captain. Mary sees Elisabeth peering in at the situation, and says, "Elisabeth, come help."

Elisabeth pushes her way through the crowd, and rushes to Mary's side, and at the same time, the officer begins clearing the people back. Captain Cannon looks at Joshua, and says, "You know her better than the others Joshua...how long before we can have pressure?"

Joshua looks at the pipe, wipes his forehead, and chin with his hands, and then says, "Got to cool down first Captain, about thirty minutes."

"Hurry Joshua...the Natchez is about thirty minutes behind us."

Thirty minutes later, in the wheelhouse of the Robert E. Lee, Captain Cannon sticks his head out the side window, looking at the smoke stacks of the Lee, with very few red embers flying out. He then looks down river and sees the Natchez torch baskets, coming upriver towards them. Captain Cannon rushes to the speaking tube with urgency, shouting, "Joshua! How much longer?"

In the Lee's boiler room, steam is starting to hiss, from escape valves. Engineers are feverishly turning valves, while stokers are stoking the eight furnaces.

Sweat drips from Joshua's brow. He rushes to the speaking tube, while looking at the steam gauge, and says, "She about there Captain, eighty pounds!"

The Lee's whistles blow, as Captain Cannon's voice radiates through the tube, saying, "Joshua, shove-off! The Natchez is several miles back!"

"Aye, aye Captain," says Joshua shouting through the tube. He then rushes out of the boiler room door.

In the Natchez wheelhouse, the pilot is at the helm. Captain Leathers is next to him, looking through his scope, through the half-moonlit night. He spots the torch lit Lee, and immediately goes to his speaking tube, and shouts, "She's stopped. The Lee is stopped!" He then goes to the engine order telegraph, and moves the lever from, one quarter, to three quarters ahead. He goes to the front window, and shouts, "Look outs, keep an eye open for anythin' in the water. We're goin' to overtake and pass him!" Captain Leathers then reaches up, and pulls the whistle ring.

On the Lee, Joshua is standing at the rail looking at the Natchez blowing its whistles, steaming up river fast. He then turns to the deckhands who are holding long poles, and with urgency, Joshua shouts out, "Alright gentlemen, shove 'em in, let's go." And in a 'call in response', Joshua says, "I don't know what ya told, ya mommas ain't here, shove 'em in, let's go!"

The deckhands are straining to push the Lee off the mud-bank, as Joshua shouts the chant, "I don't know what ya told, ya mommas ain't here, shove 'em in, let's go!" All the deckhands join in the chant, "I don't know what ya told, ya mommas ain't here, shove 'em in, let's go!" They strain against the mud hold onto the bow of the Lee, as Joshua shouts, "I don't know what ya told, ya mommas ain't here, shove 'em in, let's go!" Joshua looks, and sees the Lee breaking free of its mud hold, as he then shouts, "I don't know what ya told, ya mommas here, and she's on de go!" Joshua then looks at a roustabout, and says, "Johnny. Take over, got to see to de boiler!"

Johnny acknowledges Joshua, as Joshua runs back to the boiler room, while Johnny, using the 'call in response,' shouts, "I don't know what ya told, ya mommas here, and she's on de go." In unison with their poles, hand over hand, they continue pushing the Lee from the mud bank with their poles towards the middle of the river.

In the Lee's boiler room, steam is hissing from different points in the boiler plumbing. Joshua hurries to the steam gauge, and looks at the dial, then blows in the speaking tube, shouting, "One hundred Captain and buildin'!"

The engine order telegraph rings, and moves to slow ahead. Joshua matches the order, and hurries to a large lever coming from several pipes, and pushes the lever forward several degrees.

The Robert E. Lee comes alive again, moving forward. The engine order telegraph moves from slow ahead, to full ahead. Joshua looks to the engine order telegraph, then rushes to the speaking tube, blows in the tube, and shouts, "Captain, we'll lose pressure too fast if we go full."

In the wheelhouse of the Lee, Captain Cannon is looking at the Natchez's torch baskets and red embers coming from her smoke stacks, headed at them. He goes to the speaking tube, shouting, "The Natchez has almost caught us!"

"Aye, aye Captain. Full she is," says Joshua. The side of the engine order telegraph, rings, and goes to full ahead. Captain Cannon looks out the front window, and shouts, "Lookouts...watch for obstacles."

In the Lee's boiler room, the furnaces are coming to life, as fire stokers feed the boilers their logs. Joshua is looking at the steam gauge, and then goes to the speaking tube, blows in the tube, and shouts, "Captain, one-hundred and twenty pounds." Log after log is thrown in the boiler. Mr. Willis is standing in the doorway and looks at Joshua, saying, "Josh, you got a minute?"

Joshua, nods his head. He looks at one of the engineers, and says, "Keep an eye on the gauge, one-twenty, no more." Joshua walks out of the boiler room, as stokers pass him with fuel wood. Joshua looks to Mr. Willis standing by the railing, looking at the Natchez, almost on their stern, blowing its whistles.

The Robt. (Robert) E. Lee and The Natchez – Circa 1883
Picture by: WM. M Donaldson & Co.

The Lee picks up speed, keeping its distance, and begins pulling away from the Natchez, as Mr. Willis looks at Joshua, and says, "Good job Joshua gettin' us off the riverbank and gettin' the boiler up."

"No problem Mr. Willis...she almost caught us...that was close."

"Joshua," says Mr. Willis. He looks at Joshua with seriousness, and then says, "We'll be out of fuel by late mornin'." Joshua looks at the dwindling fuel wood supply, then looks back at Mr. Willis, saying, "Aren't we stoppin' in Vicksburg in de mornin', and so is de Natchez? Looks like we'll be gettin' fuel at de same time."

"Not really Joshua...the Natchez is a coal burner. That will be their last stop, when we have to stop one more time for fuel wood. Captain has a plan Joshua...come," says Mr. Willis. They both turn, and walk out towards the bow.

The next morning, the Robert E. Lee is entering a long stretch of water, from a bend in the river, with the Natchezs smoke not far behind in the bend. Mary, crewmembers and passengers are standing on the roof of the Hurricane Deck of the Texas Patio. Mary approaches Elisabeth, and says, "Thank ya Elisabeth...tell the cabin boy to check every half-hour, and make sure Annie May don't need nothin' else for Mr. McDermick."

"Yes Miss Mary," says Elisabeth, as she hurries off.

The Robert E. Lee's whistles blow. Mary turns, and looks at Captain Cannon in the wheelhouse blowing the Lee's whistles again, then, she looks back at the Natchez's smoke.

Mary hears another set of whistles in front of her. She turns and sees a steamboat barge fully loaded with fuel wood, from deck, to the top of the roof of the quarters, with only the wheelhouse visible. Black smoke bellows from its smoke stacks, as it builds steam leaving the wood yard, blowing its whistles again.

From the boiler deck below, Mary hears Joshua shouting, "Stand by!" Mary hurries to the railing. She looks down at Joshua standing on the starboard side, with a dozen deckhands. They are holding lashing-ropes, with the other end tied to the Lee's lashing points.

Joshua looks at the fire stokers taking the last of the Lee's fuel wood, then, he looks at the wood yard. However, instead of the Robert E. Lee slowing down, and heading for the wood yard, the Lee heads for the middle of the river, and the portside of the steamboat barge, Pargaud, which is fully loaded with fuel wood.

The Robert E. Lee heads for the Pargaud at full-speed ahead, as both steamboats blow their whistles in some type of steamboat code. The Pargaud deckhands appear along the portside, are also preparing their lashing ropes.

As the Robert E. Lee catches up to the Pargaud, the Lee's whistles blow. The Lee begins slowing, to one-quarter speed, coming along side the Pargaud, becoming parallel with the barge within several feet. Then the Lee's large ship bell rings, as Joshua shouts, "Now!"

In an orchestrated move, the deckhands from both boats jump from one, to the other, carrying their lashing-ropes. Joshua then chants his orders, "Pull 'em tight, make 'em kiss! Pull 'em tight, make 'em kiss."

The deckhands are bracing themselves, with their legs, pressing their feet against the decks. They are pulling with all their might, drawing the two boats together. The deckhands then wrap their lines around hardened structures of the boats, holding the boats in place. In the meantime, a dozen roustabouts are feverishly unloading the wood from the Pargaud, in chain-gang fashion, to the Lee, while they are both underway, near one-quarter speed against the river current.

Mary looks at this feat with amazement, and shouts, "Holy Jesus! Way to go Joshua…way to go, ain't that somethin'!"

In the wheelhouse, Captain Cannon and Herman are looking out the window opening at Captain John W. Tobin of the Pargaud, as Captain Cannon shouts, "I see you got the message Herman sent!"

"Yes, Captain and I got the best, twenty-four cords, class one oak too!" shouts Captain Tobin.

"That should last us! Thanks again, Captain!" shouts Captain Cannon.

In the Natchez wheelhouse, Captain Leathers, with an amazed expression on his face, is looking at the two steamboats through their partial black smoke wafts, steaming side by side, saying "What in the world?"

In the Robert E. Lee wheelhouse, Captain Cannon looks at the last third of the fuel wood being loaded, then, he looks at a bend in the river coming up. He pulls the rope ring, ringing the bell.

On the Main Deck of the Robert E. Lee, Joshua looks upriver to the bend in the river. He then looks at the last third of the fuel wood on the Pargaud, being transferred to the Lee, as he shouts, "Roustabouts, your momma's gettin' close, de door is closin'!"

The Roustabouts speed up their pace, just as the Lee's bell rings twice, and Joshua shouts, "Momma's home!"

Both groups of deckhands unwrap their lashing-ropes, and jump back to their respective boats. The Pargaud slows, pulling off with about one-quarter of the fuel wood still not loaded. The Lee sounds its whistles, and bell. Black ebony smoke, begins pouring out of the Lee's smoke stacks, as the steamboat paddles off towards St. Louis.

In the Natchez wheelhouse Captain Leathers looks at the two boats separating. He pulls back on the engine order telegraph, from full, to slow ahead, as the response rings. He turns the helm towards the fuel yard, looking at the Robert E. Lee, and says, "Holy shit...'damn' northerner!"

Two days later, it's morning on the Robert E. Lee. A thick fog covers the Mississippi River. The Lee slowly makes its way up river. Stokers are nearing the last of the fuel wood. Joshua walks out of the boiler room towards the railing.
Captain Cannon and Herman walk down the staircase to the Boiler Deck with worried expressions on their faces. They see Joshua and walk over to him standing against the railing, looking back into the fog. He hears them approaching, and says, "I don't hear her Captain," says Joshua.
"It don't matter Joshua...be out of fire soon, about ninety-five more miles, they win," says Herman.
"I should of stopped in Memphis. I didn't want to give them an edge," says Captain Cannon.
"Too bad Eagle Bend came up...had to stop loadin' and break loose...would of had enough fuel," says Joshua.
Mary walks down the staircase, and walks over to the group. Captain Cannon looks at her, and says, "How's Mr. McDermick?"
"Doin' better Captain. I'm good at a lot of healin'. I cleaned the burn, removed the dead skin...he'll need that doctor in St. Louis for 'em burns...the mud only make him feel better."
Captain Cannon says, "Well Mary, thank you for taking care of my close friend...looks like he got hurt for nothing."
"Why ya say that Captain?" says Mary.
With a resolved look, he sighs, then, says, "We're running out of fuel, Mary. No more fuel stops between here and St. Louis."
Mary looks at the last of the fuel wood being carried into the boiler room.
The sound of the Natchez's whistles are heard in the distant background. Everyone looks back at the sound. They now have resolved expressions on their faces. Just then, Elisabeth walks down the staircase and over to Mary, and says, "Excuse me, Miss Mary?"
"Yes Elisabeth," says Mary.
"De cook said all that meat gonna waste...none 'em passengers eatin' much. Doin a whole a lot drinkin' and gamblin' though."
Mary thinks for a second, and looks at the Robert E. Lee, then to the boiler room. She smiles and grins, then rolls up her shirtsleeves. She looks at Elisabeth, and says, "Elisabeth...ya watch out for Mr. McDermick...we got some work to do here..." Mary then looks at the

group, and says, "Captain, Joshua, Herman...I have an idea." All quickly gather around Mary.

Later, the Robert E. Lee is now going slow, fighting the river current. On the Lee's Boiler Deck, sounds of breaking wood is heard, along with the sound of the Natchez's whistles in the far background, getting closer in the fog.

Deckhands, roustabouts, officers, cabin boys, Mr. Willis and Herman are tearing apart what remains of the Lee's shell structure, breaking it into pieces.

Rooms and most of the Lee lay open, exposing some passengers. Mary along with other crewmembers, come walking from around the side of the Lee, where the galley is located, carrying knives, and portions of sides of beef, pork, and bacon, as they head toward the boiler room.

Just before Mary reaches the boiler room, she stops and points at the Lee's woodpile, saying, "Bring some of the wood."

Several of the roustabouts grab arms full of wood and follow the line behind Mary towards the boiler room.

In the Robert E. Lee's boiler room, Joshua is looking at the steam gauge. He then goes to the speaking tube, blows, and says, "Eighty and dropping Captain." Mary walks into the room, with a roustabout, carrying a quarter side of beef with meat hooks. She looks at Joshua, and says, "Alright Joshua, we's gonna have us some fun here. We goin' ta win this race...let's get this wood and meat up in the fire and get this boat a cookin'."

Some of the stokers open up the eight doors of the furnaces, showing very little fire within. Mary, stokers and roustabouts begin tossing in the wood, then cutting the meat up, and tossing the chunks into the fire.

"Ya keep an eye on the gauge Joshua, she be risin' any tine," says Mary.

"I hope we don't blow a boiler," says Joshua. He then looks at the steam gauge, and shouts, "She's risin'! Seventy-five, seventy-seven, eighty, eighty-five, ninety." The needle rises, the fire begins to roar in the furnaces. Joshua hurries to the speaking tube.

Later that morning, at the river docks in St. Louis, the fog has lifted from over a larger city. Another ten thousand spectators are gathered for the finish of the race, and for the Fourth of July celebration. They are standing on rooftops, boats, docks, and lining the levees.

Race announcements and Fourth of July banners hang from every building. It's an extravaganza. Piano and accordion music radiates out, from all parts. A spectator, hanging from a boat mast, points, and shouts out, "Here comes somebody."

The entire sea of humanity looks from the spectator, to the south in domino fashion. The spectator shouts again, "...and they're movin'...it's the Lee!" The sea of humanity erupts into cheers, as the Robert E. Lee blows its whistles far down river.

At the same time on the Lee's Main Deck, as the Lee nears the finish line, the Lee's whistles blow, and the bell clangs. Mary and the roustabouts are singing, *Shoo Fly, Don't Bother Me*, sitting on crates while the Lee steams towards the finish line. The Natchez is nowhere in sight.

The seventy-five guests and the Lee's crew are enjoying the singing, while Joshua pushes the Lee's cannon out of the hollow towards the bow, passing a very jubilant Mary and crew.

Mary stops singing, and puts her nose up in the air, smelling the air. She then looks at Joshua pushing the cannon, saying, "Joshua, the Lee gonna to be smellin' mighty good comin' across the finish-line!"

"Sure is...hoping de smell brin' more passengers and cargo too!" says Joshua. He then looks at Mary proudly, saying, "Ya know, they can now call ya, 'Queen Mary, de River Queen'. That was sure somethin' of an idea Mary." They both smile at each other. Mary then goes back to singing with the roustabouts, looking at the extravaganza.

The Robert E. Lee crosses the finish line, and Joshua fires the cannon. The Lee's whistles blow.

Herman, looking at his watch, shouts from the Texas Patio, "We beat their record...three days...eighteen hours and fourteen minutes!"

Mary and Joshua shout at the top of their lungs simultaneously, "Yahoo." They then embrace and dance in a circle. The guests on the Lee, begin congratulating the crew, and the crew congratulates each other. The celebration on the riverbanks and levees accelerates with their own cannon fire.

That night, it's warm and humid, with skyrockets and fireworks filling the sky, near the Robert E. Lee. Joshua is walking through large crowds on the docks, making his way to the Lee. Mary is sitting on the Main Deck with her legs hanging over the side, smoking her hand-rolled cigar, occasionally, looking up. When Joshua stops in front of her, she is looking up, as she says, "...That sure is pretty Joshua." She then looks at Joshua, and seriously, says, "Better to see it in the air, than it comin' at ya in a 'war'." Then excited, she says, "Hey...what ya find out?"

"Ah, de Natchez, her water pump had problem...and they tied up couple hours, cause of de fog."

"That's why they were so late gettin' in, they let fog stop 'em! Shoot...didn't stop the Captain. He got a good thin' listenin to the water, as ya move along…know where ya goin', not stoppin'." Mary takes a puff from her cigar.

Joshua, a little hesitant, looks at Mary, and says, "…Ah, Mary…I've never asked ya about somethin' before, all these years, never know how?"

"Ask me what Joshua?" says Mary.

"…When ya start smokin' cigars? Not every day ya see a lady smokin' 'em."

Mary chuckles, and smiles a little, then says, "When I was a little girl on the plantation…the slaves used herbs…things' to cure ya…like smokin' wrapped tobacco…just somethin' I've been doin' a while." Mary takes another puff from her cigar, as the fireworks finale begins, and they both look skyward.

Several moments later, the finale ends. Herman walks up holding a partially opened package, and looks at Joshua, saying, "Joshua…Captain on the stern?"

"I think so Herman. What ya got there?"

"Our new flag," says Herman. He opens the package, and pulls out, Old Glory, and holds it up for Joshua and Mary to see, saying, "Office said it was lost in the mail for three years…Nebraska is the thirty-seventh star added."

The next day in the afternoon, the American flag is whipping in the breeze from the Robert E. Lee's Texas Patio Deck jack staff. Cleaning crews go about their tasks, cleaning up after the celebrations, and repair crews are beginning to put the Lee back together.

Mary is sitting on a crate, reading a letter as Joshua walks up, and says, "Afternoon Mary."

"…Oh'…hi Josh," says Mary.

"Just came from de hospital, de doc said Mr. McDermick is gonna be fine in about three weeks. De doc said we got him there in time before infection set in. He said ya cleanin' off the dead skin, and using that river mud ya used, helped him. It kept de bugs off de burn."

"Ya, I know Josh. It also cooled the burn, on top of the bandage." Joshua smiles at Mary, but Mary looks a little sad for a few seconds. She then looks at Joshua, and says, "…Ah…sit down Joshua."

He sits on another crate and looks at Mary with concern, and says, "Ya…what's wrong Mary? Why ya all teary eye and everythn'?"

"…Joshua…remember my friend in Ohio that's a nun?"

"Ya…your friend Sister Annunciation, who ya talk about from time to time."

"Ya," says Mary. Then with resolve, she says, "Her sister Josephine died. She wants me to come to Ohio to help her at the convent."

Joshua looks in Mary's eyes, and says, "Ya...goin', huh?"
With a resolved smile, she looks at Joshua nodding her head, and says, "Ya Joshua. Tomorrow."

The next morning, at the stagecoach stop in St. Louis, Joshua is helping Mary into the coach, and as she sits down, Joshua closes the door. Mary then looks out the window, and says, "I'll write."

Joshua, Captain Cannon, Herman, Elisabeth, Johnny, and the Lee's crew are looking at Mary in the stagecoach preparing to leave, as Captain Cannon says, "If things don't work out...you're always welcome back Mary...if you like, come back as a dealer in the game room."

"Thank ya Captain," says Mary.

"Take care, Mary," says Herman.

"Bye Mary," says Elisabeth.

"Maybe I try to come and see ya one day?" says Joshua.

"I would love that Josh," says Mary. Then teary eyed, Mary looks at Joshua and everyone else as she waves.

The stagecoach driver looks back, then forward, cracking the whip. The coach rolls away, leaving all behind, waving goodbye to Mary.

TOLEDO

Several weeks later, Mary is walking along a cobbled-stone street, carrying her two carpetbags in one hand. She is looking at the letter she received on the Lee, in her other hand. She stops, and turns looking at a three-story stone and brick building in front of her. The building has a wood carved plaque hanging over the door with the words, 'URSULINE CONVENT AND SCHOOL'.

Mary puts the letter in her pocket, and walks up to the two huge wooden front doors of the convent. She sets her bags down. She then pulls on the front door rope knocker, feeling it give way with a thud at the door, from something inside. She lets go of the rope, then listens to the thud echo, radiating inside the convent.

Several moments have passed, and Mary reaches for the rope again. However, the large doors open, taking the rope knocker away from her. She looks at two Ursuline nuns, now standing in the opening, looking up, at her, reaching towards them. The nuns are startled, and they stare at her in amazement, and begin backing away from her.

Mary looks at them, and says, "Hello…my name is Mary. Does Sister Annunciation live here?"

The two nuns look at one another. Then one of the nuns, turns, looks at Mary, and says, "Why yes…Sister has been expecting you…please, come in." Mary picks up her two carpetbags, and walks in through the doorway. One of the nuns closes the door behind her. When she steps into the convent, she sniffs the air, and looks around the dimly lit cathedral room and corridors. She sees candles lit in many different places, which are surrounded by Roman Gothic furniture and décor.

It is so quiet that one could hear a pin drop. Mary is still sniffing the air and looking around, then somewhat loudly, she says, "What's that smell?" Mary's voice echoes tremendously throughout the convent. She notices her voice, with one of the nuns looking at her, stupefied, saying, "…Spiritual incense."

"Oh," says Mary.

"I'm Sister Dolores, and this is Sister Christine. Sister is busy with Mother at this moment. She asked us to show you to your room."

"Why sure thin' Sister," says Mary, a little louder, forgetting about her voice echoing. Her voice echoes throughout the convent again, as she says, "Wow, your voice sure echoes in here, and this sure is a fancy place!" Mary's voice continues to echo down the corridors.

The two nuns are astounded looking at Mary. Sister Dolores turns, walking towards a stone staircase, and says, "Please follow us." Sister Christine turns and follows Sister Dolores walking to the staircase. Mary is following, turning around in circles, amazed by what she sees, looking at her new home.

Moments later, in front of Mary's room, she opens the door and looks inside. She begins to smile looking around. She sees the room has one single bed neatly made, with a new white dress, underwear and white socks lying on top. There's also a rocking chair with new shoes on the floor in front, a chest-of-drawers with a mirror above, and a nightstand.

Mary's eyes are wide open. She walks in the room looking around. She turns in a circle, then looks back at the nuns, and says, "Ya sure this is my room?"

The nuns are puzzled because of Mary's comment. They look at one another. Then Sister Dolores looks at Mary, and says, "Why yes, this is your room. The bathtub and lavatory are downstairs at the end of the hall." Then with resolve, she says, "Supper will be at five. You'll hear five bells. There are two eating rooms. One is for the children and servants on this end of the building. On the other end is for Sisters. You are invited to eat with us tonight." She then stares at Mary with awe, and says, "Sister and Mother will see you there."

Mary quizzically looks at the nuns, and says, "Whose Mother?"

The nuns are really almost beside themselves, as Sister Dolores says, "Mother Superior, Mother Amadeus. Mother is the Superior of this convent."

"Oh," says Mary. Lifting up her eyebrows. She then looks at the nuns, and says, "Five bells?"

With a blank stare, Sister Dolores says, "Yes, five bells."

The nuns continue staring at Mary. She throws her bags on the floor, and picks up the dress. She turns the dress around, and says, "Ya got any pants?"

Both nuns gasp with surprise. They turn and leave quickly, talking to one another, walking away down the hallway, periodically, looking back over their shoulders through the doorway at Mary.

That evening, it is still very quiet in the convent, even as cooks and servants put courses of food on a large wooden planked rectangle table, with ten chairs, one setting at each end.

Sisters Dolores and Christine are seated on one side of the table, next to each other, in the middle. They are talking with two other nuns seated across from them. The nuns stop talking when they hear whistling echoing throughout the convent, which is getting louder coming towards them from the hallway. The nuns all look towards the doorway.

Mary walks into the dining room, still whistling, and wearing her chambermaid clothes. The four nuns look at her, as Mary stops whistling, and says, "Well, 'howdy' u'all! Thanks for the clothes, don't like 'em type of dresses. The underwear fit fine though."

The nuns, already astonished, look at Mary, then quickly look to one another, and begin speaking softly to their neighbor, as they look at her.

Then a voice from behind Mary, says, "Mary."

She turns around and sees her friend from a long time ago, standing with another nun. Mary says, "Mary Jo! ...I mean, Sister Annunciation!" Mary is much taller, and very excited. She hurries to her friend, embracing her, then picking her up, turning her in a circle, and then putting her back down. The nuns look at them in amazement.

Sister Annunciation is also a little taken aback by Mary's size, moreover, her outwardness.

Mary looks at her friend, and says, "It sure is good to see ya. What's it been? Golly!" Mary looks at the other nuns, whose looks' are bemused, as Mary says, "It's been about twenty years since I've seen my friend. Shoot...the letters we sent each other, the only way we keep in touch." Mary then turns and looks at Sister Annunciation, and sadly says, "I'm so sorry to hear about Josephine. The children here?"

"Yes Mary," says Sister Annunciation. She then turns, and indicates with her hand, saying, "This is Mother Amadeus, Mother Superior of the convent."

"That's what these Sisters told me." Mary turns and looks at Mother Amadeus, saying, "A pleasure meeting ya." She then puts her hands on her hips, and says, "So ya run this place?"

The nuns sitting at the table, go into a hyper whisper conversation between themselves. Sister Annunciation, a little embarrassed, says, "Yes...she is Mother Superior of the convent. Mary, the food is getting cold," says Sister Annunciation.

"Well, come on, let's sit down and eat, I'm hungry. We'll talk about mother, Josephine, and the children later," says Mary.

Sister Annunciation smiles at Mary, as she offers a chair to her in the middle. However, Mary has gone to the other end of the table, and sits down in Mother Amadeus' chair, looking at the food, with all looking at her. Mother Amadeus motions with her hand at the other nuns, not to say anything. She looks at Sister Annunciation, and says, "Sister." Mother indicates with her hand to Sister Annunciation's chair, at the other end of the table. She walks to her chair, and sits down. Mother Amadeus walks to one of the open chairs next to Sister Dolores, and sits.

Moments later, Sister Annunciation is finishing saying prayers, "Bless it our Father for which we are about to receive, through Christ our Lord, Amen." As Sister Annunciation finishes, Mary stands up and looks at the nuns, who are still bemused, looking at her. She begins serving herself on her plate, then, passes on the portions to the nuns. As the portions are passed along, Mary looks at the nuns, and says, "So like I was sayin', Sister Annunciation here, she sent letters and books. That's how I learnt to read and write." Then she looks at her friend, and says, "Isn't that right Sister Annunciation?"

"Yes Mary. Welcome to the Ursuline Convent, Mary" says Sister Annunciation.

Mary smiles, and then says, "Thank ya Sister Annunciation. I'm lookin' forward to gettin' to work...what's the first thin' ya need done."

The nuns tentatively watch Mary sitting back down. She looks at the nuns and smiles, as they smile at her. Mary then looks at her plate and begins slicing a piece of meat, then puts it into her mouth, and chews. The look on her face is, she only wishes she hadn't. The expression on Mary's face is now priceless, as she says, "...Ah...ah, ah, the first thin' I need to do is to teach the cook...how to cook!"

The nuns including Sister Annunciation, and Mother Amadeus, give big smiles to Mary, nodding their heads eagerly in agreement.

The next morning, Mary is in the kitchen, teaching the cooks how to cook. That evening, in the dining room, the nuns, having finished eating the food on their plates, are asking for seconds. The servers dish out more food, as Mother Amadeus smiles at Sister Annunciation, then looking at her plate, she wipes up the gravy with her slice of bread.

The next day, Mary is surveying the backyard of the convent. Later in the day, she is shopping for clothes in town with the cook. She is trying on man's pants, then buying several, as the cook, men, and women in the store, look at her with dumbfounded expressions. Mary and the cook then leave the store, and walk over to the feed store. At the store, Mary purchases herbs, vinegar, seeds, chicken wire, lumber, supplies, tobacco and whiskey, astonishing the cook.

A week later, Mary is finishing nailing together a chicken coop in the backyard of the convent. She then reaches into her pocket, and brings out one of her rolled cigars and lights it.

One day later, Mary is buying chickens and a rooster, and then later at the convent, she is giving herb tea to Sister Christine in her room, who is not feeling well.

Two weeks later, Mary is washing the convent laundry. After finishing, she plays with the white and Indian children in the yard.

Several months later, a push mower sits beside a newly mowed lawn, and a ladder lays on its side, near the freshly pruned trees. The front of the mission is manicured for the coming fall. Mary has just finished cutting the scrubs in front, when several mission children, come running from around the side of the mission, and right onto Mary's newly cut lawn. Mary quickly puts her tool in a wheelbarrow, and puts her hands on her hips looking at the children, yelling, "Get off the lawn! Get your damn feet off the lawn Noelle...I just cut it! Get off!" Noelle and the children, startled, basically jump off the lawn in one single leap, as if playing hopscotch. Mary is still upset and yelling, mostly at Noelle, saying, "Ya hardheaded, pigheaded and a stubborn child! How many times do I have to tell ya, don't run on the new cut grass?"

The next spring, Mother Amadeus is looking out her window at Mary in the courtyard. She is helping Sister Christine and another nun move a statue. Mother Amadeus turns, looks at Sisters Dolores and Annunciation, and says, "Mary is a blessing, Sisters."

"As I explained when she first arrived here. She became my confidant slave at a young age, always looked after me as her job. She was always courteous and polite. However, one time when I returned home for a visit from the convent, she surprised me. She actually held her own against some roughnecks, physically defending me. After my parents sent me here, Mary seems to have become even more independent in nature, seemingly, more so after slavery, and working on a Mississippi River boat. After, we took in my sister's children, plus, we needed more help here at the Convent, and from Mary's writings, I felt she could do the convent some good, especially with meal preparations."

"She took some getting used to Sister," says Sister Dolores.

Mother Amadeus looks at Sister Dolores, and says, "Yes...however, Mary is a special person Sister, as Sister suggested." Mother Amadeus then looks back out the window at Mary and the children, and says, "She is a blessing. I want her to have more interactions with the children. She will be good for them, and if she wants...she has a job here for life."

For the next year, Mary works feverishly doing her chores around the convent, reading books to the children, doing laundry, preparing the convent backyard ground for a vegetable garden, enlarging the chicken coop, and adding more chickens.

Whenever a child becomes ill, Mary makes sure they drink her special tea, and then she watches over them, until they recover.

Mary's nights are spent, reading books, and smoking her cigars in the back of the convent. When it snows, she shovels the snow off the front steps, walkways, and occasionally, in the back of the convent, behind the chicken coop, Mary enjoys her cigars, and sips of whiskey from a bottle hidden under her coat, adapting to her new life.

A year later, Mary attends to a larger chicken coop and garden in back of the convent. At meals, the cooks are now serving seconds, and some thirds, as Mother Amadeus and Sister Annunciation smile at Mary sitting at the table.

In the backyard of the convent on a bright summer day, convent children are playing. They are running circles around Mary and having a good time.

Mother Amadeus is watching, and then looks at Mary, and says, "Okay."

She looks at Mother Amadeus, then to the children, and says, "Okay children, time to eat." All the children run to several tables with benches, and sit down. Mary and the nuns bring food to the tables, as Mary says, "Alright children, quiet down now. Let's say our prayers." She looks at Mother Amadeus, and says, "Mother." The children stop talking, as Mother Amadeus steps up to the table.

That night in Mary's room, she is lying on her bed reading a book by lantern light. The light is also highlighting the calendar on her wall, showing the date, November 8, 1884. There's a knock at the door, as she says, "Come in."

Sister Annunciation opens the door. Mother Amadeus and Sister Annunciation smile at Mary, and walk in with Sister closing the door behind them. Sister Annunciation walks over by Mary, as Mother Amadeus walks over to the bed, sitting down on the edge, and with a worried look, she says, "Good evening Mary."

She sees the worried look on Mother Amadeus' face. She then looks at Sister Annunciation who has a concerned look also. This causes her to sit up in the bed and with concern, Mary says, "Good evening Mother Amadeus and Sister Annunciation...anythin' wrong?"

Mother Amadeus sighs, and says, "...Mary, it's been several years since you arrived here at the convent...you've done a very good job..."

"Did I do somethin' wrong?" says Mary.

"No, no, no Mary..." says Sister Annunciation.

Mother Amadeus, says, "Mary...the children look up to you here. The convent doesn't know how it got along without you before you came...you taught the cooks, started a hennery, a garden..."

Interrupting, Mary says, "Ah...Mother Amadeus..."

"No Mary, please listen," says Mother Amadeus, and with resolve, she says, "I've been reassigned to St. Peters Mission in the Montana Territory."

Mary looks at both, quickly, and says, "In Montana Territory! Ya both goin'?!" Then with a wanting look, Mary says, "Am I goin'?"

"No Mary," says Mother Amadeus. She then adds, "…that's what I'm trying to tell you. The convent needs you, and Sister Annunciation here…besides, where I'm going, there's no accommodations…it's very primitive conditions."

"Why they sendin' ya to Montana Territory for then?"

"The Bishop wants me to start a school for Indian girls, and territory children at the mission," says Mother Amadeus.

Sad, Mary says, "When do yah have to leave Mother?"

"As soon as I can pack-up and get on a stagecoach, Mary. Sister Annunciation will be taking my place…you two get along very well." Then Mother Amadeus looks at Mary with seriousness, and says, "Mary, Sister Dolores respects you very much…" Then she chuckles, and says, "It's just some things you do…that puzzle her and the other Sisters."

"Like what Mother!" excitedly, says Mary.

"Like wearing pants under your dresses and sipping whiskey, of course…occasionally." She then sighs, and says, "The Sisters just wished you would come to church, and all of us wish you would stop smoking."

"Mother Amadeus…God is in my heart. I've been smokin' since I was on Sister Annunciation's family's place, and drinkin' too. I ain't hurtin' nobody…I'm not gonna quit either." Mother Amadeus and Sister Annunciation both look at Mary fondly and smile, as Mother Amadeus says, "We love you Mary." They smile at Mary, and she smiles back.

The next day, the skies are blue with puffy white clouds adrift, as an intermittent cold wind blows. At the Toledo Stage-line, Mary is holding back tears as she holds hands with Mother Amadeus, who is sticking her arms out the stagecoach window. Mary says, "Mother Amadeus, ya write as soon ya can." She then looks at Mother Amadeus' bags, and says, "Ya sure ya got everythin'?"

"I hope so Mary," says Mother Amadeus. Mother Amadeus and Mary release hands. Mother Amadeus then looks at Sisters Annunciation, Dolores, Christine and the other nuns, standing behind Mary, also sniffling, holding back tears. Mother Amadeus, then says, "I'm going to miss you all." She then looks at the convent, and says, "Things look like they are coming around Sisters. Hopefully I'll be able to do the same where I'm going."

"Mother, with the Lord's blessings, you'll succeed," says Sister Dolores.

"Thank you Sister," says Mother Amadeus.

The shotgun rider closes the opposite door of the stagecoach, and then climbs on board rocking the coach. Mary looks at Mother, and says, "Mother Amadeus, ya make sure ya write, as soon as ya get settled."

"I promise Mary...I promise," says Mother Amadeus.

Months later, Mary is sitting at the dining room table reading a letter to the nuns, saying, "...Mother said, 'it's also 'very' cold, about forty below zero. The wind wants to blow ya sideways.' She then says, 'there are twenty saloons, and thirty houses of ill repute. We're livin' in log cabins'." Mary looks even more intensely at the letter, telling the nuns what Mother wrote, "'There are only three of us and thirty girls. We have very little food...only what people brin' us from town and hardly any medicine'."

"Let us pray," says Sister Dolores. Mary and the Sisters bow their heads.

Five months later, in the spring of 1885, Sister Annunciation is standing at the front door of the convent, reading a message, as a messenger stands outside the door in the snow. She looks at the messenger quickly, and then begins breathing fast. She turns her head into the convent, and urgently shouts, "Mary! Mary...Mary, Sisters!" She quickly looks back at the messenger, and says, "Thank you." Sister Annunciation closes the door and quickly hurries towards the staircase still shouting, "Mary, Sisters...Mary, Sisters...Sisters!"

Mary and some of the nuns come running down the staircase looking at Sister Annunciation with urgency, "What's wrong Sister!? What's wrong!? What is it!?" says Mary. As she nears the bottom of the stairs, she jumps from a step, and lands in front of Sister Annunciation, asking, "What's wrong Sister!?" The other nuns gather.

"Mother is gravely ill. They say she has pneumonia, and she is asking for you Mary," says Sister Annunciation.

Mary looks at Sister Annunciation with urgency, saying, "Sister, I'm gonna leave on the first stagecoach out of here for Montana Territory! Gonna be takin' a few things' with me."

Sister Annunciation says, "Whatever you need Mary! I'll have Sister Christine make your travel arrangements, and I'll get Sister Dolores and the other Sisters to help you pack."

"Thank ya Sister Annunciation. I'm gonna build two crates, gonna take two roosters and two chickens with me. Have the Sisters pack my bags, get the cook to give me, two bottles of vinegar, half the healing tea I made, some herbs and vegetable seeds, pack 'em in also..." Mary and Sister Annunciation head out in different directions with the other nuns following Sister. Mary looks back at Sister Annunciation, and says, "Tell him leave enough seeds for ya to get growin' in the sprin'."

The next day, the ground is partly covered with snow. Mary, dressed for the cold, is helping the shotgun rider tie down the rocking chair that was in her room to the top of the stagecoach, with part of the legs protruding from under the cover.

"Please cover the legs," says Mary, pointing up at the legs of the chair, looking at the shotgun rider up top. Mary finishes tying her knot, then, walking back to the rear boot of the stagecoach, she checks the other leather straps holding the cover. Then she turns and looks at Sisters Annunciation, Dolores, and Christine, then to the other nuns with the children, and the cook, and says, "Hope 'em chickens make it...kinda' cold." Mary smiles, and then says, "Sisters, I'm grateful, thank ya so much for the rocker." She then looks at the chair, and says, "I'll enjoy it forever."

"You're welcome Mary..." Then with resolve, Sister Dolores says, "Mary...please bring Mother back to good health."

"I'll do my best Sister...I'll do my best."

"Remember Mary, you'll transfer to a train in Omaha, then back to a stagecoach in Ogden, till you get to Gorham in Montana Territory. A buckboard will meet you in town and take you to St. Peter's Mission. It should take you nine days. Make sure your luggage, chickens and the rocker stays with you every time you transfer," says Sister Christine.

"I will Sister," says Mary. She walks to the other Sisters and hugs each one, then hugs the cook, then all the children. Finally, she turns and climbs up into the stagecoach, closes the door behind her, and says, "Good-bye everyone."

The stagecoach driver looks down, on both sides, then forward, cracking the whip. The coach rolls away, with all waving goodbye to Mary.

St. Peter's Mission / United States Postal Service

In the morning, nine days later, the stagecoach approaches a wooden bridge. Big blue skies are abundant, and white puffy clouds overlay the patchy snow that covers the ground, in the Montana Territory. The stagecoach, being pulled by four horses, crosses over the bridge that spans the Missouri River, coming into Gorham, Montana, a small fast growing wilderness town, on the eastern edge of the Rocky Mountains.

A chilled cold wind blows sporadically, whipping dust, and blowing several tumbleweeds down the middle of the road. The stagecoach rolls into the middle of town, coming to a stop in front of the Wells Fargo Overland Stage & Gorham Stage-line Offices. The driver, wearing his wilderness coat, applies the brake. The shotgun rider puts his shotgun down in the foot-box, and jumps from his perch, landing both feet on the ground, and dusting himself off. At the same time, the shotgun rider's side door opens into the middle of the town's road, and out steps Mary. Wearing a heavy coat, she shakes off a chill, and, systematically begins looking at each of the buildings across from her, and then at the people of the town. Several cowboys pass by on horseback looking at her. Mary looks at the cowboys, and grins, and then looks at the townspeople, at the men wearing buckskin, and most, are wearing their side arms.

Mary then looks at the few women, who are dressed in heavy coats, covering their conservative dresses, and holding their bonnets on their heads from the gust of wind. They are going about their business, except for two women who stop in their tracks. They stare at Mary from across the town's road, standing on the buildings wood-plank walkway, as Mary stares back.

A buckboard rolls up fast, throwing dust in front of Mary, and stops. A young 'white' gentleman, somewhat meek looking, looks at Mary with urgency, and says, "Are you Mary?"

"Yes."

"I'm Joseph Gump. Mother is very ill...please hurry, please...do you have any bags?"

"Yes," says Mary. She points to the top of the stagecoach. The shotgun rider is untying the rope that's holding the cover, throwing it off, revealing the rocking chair and the other baggage on the top of the coach, as Mary says, "That chair, those two carpetbags and the chickens in the rear." The shotgun rider hands down the chair to Mary, she takes it, putting it into the buckboard.

Later that evening, on the road to St. Peter's Mission, the buckboard, carrying Mary and Joseph, is traveling through ankle high snow, coming around a bend in the road and into a small valley. The valley has sporadic cottonwood trees growing about, unusual rock formations, and buttes that surround the little white mission church in the middle of the snow-covered valley. The church is L shaped, with a portable steeple placed in the middle of the L, which has a cross at the top. The smaller structure of the L, protrudes to one side of the steeple, that also has a cross placed in the middle of the apex, at what appears to be the mission church. The long-gated structure of the L, is what appears to be the cabin, with smoke coming from its chimney.

St. Peter's Mission – Circa 1885

Mary looks at the mission in the distance, then looks at Joseph, saying, "Can't this thin' go any faster? We've been on the road all day."

"We're almost there. The mission is sixteen miles from town. It's almost a day's trip by buckboard," says Joseph.

Mary looks at Joseph with determination, taking the buckboard reins from him, and then whipping the reins, shouting, "HAH! Giddy-up! Hah...hah!" The buckboard takes off down the road, kicking up snow, and thank God, everything is tied down in the back, including the bouncing chickens in their crates. Joseph is holding on, with his eyes wide open.

Several minutes later, the buckboard nears the church and cabin with several doors. Mary pulls on the reins, shouting, "Whoa! ...whoa...whoa..." The buckboard comes to a stop. Mary looks at Joseph with urgency, saying, "Which door?" Joseph points to a door, but before he can say a word, Mary is already headed towards the door, as she looks back at Joseph, and says, "Joseph brin' my bags!"

Mary opens the door and looks at Mother Amadeus laying on a cot. She is barely conscious, covered with blankets and animal skins. Two nuns are kneeling by her, who are dressed in animal skins, that cover their convent attire. One of the nuns is wiping Mother Amadeus' forehead with a cloth. Mary's face grimaces, almost breathless, she says, "Mother!"

Mary rushes to Mother Amadeus' side. The nuns, stand, and give her room. Mary puts the palm of her hand on Mothers' forehead, and then puts her ear to her chest, as Mother Amadeus barely breathing, says, "...Mary..."

"I'm here, I'm here...I'm here!" says Mary. Joseph walks in carrying Mary's bags. She looks at him, and says, "Over here Joseph!" She then looks at the nuns, and says, "I need a lot of hot water and some old clothes..." Then she looks at Joseph, and says, "Joseph, I know the ground be hard, but I'm gonna need dirt that will make good mud, and as much ash from the fire as ya can get."

Joseph lays the bags by Mary and goes to a corner of the cabin with a hole in the floorboards, and begins digging. One of the nuns that was wiping Mother Amadeus' forehead is pointing to the fireplace, and whispering to the other nun.

The other nun goes to the fireplace. The nun, standing near Mother Amadeus, looks at Mary, astounded while Joseph is digging dirt, and says, "Joseph, I take it...this is Mary?"

Joseph looks at the nun, and says, "Yes Sister Gertrude, this is Mary."

Sister Gertrude sighs, and looks at Mary, and with resolve, she says, "How is Mother? We believe she has pneumonia."

Mary is looking through her bags. She brings out a leather pouch, a bottle of vinegar, and a bundle of tied sage, then with a worried look, Mary looks at Sister Gertrude, and says, "She has poison in her lungs...not good, Sister." Then Mary, with determination, says, "I'm gonna do my best to brin' life back into her lungs. First, I'm gonna give her some hot tea, then I'm gonna draw the poison out of her lungs."

The other nun brings a pot of hot steamy water over to Mary, and sets it down. Mary gets up, walks over to the fireplace and lights a piece of sage on fire, blowing the fire out, letting it smolder, then looking back at Joseph, she says, "Joseph, how's the dirt comin'?"

"Almost got this pot full," says Joseph.

Mary walks back to Mother Amadeus, kneels with the sage smoldering in her hand, looks at Joseph, and says, "That's enough, brin' it here...get me some ash, then ya gotta leave Joseph...ya can feed 'em chickens for me, and put 'em under some cover." Mary then looks at the nuns, and says, "Sisters, first thin' we gonna do, is give Mother some tea...I need a cup."

Moments later, Joseph brings the dirt and ash over to Mary, then, he leaves walking out the door. Sister Gertrude walks over to Mary. Looking at Sister Gertrude, Mary hands the smoldering sage to her, as the other nun hands Mary a cup. Mary pours a green powder out of the pouch and into the cup. She then pours in the hot water from the pot, stirring and mixing in the herbal ingredients.

Mary reaches into her bag and brings out a bottle of whiskey. This causes both nuns eyes to widen, as Sister Gertrude, says, "You're giving Mother Whiskey?!"

"Ya want Mother to get better don't ya?!" Mary says seriously. Both nuns look at each other, then at Mary nodding their heads. Mary pours in the whiskey, then takes a couple of sips herself, causing both nuns, again, to take notice, as Mary says, "Help me sit her up so I can get this in her, then help me take off her night gown."

The other nun walks over and kneels next to Mother Amadeus, lifting her up, as Mary begins feeding her the tea.

Moments later, a smoky haze hangs in the air in the Ursuline nuns cabin. Mary is putting the ash in the pot of dirt, then, stirring in hot water. Sister Gertrude, and the other nun, tuck a torn piece of cloth around the top of Mother Amadeus. Mary looks at them. They nod their heads that they are ready, and Mary begins spreading large amounts of the steamy muddy mixture on Mother Amadeus' chest. Mother begins moaning and moving, then coughs slightly, as Mary smears the rest of the paste on Mother Amadeus.

Several days' later, large burning candles are placed about the inside of the small cabin. Mary is asleep in a chair next to Mother Amadeus, when Mother begins moving on the cot, restricted by what's on her chest. She slightly opens her eyes, grabs the end of the blanket near her face, and barely throws it off her, only to see a clean cloth, laying over her larger chest cavity area, with cracked caked mud drying around the sides. She then looks at Mary asleep in the chair, and calls out softly, "Mary," she coughs. "Mary," she coughs again, "Mary, Mary."

Barely opening her eyes, Mary, looks at Mother Amadeus. She sees Mothers' eyes, and begins to smile, and immediately jumps up, and shouts, "Sisters! Sisters! Sisters!"

An hour later, Mary is pouring green powder from her pouch into a cup of hot water. She takes the whiskey bottle out of her bag, and adds a splash into the cup, then hands the cup to Mother Amadeus.

Sister Gertrude, seated at the foot of the cot, clears her throat, looking at Mother Amadeus, saying, "Mother, I wished there was a doctor in town...are you sure you want to keep drinking that..."

"Sister Gertrude, excuse me. Do ya want Mother to get better? I told ya, the whiskey and tea, make ya have a fever, make ya sweat...kill the poisons in ya...the hot mud, makes the poison come out," says Mary.

Mother Amadeus coughs, as she says, "Sister, Mary knows what she's doing. I've known Mary awhile..." She coughs, and then says, "...That's why I had you send for her...she has always been very loyal, strong and smart."

"Uh," says Sister Gertrude, as she then says, "Perhaps you're right Mother. She has brought you back from near death...she really hasn't left your side since she arrived." Then she looks at Mary, and says, "...I'm sorry...it's...it's..."

"Sister, ya not the first, and won't be the last, apology accepted." Mary stands up with her arms open and the two women embrace.

Later in the cabin, Mary is applying another round of mud on Mother Amadeus' chest, as Mother says, "...It was Father Giorda who started St. Peter's Mission here, through its troubled past, Indians, raids, and bandits..."

"Mother, says Mary interrupting. Then with a sidelong look at her, she says, "There's nothin' out here...why Joseph was tellin' me, there's bears, wolves, Indians, outlaws, and a mess of other things'." Then Mary looks around, and looks at Mother Amadeus. Her eyes are wide open, nodding her head speaking softly, saying, "I think they done made ya crazy?"

Mother Amadeus smiles, and coughs into a rag, spitting up phlegm, then looking at Mary, saying, "No Mary, they didn't make me crazy...there is a reason why I'm here...the Lord knows. Next week the children will return for school, and you'll see." There's a knock on the door. Mother Amadeus looks at the door, coughs, and says, "...Come in."

Joseph opens the door, for the other nun to enter, with Joseph following, closing the door behind them. They both walk into the room looking at Mother Amadeus, as Joseph says, "Mother, you look better. You feeling better?"

"Yes, thanks to Mary, thank you Joseph for bringing her," says Mother Amadeus.

The other nun says, "Mother, glad you are feeling better." Then she looks at Mary, and says, "Thank you for healing Mother, Mary."

"Don't thank me." Mary looks at the ceiling of the cabin.

The other nun looks up also, saying, "Yes Mary, Praise the Lord." The nun then looks at Mother Amadeus, and says, "Mother, we're running out of supplies. We may not have enough to start school...we need to go into town soon."

"Yes Sister Clara, however, we are still short of funds. I was hoping Father Landesmith would have sent more funds by now," says Mother Amadeus.

"I have some money I made, Mother Amadeus," says Mary.

Mother Amadeus smiles at her, as she says, "No Mary, thank you. This is the Missions' problem." She then looks at Joseph, coughs, and says, "...Joseph take what we have, you and Mary go into town tomorrow." Then she looks at Sister Clara, and says, "Sister, please make a list for them." Then she looks back at Mary, coughs again, and says, "I guess I should ask you, if you want to stay on and help?"

Mary looks at the small cabin, then, she looks at Sister Clara, Joseph, then at Mother Amadeus, smiles, and nods her head.

Later that next morning, on the road to Gorham, Mary wearing her heavy coat, is driving the buckboard, approaching the bridge that she came across in the stagecoach. Joseph is sitting beside her, talking, and as the morning cold meets their warm breaths, it creates vapor clouds, trailing behind them. Joseph is pointing, saying, "That's the new bridge you came over, we're comin' to, over the Missouri, that replaced the ferry...couple of more years, the railroad will come, that's when Father Landesmith from Fort Koegh plans to build the new mission, once the railroad is built."

"Mother needs a new mission...the railroad comin' means the town gonna grow. Is that good Joseph?" says Mary.

"I don't know Mary, it's already started. Stop here Mary, we don't need to go over the bridge, the town is over there." Joseph points, and Mary slows the team of horses, turning them pulling the buckboard towards town.

As the buckboard nears the center of town, most of the people stop, and look at Mary, driving the buckboard to the Gorham General Store.

When the buckboard nears the front of the store, Mary slows and stops the team of horses pulling the buckboard, saying, "Whoa...whoa..." Mary then applies the brake, and ties the reins to the buckboard. She looks around the town. The townspeople who noticed her, slow in their pace, staring at her, as Mary looks at Joseph, and ask, "Got the list?"

"Yup." Joseph looks around town, then looks at Mary, and says softly, "Ah Mary...ya kinda notice people a lookin'?"

"Ya, they always do Joseph...come on, we got some supplies to buy," says Mary. Joseph and Mary jump off the buckboard and walk to the door of the Gorham General Store. Joseph opens the door for Mary, as Mary says, "Why thank ya Joseph." He bows his head to Mary. She enters the store, and Joseph follows her.

As Mary enters the store, all is very quiet even though there are several patrons, more women than men shopping, frozen in their tracks, staring at Mary, along with the store clerk behind the counter.

Mary sees the stares. She looks at Joseph who shrugs his shoulders, and begins gathering their supplies. Mary turns around, and looks at everyone in the store, saying, "Well, howdy everyone."

Everyone just about jumps out of their skin from Mary's voice, waking them out of their gaze. They nervously, and quickly, go back to their shopping, looking at her indirectly. She looks around the store, then at the store clerk, and says, "Excuse me, mister."

Hesitant, the store clerk says, "...Yes...may I...help you?"

"Ya sure can." Mary then points, and says, "Need to buy about four yards of that wool, five yards of buckskin, an apron..." Then she points, and says, "Three yards of that material, and that pullover wool cap..." Then she looks around, and says, "That wool coat."

"That's a man's coat...ah, ma'am."

With a look at the store clerk, Mary says, "Well ya ain't got nothin' else that will fit me, do ya?!"

Everyone in the store begins whispering, looking at Mary, except for Joseph, who is putting blankets on the counter. The store clerk looks at Mary, and says, "...Ah, ah...no ma'am."

"Fine," says Mary. She points at Joseph, then says, "This gentleman will pay for it when he's done gettin' supplies." Mary looks towards the outside windows, only to see the townspeople peering through the windows at her, then, moving away quickly when they see her looking at them. She then says, "What's the best saloon in town, and where can I buy a gun?"

The whispering in the store, suddenly goes to a loud murmur. The store clerk, shocked, and nervous, stutters, saying, "...Ya...ya, ya...want to...go to a...saloon?"

"Bugs got your hearin'...ya, and I want to buy a gun too!"

Nervous, and stuttering even more, the store clerk says, "...Ah, ah, ah...there's several, ah...The Silver Dollar Saloon...across the road."

"What about a gun?" says Mary.

The store clerk, more nervous, stutters, shaking as he points, saying, "...Ah...over there...in the...display cabinet."

Mary walks to the front of the display cabinet.

The store clerk hurries around the corner to the back of the cabinet where the guns are located, standing in front of Mary.

The entire store is watching, pretending not to, as are the townspeople, peering back through the windows at Mary, as she says, "What kinda' guns ya got?"

The store clerk really stutters now, saying, "...Ah...ah...are you...sure you...want to buy...a...'gun'...ah, ma'am?"

"Ya, and I want that scattergun too..." says Mary, as she points up at a shotgun hanging on the wall behind the store clerk. The store clerk's eyes, just about fall out on the floor. She looks back at the gun cabinet, and then says, "...I want...that one." Mary points at one of the pistols in the cabinet. The store clerk nervously points at the gun, then, looks at Mary, who is nodding her head in acknowledgement.

The store clerk reaches in the cabinet, and brings the pistol out, holding it in front of him, slightly shaking, stuttering, and saying, "...Ah...ah, this is...a thirty-eight Smith & Wesson."

"Ya make a separate bill with that holster too." She points at a holster next to the pistol, then she looks up, back at the shotgun, above the store clerk, and says, "And with that scattergun, give them to that gentleman," says Mary.

Surprised, he stutters, saying, "...You want the...you really want the...Crescent brake-action...side-by-side...shotgun... too?" says the store clerk.

Mary, giving the store clerk a look, reaches inside her coat pocket. The store clerk quickly hurries to a ladder, putting the ladder up towards the shotgun. She brings out a fat elongated leather pouch that jingles. She opens the pouch and pours silver dollars into her hand, looking at the store clerk, bringing the shotgun down, she says, "This should cover it and some of the items that gentleman is gettin'." She puts the silver dollars on the counter. She then looks at Joseph carrying grain sacks to the counter, and says, "Joseph." With the list in his mouth, Joseph is putting the sacks down on the counter top, and looks at Mary walking towards the door, as she says, "I'm goin' over to the saloon. Make sure the gentleman there, puts my material, scattergun, holster and pistol in with the supplies...get some bullets and buckshot too. I've already paid him, should be enough, and some extra to help St. Peters. Meet me across the road at the saloon."

Joseph acknowledges with a nod of his head, and mumbles with the list in his mouth.

Mary opens the door. Townspeople quickly turn from the outside windows, and begin walking, pretending that they are going about their business. She walks out, closing the door behind her. Some of the patrons inside the store, rush over to the windows, looking out, trying to get a look at Mary through the curtains, while others rush over to Joseph.

Mary is standing on the wood-plank walkway, outside the store, looking at the town. Cowboys on horseback and townspeople on foot, are staring at her, going about their tasks...She reaches in her pocket, and brings out one of her hand-rolled cigars, that's already been partially smoked. She brushes away some of the old ash, and puts the cigar in her mouth, then taking out a match from her pocket, she strikes it against her back side, lighting the match.

Mary then looks around town, with the cigar in her mouth, her eyes focusing on the townspeople staring at her. She brings the match up, cupped in her hand, to the cigar, taking several puffs, then blowing the smoke out of her mouth, extinguishing the match, and flicking it away. She steps out onto the road, walking towards the Silver Dollar Saloon smoking her cigar.

Moments later, music radiates out through the smoke filled saloon air, as Mary walks up to the swinging doors, and looks into the saloon. She sees mustache and bearded gun toting patrons enjoying themselves, and some standing at the bar, drinking their spirits, and conversing. Saloon girls are entertaining many of the patrons, while poker games abound at the tables, however, there are no women drinking socially, or gambling.

Mary grips the cigar with her lips. She pushes one of the doors open and walks into the saloon. The saloon murmur and music slowly quiets to a complete silence. Everyone looks at her, walking to the bar, un-phased by the stares.

When Mary reaches the bar, she stops, taking the cigar out of her mouth, and looking at the bartender, saying, "Whiskey."

The bartender is already staring, looking at Mary, as he says, "We don't...serve..." He then looks at Mary with a quizzical expression, and says, "...women in here."

"Why not!" Mary says upset.

Stuttering, the bartender says, "Be...Because..."

"Give the lady a drink, Harry, it's on me," says a man interrupting, sitting at a poker table in the corner. Harry the bartender, the patrons, and Mary all look at the table. The man stands up wearing two fancy pearl side arms, one holstered on each side of his fancy clothes. He walks over to the bar, towards Mary. The room begins to murmur, looking at her. The piano player begins slowly playing again. The man approaches Mary, tips his hat, stops beside her, and says, "Hello, my name is R. B. Glover, you can call me Mr. Glover, I'm the owner of the Silver Dollar..." The bartender puts a glass of whiskey in front of Mary, as Mr. Glover puts his hand out to shake Mary's hand.

Mary smiles, and grips his hand, greeting him, as Mr. Glover says, "Wow, that's some grip you got there. What's your name...ma'am?"

"Mary...Mary Fields, and thanks for the drink."

"You're welcome," says Mr. Glover.

Mary takes the glass of whiskey off the bar, looks at it, and then downs the liquor, putting the glass back on the bar. Everyone in the saloon looks on in amazement. She then takes a puff from her cigar, blowing out the smoke.

"You're new around these parts, aren't you," says Mr. Glover.

"...Ya, ya can say that...got here five days ago...be workin' at the mission."

"St. Peter's?" says Mr. Glover.

"Yah," says Mary.

Some of the patrons have gone back to what they were doing before Mary walked into the saloon. She looks around the room, then, she looks at the poker games in progress. She looks at Mr. Glover, and says, "Can a woman play cards here, Mr. Glover?"

"You know how to play poker, Mary?"

"Worked on a riverboat several years, Mr. Glover."

"Well, let's see if we can find you a table." Mr. Glover looks around the saloon and sees an open chair, as he says, "Here Mary...that table over there." Most of the saloon patrons are still staring at Mary, including those outside peering through the windows, under, and above the saloon swinging doors. Mary follows Mr. Glover over to the poker table, with three men sitting at the table. They look Mary up and down, as she puts the cigar up to her lips, gripping it with her teeth, smiles, and then stares back at each man, as Mr. Glover says, "Gentlemen, this is Mary Fields...she wants to try her hand at poker..."

Some of the saloon, chuckles. The card player on Mary's left, throws his cards down on the table, stands, gathers his money, and looks at the card players at the table, saying, "I'm out!" Then he looks at Mr. Glover, and says, "Damn you R. B., I ain't sittin' down at no table with no cigar smokin' Nigger..." Then he looks at Mary, up and down, and says, "woman!"

The angry card player looking at Mary, hurries away through the swinging doors, moving the peering townspeople out of the way. She looks at Mr. Glover, and says, "Must'a been loosin'?"

Mr. Glover chuckles, and says, "Don't mind him none Mary...please sit."

Mary looks at Mr. Glover pulling the chair back for her.

The gambler on Mary's right looks at her, and says, "Ya know how to play Five Card Draw, three card limit, no wild cards, three..."

"Deal!" says Mary interrupting.

Everyone at the table looks at Mary, astounded. Most of the saloon now gathers around the table. A new gambler quickly sits at the empty chair to Mary's left, placing several stacks of silver dollars on the table in front of him.

Mary rolls up her sleeves, and then takes the cigar out of her mouth, putting it on the edge of the table. She takes out her money pouch from inside her coat pocket, and empties a hand full of silver dollars into her hand, putting the pouch back in her pocket. She puts the money on the table, settling into her chair, as the gambler on her right, shuffles the cards.

One hour later, it's very quiet in the Silver Dollar Saloon. No piano music is playing. Faces are peering in through the windows and swinging doors. The tension in the saloon, is as thick as the tobacco smoke, it could be cut with a knife. The saloon patrons' faces show their uneasiness while Mr. Glover stands behind Mary, with Joseph to his left, smiling.

Mary has more silver dollars in front of her than her three opponents once had, especially, the new gambler to her left, who only has a quarter of the stack of coins he had in front of him. He looks very uncomfortable.

Mary is dealing the last round of cards of the new game, as she deals herself the last card. She then puts the deck in the middle of the table, next to the game bets, placing a coin on top of the cards.

Everyone looks at their cards. Mary looks at her hand, slightly bringing her cards off the table, cupping her hand around them. She then picks up her cigar from the table's edge, looks at it, then puts it up to her mouth, gripping it with her lips, puffing, till the end begins to glow red, and smoke emanates.

Mary then blows out a puff of smoke with the cigar still in her mouth, as she looks at the new gambler. The new gambler grabs several coins from his dwindling stack, and looks at the table, tossing them in the center. The quiet gambler across from Mary tosses his coins into the pot, as does the gambler.

Mary then looks at her cards, looks around the table, and picks up several of her silver dollars, tossing them into the pot.

The new gambler looks around the table till he gets to Mary, giving her an evil eye. Mary looks at him, and says, "What's wrong mister, don't like ya cards?"

"No, don't like how ya dealt 'em...three cards." The new gambler takes three of his cards from his hand and tosses them towards the middle. Mary picks up the dealing deck, taking several puffs on her cigar, and deals the new gambler three cards.

The quiet gambler tosses in three cards. Mary deals him his three.

The gambler studies his cards for a few seconds. He looks at Mary, putting her cigar back on the edge of the table, as the gambler, says, "I'll take...two." The gambler tosses in two cards. Mary deals him his two. She lays the deck back down, towards the middle of the table, then picking up her cards.

Mary looks to each players' eyes, staring at her, starting with the new gambler, then the quiet gambler, to the gambler, then, back to her cards cupped in her hands, as she says, "Three cards."

Mary discards three cards from her hand into the other discarded pile, putting her other two cards down. She picks up the deck and deals herself three cards. She lays the deck back in the middle of the table, putting the coin back on top.

The new gambler is looking at his cards, then looks at Mary with an unkind look, smiling, then at the other players, saying, "I raise ya..." The new gambler picks up several coins from his dwindling kitty, tossing them into the pot, then looking at Mary saying, "Two."

The new gambler then looks at the quiet gambler who tosses in his cards, whereas, the gambler is looking at his cards, then looking at his kitty, picking up his coins, tossing them into the center of the table. "I'll see your two," says the gambler.

Everyone now looks at Mary, looking at her hand. She smiles and looks at the new gambler. She picks up a hand full of her coins, counting them, then, tosses the silver into the pot. She looks to the gambler, then to the new gambler, and his kitty, and says, "I see ya two...raise ya nine."

A quiet murmur settles in the saloon. The new gambler looks at his hand, then to Mary's eyes, to the gamblers' eyes, then back to his hand, finally he picks up the last of his coins from his kitty, saying, "I'll see ya nine...raise ya three."

The gambler studies his cards for a couple of seconds, and then looks at Mary, and the new gambler, saying, "I'm out." The gambler tosses his cards in the middle.

The murmur picks up in the saloon. Everyone looks at Mary. She looks at her single opponent, the new gambler, and says, "I'll see ya three...what ya got?" Mary picks up three silver dollar coins, and tosses them into the kitty.

The new gambler looks at his hand, then looks at Mary, laying his cards on the table, face up, spreading his cards out, slowly, looking at her, saying, "That there is a flush...you've been lucky so far, gettin' all those three of a kind, and pairs all the time...I know ya can't beat a flush!"

Mary looks down at the new gamblers' cards and sees, Ace of Hearts, Jack of Hearts, Seven of Hearts, Five of Hearts, and Four of Hearts. The new gambler reaches for the pot.

Mary looks at him with a determined look, and says, "Not so fast mister!"

If the look on the new gambler's face could kill, Mary would be a dead woman now. The new gambler, stops reaching, and looks at her, saying, "What ya goin' tell me...ya got better!?"

"Yup...flush!" Mary slowly spreads her cards out on the table, showing an, ace of spades, four of spades, five of spades, nine of spades, then Mary slowly reveals her last card, the queen of spades.

The new gambler slowly stands up in anger, and looks down at Mary, shouting, "Ya cheated...I don't know how, but ya cheated...Niggers ain't smart enough to win nothin'!"

Mary stands up, pushing her chair back. She backs away from the table looking at the new gambler, saying, "...Mister...I ain't got to cheat, and I ain't lookin' for no trouble. I just want to win some money." Mary slowly walks to the table to collect her winnings. The new gambler quickly steps towards the table, grabbing Mary's left arm with his left hand. Mary then says, "I wouldn't do that if I was ya mister...let me go!"

"Nigger...ya ain't touchin' that money!" says the new gambler.

Mary throws her left arm up in the air causing the new gambler's hand to fly up, letting go of Mary's arm. He then steps towards her and swings his right fist at her. Mary dodges the new gamblers' swing. She then hits him with a glancing right cross, causing the new gambler to begin falling backwards, reaching for his gun.

Joseph yells out, "He's goin' for his gun!"

No sooner than Joseph yells 'gun', Mary looks quickly to Mr. Glover standing to her right, grabbing his left sidearm, fast, pulling the hammer back, and pointing the gun straight at the new gambler, hitting the floor, barely un-holstering his gun.

The whole saloon goes quiet, looking at Mary. She is pointing Mr. Glover's gun at the new gambler. The new gambler, lets loose of his gun handle, letting the trigger guard swing by his forefinger, then laying the gun on the floor.

All of a sudden, another gun-hammer clicking sound is heard, as Mr. Glover says, "I wouldn't do that, either...mister, put your hands up!"

Mary still pointing the gun at the new gambler on the floor, quickly looks at Mr. Glover pointing his other gun at a cowboy with his hands in the air. Mr. Glover quickly looks and smiles at Mary, and says, "Mary get your money...don't worry about anythin', you won fair and square..." Then proudly, Mr. Glover says, "The card game, and the draw. I'll take care of things', get out'a here!"

Mary releases the hammer, and gives Mr. Glover his gun back. She and Joseph quickly begin collecting her winnings from the table, putting the silver dollars into her pouch and pockets. Joseph then hurries towards the front door with Mary following. She is backing out, putting the pouch into her inside coat pocket, looking at everyone, then looking at Mr. Glover pointing his guns at the patrons, as Mary says, "Thank ya, Mr. Glover."

"You're welcome Mary…oh, by the way…I heard Mother Amadeus is doing better. She told me all about you before she took sick…you're always welcome in here Mary."

She is a little surprised by Mr. Glover's statement. Mary smiles at him, then turns and walks out through the swinging doors. Some of the saloon patrons hurry over to Mr. Glover while others hurry to the windows and the swinging doors, looking at Mary, as Mr. Glover pointedly says, "Don't go outside gentlemen!"

Moments later, Joseph climbs onto the buckboard. Mary approaches the buckboard, looking back over her shoulder at the saloon. She looks at all the supplies in the back of the buckboard, then, she looks at Joseph, saying, "We got everythin' Joseph?"

"Ya, Mary. Your shotgun, pistol and ammunition are wrapped in the missions' blankets."

Mary climbs on the buckboard, grabs the reins, releases the brake, and shouts, "Yah…yah, yah!"

The buckboard rolls away with the townspeople looking at them. Joseph smiles, and looks at Mary, saying, "…'Wow' Mary, that sure was somethin'…you beat that cowboy in poker, then you out 'drew him'…'wow'. Never seen anythin' like it! Where did you learn to play poker, fight, pull a gun that fast, especially one not strapped to you?"

"Years of experience, Joseph. Here…" Holding the reins in one hand, Mary reaches in her coat pocket and brings out her pouch of money, handing the pouch to Joseph. Take the money out of the pouch Joseph, give it to Sister Clara. That should pay for their supplies and more."

"Where am I going to tell her the money came from?"

Mary smiles, and then says, "Tell her it came from the Black fairy."

Joseph smiles at her. Mary smiles back, driving the buckboard out of town.

Gorham, two years later, in 1887, an early spring morning, the store clerk has finished nailing a wood carved sign in front of his store, with the words, 'Cascade General Store'. A small band is marching through the middle of a slightly larger town, playing their instruments, marching under the banners that are strung across the road, from almost every building.

Town spectators, ranchers and cowboys are standing on the wood-plank platforms, and the road, watching, and waving at the band, walking under a large banner stretched across the middle of town, with the written words, 'Welcome To The New Town of 'Cascade – Montana'.'

A photographer is standing on the wood platform. He notices Mary walking towards him. He stops her, and takes her picture.

Mary Fields aka Stagecoach Mary
In front of The Mint Saloon, Cascade, Circa 1887

Moments later, at the Cascade Train Station, a train whistle is heard in the distance, as Mary walks up to the supply wagon, putting a bag behind the wagon seat, in the bed. She climbs aboard, and sits on the wagon seat next to Joseph. She is dressed in her wilderness clothes, a wool skirt that's hiked-up enough to show her buckskin pants and leather boots under the skirt, with a white apron, cotton button down blouse, and coon cap, with her shotgun laying upright against the front panel of the wagon, between her and Joseph.

Most people that pass the wagon say 'hi' to them, and they greet them back. Joseph notices Mary's attention is distracted. He sneaks his hand in the back of the supply wagon, reaching into the bag, that she just put in the back. She sees his hand, and kiddingly slaps Joseph's arm. He quickly brings his hand out of the bag empty, with Mary looking at him, saying, "Joseph...stay out of that bag! Ya know that candy is for the children!"

"Sorry, Mary...I sometimes wish I was a kid again around you. You treat those children real good."

"Those children need love Joseph...the Indian children and the orphans."

The train-whistle blows, when the engine slowly comes into town rolling up to the station, ringing its bell. As it approaches and passes the station, the engine steam coming from the engines escape vents, blows across the wooden train platform. The engine passes the station, coming to a stop. The end of one of the passenger cars has stopped near Mary and Joseph. The conductor opens the door, and the passengers begin walking out of the car, and down the steps onto the platform. Mary looks at a small group of Chinese women and men, stepping onto the train platform. They begin looking around the station, then spotting Mary, and staring at her. One of the Chinese women looking at her, says in Chinese, "Look," pointing at Mary.

At the same time, Mary says, "Look," to Joseph, pointing at the Chinese.

Joseph looks at the Chinese, then to the sound of the freight car door opening. He looks at Mary, saying, "This is the first shipment of building material for the new mission."

Mary looks from the Chinese to the freight car, and says, "Can't wait till we start Joseph. The children and nuns need a new place real bad." They both jump off the lead wagon and walk towards the conductor, and train personnel.

Later that evening, Mother Amadeus, Sisters Gertrude and Clara, and five men, are standing outside the mission with ten Blackfoot Indian girls, dressed like 'white' girls. They are wearing white dresses, with white bows tied in their jet-black hair.

The girls are watching Mary driving the freight wagons towards the mission fully loaded with building supplies, and Joseph sitting beside her.

She slows the team of six horses pulling the wagons, rolling to a stop in front of them, saying, "Whoa..."

Mary pulls the brake handle. Joseph jumps down and begins untying the load. The men begin unloading the building supplies from the wagons. All the Indian girls run up to Mary greeting her. She greets them back, with, "Children, children, children, hello."

One of the older Indian girls, is looking at Mary, as Mary looks at her, saying, "Leona, I'm goin' to give ya this bag of candy...ya make sure all the other girls get a piece now, ya hear."

"Yes Miss Mary," says Leona. She takes the bag and begins passing the candy to the other girls, eagerly gathering around her.

Mother Amadeus walks up to Mary looking at the wagons, saying, "Well Mary...this is the first of many deliveries of building supplies...we are finally going to get our new home for the girls. The boys' mission will be on the other side, which we will make sure, the boys and girls are kept well apart."

Mary looks at Mother, and says, "Good luck with that, keep 'em boys away from girls." Then Mary looks at the old mission, and says, "We sure do need one Mother...these winters are very rough and cold...these old wood sheds ain't keepin' the cold out."

St. Peter's Mission with weeds growing on top of roof – Circa 1887

Sisters Clara and Gertrude walk up to the lead wagon looking at Mother Amadeus, and then to Mary, saying, "Mary, can you bring some eggs in from the hennery for tomorrow morning."

"Sure thin' Sister," says Mary. Then looking at Mother Amadeus, she says, "Oh Mother, I forgot...there's a package addressed to St. Peter's Mission." She reaches in the back of the wagon, and picks up the package, handing it to Mother Amadeus. Mother puts out her hand, and stops her, saying, "Open it up Mary." She looks from Mother Amadeus, then to the package, tearing open the package and revealing a new American flag. She pulls the flag out revealing a blue pattern with 'thirty-eight' stars. Mother Amadeus looks at her, and says, "Good, now we have a flag to put on the new flagpole."

"I forgot," says Mary. She looks at the new flagpole beside the steeple, and then says, "Was there a new star Mother?"

"Yes, Mary, I think it was…for Colorado, eighteen seventy-six, eleven years ago?"

"How many more states can there be Mother?" says Mary.

"Don't know Mary, I read that several more will be added in a couple more years. A great part of the Montana territory will probably be the state of Montana."

Joseph walks over to the lead wagon and pushes the last sacks towards the back. The helpers grab the last sacks, as Joseph looks at Mary, saying, "The lead wagon is unloaded, Mary. You said the new chicken feed bin is ready?"

"Yah Joseph. Unhook the lead wagon from the others and hop on," says Mary. She then looks at Mother Amadeus, and says, "Excuse me Mother, got chores to do."

Mother Amadeus smiles at Mary. Joseph climbs aboard. Mary whips the reins, the wagon rolls away, with the children waving good-bye to her.

Later that evening by lantern light, Mary and Joseph are pouring chicken feed into the chicken bin, with several hundred chickens running about, as Joseph says, "Mary, how many more chickens you plan on raisin'?"

"Don't know Joseph. With the new mission being built…we goin'a get more children…we goin'a need a lot of eggs…plus, I'm goin'a be sellin' 'em eggs to the ranchers to raise money for the mission."

"You know Mary, it's funny, the Blackfoot Indians don't bother us no more, kinda since you've been here. Word I hear is, many moons ago, there was a Negro man that went through here on the river with several 'white' men. It was the first time the Indians saw a Negro, and they tried to wipe the Negroes skin away thinking it was paint. When the skin color didn't change, they looked to this Negro man, as a God. I believe that's what the Blackfoot think about you, leaving us and you alone."

"A God huh, Joseph." Mary smiles, then says, "I'm not God, and I'm not afraid of anythin', man or beast."

"You know Father Landesmith is coming tomorrow to lay the first stake for the mission...word is, you did real good here Mary...he wants you to start henneries at other missions."

"Joseph...I ain't goin' no place else, unless Mother Amadeus does."

The next day, Mother Amadeus, an Indian girl, and a photographer with his camera equipment, walk out of the old mission, into a festive celebration. Several townspeople, ranchers, cowboys, dignitaries and guests, are waiting to take a ground breaking ceremony picture, posing with Sisters Gertrude, Clara, and several new Catholic nuns and priests. Mother Amadeus walks over to the group, and stands by Father Landesmith, with his foot on a spade shovel, and the handle in his hand. Mother Amadeus puts her hand under Father Landesmith's, preparing for the ground breaking ceremony picture, as the cameraman's strobe flashes.

"Okay, everyone, Sisters, children, gather over here," says Mother Amadeus waving her arms towards herself. She then looks at Mary, and says, "Mary, you too." Mother Amadeus continues waving everyone to her. As everyone gathers, she says, "Okay, spread out here." She points at the front of the church and quarters, and then says, "I've arranged for the photographer to take a picture of all of us, spread out." Mary climbs on a hay rake wagon, as everyone else goes to a spot. The photographer says, "Ready."

Nuns and children of St. Peter's Mission, and Mary seated on hay gatherer, right St. Peter's Mission – Circa 1887

Split picture from previous page...left side

Split picture from previous page...Right side

"Okay, quickly Sisters, children and Mary, let's take one more picture, everyone, over here." Mother Amadeus walks to where she's pointing. The photographer repositions his camera. Mary moves the hay gatherer. Mother Amadeus points to two other nuns, saying, "You two Sisters, go into the steeple, and look out the windows at the photographer." The two nuns run towards the steeple, as everyone gets in position.

Moments later, the photographer, says, "Ready." The flash goes off, taking the picture.

Mary Fields on wagon left, children and nuns are standing right, with nuns in the steeple
St. Peter's Mission – Circa 1887

Everyone then disperses after taking pictures into groups, conversing. Sisters Gertrude and Clara are with Mother Amadeus who is talking with Father Landesmith, saying, "This is a great day, Father Landesmith."

"Yes, it is Mother. In four years, St. Peter's Mission will offer the little Indian, ranchers', and orphan children, shelter and education. That's why we are taking these pictures, to promote the mission."

"And Father, we are very blessed that the stone for the mission can be quarried from the local hills north of here," says Mother Amadeus.

About an hour later, some of the groups are eating snacks and talking. However, they begin backing up in horror, with their eyes wide open, and pointing. They are pointing and looking at Mary walking towards them carrying, what appears to be a dead skunk by the tail, at arm's length, to the side of her, while carrying a shovel in the other hand.

Sister Gertrude looks at Mary in shock and disgust. Mary approaches, and at the same time, other people back away quickly. She stops in front of them, holding the skunk away from her.

MARY FIELDS aka STAGECOACH MARY

Mother Amadeus and Father Landesmith approach Mary slowly, holding their noses looking at the skunk, then looking at Mary, as Mother Amadeus says, "...Mary...what happened...where did you get the...dead...skunk?"

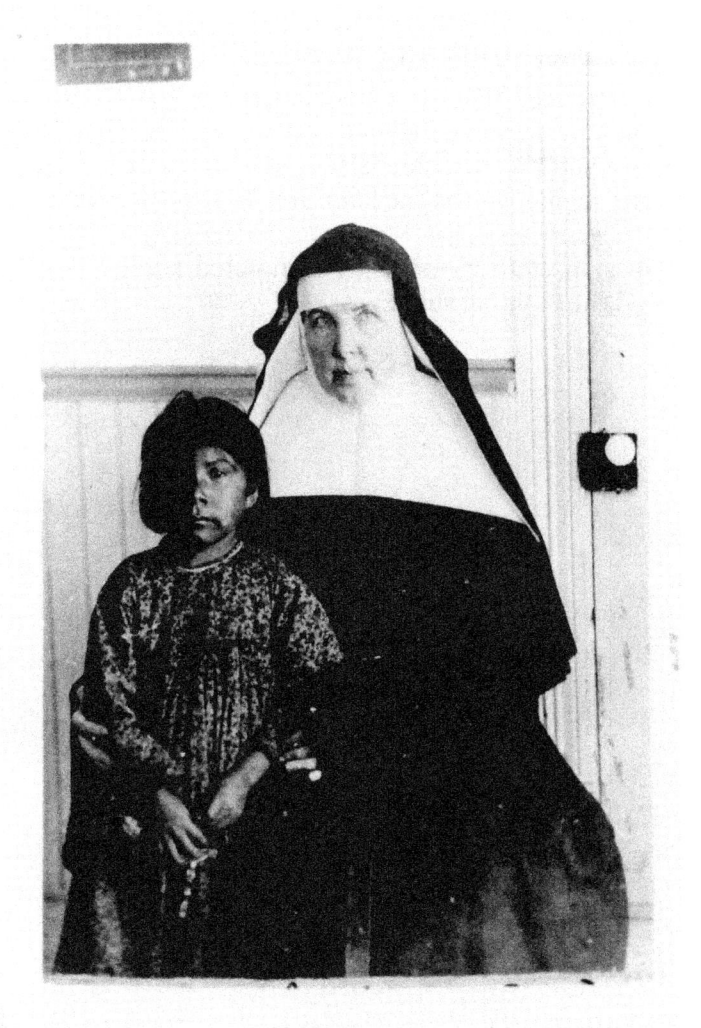

Mother Amadeus and Blackfoot Indian Girl – Circa 1887

Mary holds up the skunk and looks at it, saying, "Damn varmint killed sixty little baby chicks and sprayed the whole place up!" Then she turns and looks at Mother and Father Landesmith, saying, "...Oh'...we went round and round."

"Mary! How did you avoid being sprayed?" says Father Landesmith.

"Why father...I attacked the varmint from the front."

Mother Amadeus and Father Landesmith look at each other, then at the dead skunk in Mary's grip, then at her.

The next day, Joseph and the workers begin digging the building foundation of the girls' mission school and dormitory. Mary, Sister Clara and several other nuns, attend to the builders' needs, serving meals, and mending cuts and wounds, as they do for the next four years of building.

At the quarry, Mary helps the men load the stones on the wagons, and then assist them tying down the loads, and drives the wagons out.

At the train station, Mary loads supplies on a single wagon, from the train platform, then, securing the load, and driving the wagon away.

At the mission, with its partially completed second floor, Mary and Joseph unload the building supplies.

Nuns and construction crew standing in front of mission construction
St. Peter's Mission – Circa 1890

After Mary and Joseph finish unloading the supplies, Mother Amadeus walks over to Mary with a photographer, holding his noisy clanking equipment, and says, "Mary, this photographer is here from the Cascade Courier. They want to get a picture of you, the freight hauler for the mission."

MARY FIELDS aka STAGECOACH MARY

"Sure Mother."

"I heard you carry a shotgun?" says the photographer.

"Ya, a twelve gauge."

"Why don't you get it, and stand in front of the mission for the picture over there."

Mary walks over to the wagon, and picks up her shotgun. She walks to where the photographer pointed. The photographer says, "You ready?"

Mary holds her shotgun, upright, against her right shoulder, and nods her head.

The photographer flashes his strobe.

Mary Fields with her Crescent Firearms Side by side 12-gauge shotgun
Sold and distributed by Sears, Roebuck & Co. - Circa 1890

In the summer of 1890, the new mission continues to be built. Mary plays with the Indian and 'white' children in the yard of the old mission. She then tends to a mature vegetable garden, then to the hennery, collecting eggs.

The next afternoon, Mary is in Cascade selling the eggs. She then visits the Silver Dollar Saloon, having a drink with Mr. Glover at the bar, as Mr. Glover says, "Mary, I need a shipment picked up, that ended up at Fort Shaw. If you have time in your schedule, can you pick up my shipment? I'll pay ya to pick it up."

"Sure Mr. Glover, I'd be glad to get the shipment for ya...just a couple of days to Fort Shaw from here...I have to go to Great Falls anyways, a day out."

"Good. When you get there, see Lieutenant Colonel J. K. Andrews."

"Sure, no problem Mr. Glover. I can come back to the mission, the back way from Great Falls, but I wouldn't be able to get your shipment to ya till...four to six days from now."

"No problem, Mary."

She then smiles at Mr. Glover, and says, "Give the money to St. Peter's." Mary downs her drink and puts the glass on the bar. She extends her hand to Mr. Glover. He smiles and shakes her hand.

Two and a half days later, in the early morning, Mary is driving a single freight wagon towards Fort Shaw, which is now within sight. A group of soldiers are marching out beyond the imaginary post boundary, with their rifles at 'right shoulder arms', and wagons following. They are marching towards Mary.

Mary is looking long and hard at the soldiers marching towards her, carrying the American flag, and their red and white guidon with the number, '25', setting above the letter, 'K'. As Mary and the troops approach each other, she sees the troops are Negro troops, and begins smiling, thinking to herself. She thinks back to the Civil War when she saw the Negro troops chasing the Confederate soldiers.

As the soldiers near, the 'white' officer in the lead shouts his orders, "Troop halt." The soldiers come to a stop. When Mary nears, she pulls up on her reins to the team of horses pulling the freight wagon, and says, "Whoa." The wagon comes to a stop. She looks at the soldiers in awe, and then she looks at the officer, and says, "I'm lookin' for Lieutenant Colonel J. K. Andrews."

The officer says, "Who may I say is looking for him?"

"My name is Mary Fields. I was sent by Mr. Glover from Cascade."

"Yes, we received a wire to expect you," says the officer. The officer points to the post, then says, "Just go to that building over there. That's his office."

Mary looks to where the officer is pointing, then looks back at the soldiers and then to the officer, saying, "I remember Negro soldiers in the last part of the Civil War. They were chasing Confederate soldiers in Mississippi."

"Yes, Mary. They were called, 'Colored Soldiers' then, but now they are called, 'Buffalo Soldiers'." The officer points at the troops, and then says, "This is the 25th Infantry, 'K' Troop of Fort Shaw."

Mary is very elated and smiles. She turns her look from the officer to the soldiers, and says, "A pleasure, and thank ya sir." She whips the reins of the wagon. The wagon rolls away, as she waves good-bye to the officer in back of her, then she looks at the two columns of soldiers as she passes them.

The officer, waves good-bye to Mary. The soldiers try not to look at her passing them. However, they do, from the side of their eyes. Some, kinda turn their heads, trying to get a glimpse of her, as their officer shouts his orders, "Forward, 'Hooo'." The Buffalo Soldiers march off, passing Mary, as if two ships in the night.

One year later, Mary is giving money to Mother Amadeus, and then plays hopscotch with the old and new children of the mission.

A week later, Mary is driving the freight wagons up to the mission construction. She jumps off the lead wagon, and helps the men unload boulders and stones.

Several days later, Mary is tending to the year's new garden. Joseph walks up to Mary, handing her a paper. She looks at the paper, and says, "This is the shipping statement Joseph. This is great, the mission bell will be arrivin' Helena. The new mission is almost complete, we're gettin' the mission bell!"

"Good Mary, I'll pack food for us, for three days to Helena and back, can't wait."

Three days later, Mary and Joseph are at the Helena Train Station, helping several men load a giant crated bell onto the back of the freight wagon.

After the crate is placed on the wagon, Joseph picks up a rope laying by his feet. He ties one end of the rope to the wagon rail, and shouts to Mary on the other side of the crate, "Mary, here's the other end." Joseph tosses the rope over the crate to her.

Mary catches the rope, and pulls it, cinching the rope tight on the wagon rail, then tying off the end, as she shouts, "Okay Joseph, it's tied."

At the mission, days later, Mary and Joseph are helping the men unload the bell from the wagon. She breaks open the top of the crate with a hammer, and Joseph unties the bell from the crate. The men on top of the tower, lower a hook on a hoist rope to Joseph. He attaches the hook to the bell. He looks to the men on top of the tower, and shouts, "It's hooked." The bell begins to rise, as Joseph and Mary guide the bell, out of the crate, and off the wagon, as Mary says, "It's clear." They watch it go up into the air, then over the bell tower, and lowered into place.

January 1892, Mary and Joseph are putting the final touches around the new mission. They have planted trees, scrubs and preparing the ground for grass seeds after winter. She has just finished tapping down the earth when several of the missions' children run across the prepared ground, that she and Joseph just finished manicuring, as Mary yells, "Get off the damn dirt! Your feet are leaving foot prints in the ground, and the grass won't grow even!"

The children quickly run off, leaving their well-told footprints in the soil. Joseph shrugs his shoulders, looking at Mary, as he says, "The children are much more behaved when Mother is here."

"I wish Mother was here so she could tell me where she want her things' when we move in, in a week," says Mary.

St. Peter's Mission – Girls School with grass and scrubs – Circa 1892

MARY FIELDS aka STAGECOACH MARY

A week later, it's a sunny cold day, in front of the new mission. A half dozen nuns, including Sisters Clara and Gertrude, several ranchers, their wives, Joseph, Mary, and priests, are looking at the new stone mission in front of them. Mary is holding onto a wheelbarrow, looking at Joseph, and another priest, as she says, "I'm responsible for all of Mother Amadeus' belongings, that's it! I'll move 'em!"

"But Mary, like Bishop Brondel said, that's at least a quarter mile distance from here to the old quarters, and Mother has a lot of items. Let us help you. Mr. Moran and Mr. Senecal are here with their wagons," says Joseph.

"Mary, listen to reason," says Bishop Brondel. He reaches for the wheelbarrow, and says, "Let the men with the wagons move the items. You help Mrs. Senecal and the Sisters with meals."

Mary moves the wheelbarrow from Bishop Brondel's reach, as she pointedly says, "Bishop, ya help the Sisters with the meals. I'm movin' Mother Amadeus' belongins'."

Mary heads off to the old quarters, pushing the wheelbarrow, as several wagons, Joseph, and all follow.

That evening, Mary is rolling the last of Mother Amadeus' personal belongings in the wheelbarrow, up to the steps of the new mission.

Several months later, it's a beautiful bright spring day, in back of the new mission, in front of the newly built opera house of St. Peter's Mission.

St. Peter's Mission Opera House

Leona, and twenty-four other Indian girls are clapping their hands, and dancing in a circle around Mary, singing *Happy Birthday*. Mother Amadeus, Sister Clara and several new nuns and priests are also clapping their hands, and singing whereas, Sister Gertrude only lightly claps.

The children finish singing. They all guide Mary by her hands and arms over to a table with a birthday cake on top. Mother Amadeus, Sisters Gertrude and Clara, the other nuns and priests follow. Mother smiles, looking at Mary standing next to her, saying, "...Happy Birthday Mary."

"O' thank ya Mother."

"Happy Birthday Mary," says Sister Clara.

"O thank ya so much Sister Clara," says Mary.

Grudgingly Sister Gertrude says, "Happy Birthday."

"Why thank ya Sister," says Mary.

The girls are standing around the table shouting, "Cut the cake. Cut the cake." Mary smiles, looks at them, and says, "Okay, okay children, please wait...ya have to eat first and we are not cuttin' the cake here." Mary smiles at the children, and says, "We have a little surprise for ya."

All the girls look at Mary covering the cake.

Joseph coming from the barn shouts at Mary, "Mary, the wagons are all hitched and full of hay."

"Thank ya Joseph," shouts Mary. She then turns and looks at Mother Amadeus, and says, "I'm sure the girls are gonna like where we are goin'."

Mother Amadeus smiles at Mary putting the cake in a picnic basket. Mother Amadeus and Sister Clara then gather blankets from the porch banister of the opera house.

Leona is standing with the rest of the girls looking at all the commotion. Mother Amadeus looks at the girls, and says, "Children, let me have your attention." All the children stop talking and look at Mother, as she then says, "Mary is going to take you on a hay ride."

All the girls shout, "Yes!"

Mary looks at Leona, and says, "Leona, gather the children down by the barn, okay."

Leona smiles, and says, "Yes, Miss Mary." Leona leads the happy children, skipping towards the barn.

Later in the day, Mary is singing, *Wade in the Water*, driving the lead freight wagon, lined with hey, pulling two other hey lined wagons along the trail, leading to the top of the mountain. Joseph is sitting beside her with the shotgun between them.

Mother Amadeus, Sister Clara, Leona and several girls are seated in the second wagon, while several other nuns and girls are seated in the third wagon. They are all singing along with Mary, as she sings,

"Sometimes I'm up lord and sometimes I'm down. Ya know my God's gonna trouble the water. Sometimes I'm level to the ground. God's gonna trouble the water. Wade in the water...wade in the water...God's gonna trouble the water." As the wagons near the top, Mary stops singing. She slows and stops the wagons, saying, "Whoa, whoa..." She pulls the brake handle, then looks back to her passengers, and says, "Okay everyone...we're here."

All look down on St. Peter's Mission, to the old and new buildings for a few moments. Mother Amadeus smiles, then looks at everyone, and says, "St. Peter's is growing."

"Sure is Mother," says Mary.

Mary and Joseph then step back onto the lead wagon bed and begin unloading picnic tables. Mother Amadeus and Sister Clara take picnic baskets, and blankets off their wagon, then laying the blankets on the ground, as do the nuns in the third wagon. Mother Amadeus then looks at the girls, and says, "Okay, children."

All the girls jump off the wagons, and rush to the blankets, sitting quietly. They look at Mary and Joseph setting up the picnic tables, as Leona says, "Miss Mary. Tell us the meaning of that song we were singing again."

Mother Amadeus and the nuns set the picnic baskets on the tables, as Mary says, "Well, children...we slaves used song's and drums to talk to one another, sometimes over great distances...like your people. The words meant 'of safe travel', like, 'Wade in the Water' to hide your footprints, the direction to go...sometimes the words meant to fight back, and escape."

Later that year, at night, Mary is in her new quarters, on the first floor, when desperate shouts of, 'Fire' is heard. She quickly throws her book down, opens the door, blows out her candles, and rushes out, looking and smelling the air. More shouts of, 'Fire' are heard, coming from the basement below, where smoke is rising from the doorway. She runs towards the stairs, and then down the stairs towards the basement, as do, several other nuns, older children, and hired help running in through the front and side doors.

When Mary reaches the basement, she sees Sister Clara, still panicking and yelling, "Fire," pointing at the Bolton Heater, with flames coming from around back, and out of the exhaust pipe.

Mary quickly goes to a cabinet and grabs several bags of salt, she turns and while rushing towards the fire, she rips open one of the bags. When she reaches the fire, she throws hands full of salt on the heater and fire rising on the wall, while water begins pouring down, in through the exhaust pipe above, extinguishing the last of the fire.

That winter, a team of two horses, is pulling a single freight wagon, through blowing snow, at dust. Mary wearing her buckskin coat, is driving the wagon with three nuns, all are wrapped in blankets. One nun is sitting beside her on the wagon seat, and the other two are in the back, sitting on a pile of hey. One of the nuns sitting in back, is holding her head low, with a twisted rag wrapped around her jaw, to the top of her head. She is holding one side of her swollen face, with her hand, while being held and comforted by the other nun.

Mary is whipping the reins, when she looks at the nun next to her, and shouts over the noise of the wind, "Must of missed the turn to the mission, this don't look right. This sudden snow storm came out of nowhere, can't tell what's what."

The nun looks at Mary, and says, "We have to get Sister Catherine out of this weather."

"I know Sister." Mary looks back over her shoulder at Sister Catherine, then, looks back at the nun, saying, "Don't understand Sister Angela, why the Army Doctor don't have tools to pull your teeth?"

"The officer said, they are closing the post. All government equipment had to be sent back to Washington, before the closing. They have to send their soldiers to Great Falls," shouts Sister Angela.

"Wish we knew that before goin'. We's goin' to Great Falls tomorrow, to take Sister, if I can find our way back to the mission, it's gettin' dark," shouts Mary.

An hour later, it's still blowing snow, and total darkness is setting in, as the wagon slowly rolls along. Mary, driving the wagon, is looking towards the horizon, when she points, and says, "Look, I think I see a light?"

All the nuns look to where Mary is pointing. Sister Lucia, sitting with Sister Catherine in the back, shouts, "I see it!"

"I see it too," shouts Sister Angela.

Mary quickens the pace of the horses, pulling the wagon towards the light...

Moments later, Mary is knocking on the front door of a cabin, with a light coming from windows in the front. Sister Angela is standing to her side. A man opens the door slowly, with a pistol in his hand, and a woman peering over his shoulder. He looks at Mary, then, to Sister Angela, then back to Mary, looking at her, up and down, then, saying, "What ya want?"

"I'm Sister Angela. We are from St. Peter's Mission, and we seem to be lost in this snow storm."

The man looks from Mary, to Sister Angela pointing, then, saying, "The mission is several valleys over, in that direction."

"How did I miss the turn?" says Mary.

"Easy to do in this weather," says the man. He then looks out at the wagon, and sees the other nuns, and says, "No sense tryin' to get there in this weather. Brin' your friends in…I'll take ya there tomorrow. My new wife and I were just talkin' about religion…then you come a knockin'. Well, I'll be…my name is Mr. Farrell," as he opens the door.

The next year, Mary, holding her shotgun at her side, is having an argument towards the back of the mission with a hired hand holding his rifle, at his side, as she says, "I'm the freight hauler, and ya don't damn tell me what to do!"

"Who made ya Queen, black woman!?" says the hired hand.

"The hell with ya, Mosney!" says Mary.

The shouting has brought Sister Gertrude to an open window. She looks down at the arguing between Mary and Mosney.

"Ya think ya tough!?" says Mosney.

"I don't think I'm tough, Mosney…I know I'm the freight hauler, and ya can't and won't tell me what to do!"

Mosney eyes Mary, and then slowly, he brings up his rifle, as a gesture of truce. Mary seeing Mosney's actions, brings her shotgun up. She eyes Mosney, and they touch the barrels of their weapons, in mid-air. Sister Gertrude withdraws back inside.

Two years later, in 1895, it is an early spring day at the mission. Puffy white clouds dot the beautiful big blue skies, as Mary dances with her rake, in back of the mission, working outside the garden, singing, *"…Free at last, free at last, thank God Almighty we's free at last. Free at last, free at last, thank God Almighty we's free at last…"*

Sister Clara is hanging up several pairs of men's drawers on a clothesline near the mission's well. She looks at Mary, then shouts, "Mary…please check on the Bishop's new under-clothes here, to see if they're dry before you come in for me, okay?"

"Sure thin' Sister Clara," says Mary. Sister Clara picks up the clothesbasket and heads towards the mission. Mary goes back to raking, dancing, and singing, *"Free at last, free at last, thank God almighty, we's free at last. If ya get there before I do…thank God Almighty, we's free at last. Tell all my family and friends I'm comin' 'too', thank God Almighty, we's free at last."*

Mary stops singing, and kneels down on one knee, picking a weed from the ground, as she hears a male voice from in back of her, say, "Did I hear ya say ya 'free' Nigger?" Mary pivots on the ball of her foot, and looks up at two gun strapped frontiersmen, chuckling, walking towards her, and stopping several yards away. One of the frontiersmen begins to chuckle even louder. He looks at Mary, and says, "Niggers ain't free!" He looks at his friend, then looking back at Mary, he says, "Ya better quit all that singin' and dancin' for the overseer here see ya and put the whip to your back!" Then, the frontiersman looks around the area, saying, "...Hey Nigger, we're lookin' for work...where's the boss." The frontiersman looks back down at Mary, who's looking up at him, as he says, "Since ya can sing, ya do know how to talk, don't ya...Nigger!" Mary stands up and looks up at the sky, shrugging her shoulders, and sighing. She then lays her rake on the ground, and walks over to the frontiersmen. The frontiersman is somewhat astonished. He looks at his friend, and says, "They make 'em big around here, don't they!"

The frontiersman's friend nods his head up and down, rather nervously with an astonished expression on his face. He is looking at Mary's size, as she approaches, and says, "Mister..." Mary stops in front of the frontiersman, looking at him, then looks at his friend, saying, "I'm the 'overseer' of the labor here at St. Peters'...'boss', my name is Mary and I'm very 'free'...and ain't nobody goin' to put a 'whip' to Mary!" Then pointedly, she says, "'Now'...if ya wanta get paid, ya gotta work...go down to the barn and see Joseph."

"Okay...NIGGER Mary," says the Frontiersman, as he spits at Mary's feet, then gets in her face, saying, "No NIGGER is goin' to tell me what to do!"

"Mister...I think ya best be goin' now!" pointedly, says Mary.

"No Nigger goin' to tell me when to leave either!" angrily, says the frontiersman.

Mary, seeing the frontiersman is looking for trouble, attempts to step back from him. However, he pushes her. Mary begins to fall backwards, but she catches herself, stepping back, then lunging forward with a left cross, into the frontiersman's jaw. The frontiersman falls back to the ground. His friend, seeing the tenacity of Mary, steps back not wanting any part of this wildcat unleashed. Mary looks at him quickly.

The frontiersman she hit, goes for his sidearm, whereas, Mary seeing the frontiersman's action, pulls her pistol from under her coat and apron top, pulling the hammer back, methodically aims and fires one shot at the frontiersman. He rolls out of the way of the shot.

The frontiersman gets to his feet. Another shot rings out, hitting where he was lying. He pulls his gun, but it is shot out from his hand. He looks at Mary pulling the hammer back again, and aiming at him. Both frontiersmen take off running through the clothes hanging on the clothesline. Mary fires at him, hitting several of the Bishops drawers, just missing the frontiersmen.

She pulls the hammer back again, taking aim, and click. Mary looks at the pistol, and then says, "Damn, always leave that one out for safety!" She looks at both frontiersmen running to their horses, looking back over their shoulders. They mount their horses, and head down the road at a full run, away from the mission. She reloads her gun, looking at them headed towards town. Joseph comes running towards Mary, looking back at the frontiersmen, leaving dust in their escape.

Heads begin to pop out of the windows and doorways of the mission, and any other cover there is to hide behind. Sisters Clara and Gertrude slowly peek round the doorway.

Mother Amadeus is at the second floor window looking out from around the lower corner of the window, making sure the coast is clear before she raises her head.

Sister Gertrude rushes out the door, looking at Mary reloading her pistol, shouting, "Have you lost your 'mind' woman!?"

Mary says, "Sister..."

Interrupting, Sister Gertrude says, "I'm going to talk to the Bishop about this!" She quickly turns around and storms back into the mission.

Mother Amadeus appears from behind her window looking down at Mary. Looking up at Mother, Mary shrugs her shoulders.

Several weeks later, Mother Amadeus is seated, writing at her desk, when there is a knock on her door. She looks at the door, and says, "Come in." The door opens, and Mary walks in, closing the door behind her, then, looking at Mother. Mother Amadeus looks back at her, and says, "Good morning Mary."

"Good morning Mother." Mary then looks into Mother Amadeus' eyes, and then says, "I guess ya heard back from the Bishop?"

Mother Amadeus nods her head, saying, "Yes Mary...sit down please."

Mary sits in a chair in front of Mother Amadeus' desk. She looks at her somewhat excited, saying, "Mother...ya know it wasn't my fault, that man 'attacked me', I defended myself! He was pulling his gun first...Mother ya know if I wanted to hit him, I could of!"

"Yes Mary I know, but shhh..." Mary looks at Mother Amadeus, and calms down. Mother Amadeus seeing Mary has calm herself, says, "Mary, I know the man attacked you, you defended yourself, and you had every right to, however..." Then saddened, she sighs, and says, "The Bishop wants you fired, off the property, Mary."

She swallows her heart, looking at Mother Amadeus, with tears welling up in her eyes. Mary then says, "Mother...that's not 'fair'...can't ya say somethin', to change his mind?"

"I already tried, very hard, Mary...some of the Sisters have talked to the Bishop about other situations. About you, with Mr. Mosney, your drinking and smoking, he absolutely refuses." Then with resolve, she says, "Mary, it wasn't the fact you fired the gun at the men, even though that's the reason he's given...I think the Bishop was more angry about his...new 'darn' fangle under-clothes being perforated, more so than anything else...he had been waiting months for 'em...underwear." She then smiles, and says, "Some fancy silk material from Europe."

Mary quickly stands up, and says, "Mother, I'm goin' to go talk to him. I'll change his mind. I'm going to Helena!"

Mother Amadeus stands quickly, and says, "No Mary!" Then with resolve, she says, "I'm sorry...please...please sit back down."

Mary and Mother Amadeus look at each other, then both sit back down in their chairs. With a concerned look, Mary says, "What else can I do around here, Mother?"

"Mary, in less than six years, a new millennium will be here...things hopefully will change with time, people will look at 'you', and your people as equals in God's name."

Mary looks into Mother Amadeus' eyes, and says, "Don't think so Mother. One would of thought things' would change after the war...they haven't much...well, at least up here, I haven't seen any 'Negroes' hangin' from trees."

Mother Amadeus says frantically, "I hope not Mary!" As she then smiles, chuckles, and says, "...You are the only Negro in these parts, except for those soldiers that were at Fort Shaw for a couple of years, before they closed the post, in ninety one. They called them Buffalo Soldiers."

Mary thinks for a quick second, smiles, and says, "Yes, I remember meetin' 'em."

Mother Amadeus looks at Mary, and smiles, saying, "Mary, you have accomplished a lot for St. Peter's since you've been here. You've helped bring the building materials that built the mission, you started the hennery, the mission's garden, you've been great with the children...you've taught the cooks." Then with resolve, she says, "Mary you're very good in the kitchen. Joseph said one of the restaurants went out of business in Cascade a couple of months ago. When I went into town yesterday, I spoke with Mr. Glover...Mary I gave him a deposit...you can have your own business, and it's got a room in the back."

Mary pauses, and then says, "...My own business? Mother, I rather stay here and work for the mission."

Later, early fall, it's pouring down rain outside Mary's restaurant. Inside, she is serving a hot delicious plate of eggs, bacon, and biscuits to a cowboy drinking coffee, sitting at the counter. Another customer waves at Mary, as he's leaving, closing the front door behind him.

Mary walks over to the fireplace, and puts a mitten on one hand, and grabs a spatula with the other. She reaches into the fireplace, pulling out a skillet, she turns over two eggs with the spatula, and puts the skillet back into the fire. She takes off the mitten, picks up the coffee pot, turns and begins pouring coffee into a cup on the counter. Joseph is finishing his food, as Mary says, "How's breakfast this mornin', Joseph?"

"Thanks for the refill. Fine, very good as usual, Mary." Joseph reaches in his pocket, and brings out a silver dollar, and placing it on the counter. A customer then walks over to Mary, stands next to Joseph, and says, "Thank you, Mary. As soon as spring gets here, I'll pay ya back...keep that tab goin' for me."

"No problem. Tell the Mrs. I said hello."

"Sure thin', Mary."

The customer turns and leaves. Joseph looks around the restaurant, then looks at Mary, speaking softly, saying, "Mary, how many people you letting pay later?"

"Not many Joseph. Those poor sheepherders...they barely makin' enough to keep their poor families fed. I'm just makin' sure they stay strong, feedin' 'em. They'll pay me end of spring."

"Mary, since I've been here, you've let two customers go without paying...don't let them take advantage of you."

"I'm not Joseph. I'm just tryin' to be a good neighbor."

That winter, a cold chilled wind blows, and tumbleweeds roll down the towns' road. Townspeople are going about their daily tasks. Mary and Joseph are nailing up a sign in front of the restaurant, with the words, 'Out of business'.

Mother Amadeus, Mr. Glover and Mayor Monroe approach the wood plank walkway of the restaurant, as Mary finishes nailing her side of the sign. Mr. Glover, the Mayor and Mother Amadeus stop, and look at Mary, as Mother Amadeus says, "Mary."

She turns, and looks at them, saying, "Oh'...hi everyone."

Simultaneously, Mr. Glover says, "Hi Mary," and the Mayor, says, "Good morning Mary."

Joseph finishes nailing his side, then turns and looks at Mother Amadeus, and the others, saying, "Mother, got all of Mary's things packed-up in back on the freight wagon."

"Thank you Joseph," says Mother Amadeus. She looks at Mary, saying, "Mary, Mr. Glover and the Mayor have something to tell you."

"Mary, the Mayor and I put our heads together...we got a little cabin for ya just outside of town," says Mr. Glover.

Mary looks at Mr. Glover and the Mayor with gratitude, saying, "Mr. Glover, Mayor Monroe...thank ya, thank ya...but, how can I pay ya back?"

"Mary, as 'duly' elected Mayor, and sheriff, consider this a gift from the town of Cascade, for all your 'kindness' you have shown to the children of St. Peter's, and to the town of Cascade."

"Mayor, thank ya," says Mary, as tears well up in her eyes.

"Mary...there's some more good news," says Mother Amadeus.

Mary, wipes the tears from under her eyes, and curiously looks at Mother Amadeus, as Mother says, "Next week, The 'U. S. Postal System', is starting a new mail route past the mission to the settlements in the back country. They are taking over from Wells Fargo."

"Yah, I heard they had cut a new road past the mission...they call it the Mullen Road," says Mary.

"Tomorrow morning Mary, they are having a contest to see who's the fastest in hitchin' horses to a wagon, then racing the wagon around the town for the job," says Mr. Glover.

"I talked to the Wells Fargo Agent, Mary. At first, he refused...however, Mr. Glover here, convinced him," says Mother Amadeus.

"Convinced him what?" says Mary.

"For you to compete for the postal job, delivering the mail," says Mother Amadeus.

"Ya mean, me...apply for the job?"

Everyone nods their head. Mother Amadeus looks at Mary, and says, "Yes Mary. This way, no one can tell you what to do...you are your own boss."

"Mary, you can do it...you hitch horses and wagons pretty quick...you know how to handle a team, you should win," says Joseph.

"You'll be competing with some of the best Mary...all you have to do is hitch two horses to the wagon tongue, drive the wagon around town once, and be the best time," says Mr. Glover.

Mary smiles, and looks at everyone. The mayor looks at Mary, then looks at everyone also, saying, "Even if Mary wins...that's still pretty rough country for a woman up there, who sometimes will have to carry important documents...about fifteen miles to the mission post office, and another twenty-five past there."

"Mayor, Mary won't have any problems...she's been in that part of the country before, she can take care of herself," says Mother Amadeus. She smiles at Mary, and Mary smiles in agreement.

The next day, at the Wells Fargo Overland Stage & Cascade Stage-line Offices, there's a quiet murmur. The crowd of townspeople along with frontiersmen, ranchers and cowboys, are encircled around the front of the office and stables. They are looking at the Wells Fargo Agent, writing on a tablet, as he then looks at the crowd, and says, "This is the new Postal System position of mail carrier, northwest, Montana Territory. The fastest time so far is..." He looks at the tablet he's holding, and says, "Laliberty, nine minutes, twenty-five seconds. The next, and last contestant, Mary Fields."

The spectators' murmur increases. Mary wearing her buckskin coat makes her way through the crowd while the quiet murmur settles.

The Wells Fargo Agent waves at the blacksmith, who brings a wagon by the tongue from around the front of the stables. Meanwhile, Joseph and a stable boy are bringing out two horses from the stable by their harnesses that Mary will use for the race. The Agent then looks at Mary putting on her gloves, walking over to Joseph, who's tying the horses to the hitching rail near the front of the wagon, as the Agent says, "Miss Fields, you know the rules?"

Mary stops near Joseph. She turns, looking at him, and shouts, "Yes Sir, Agent Harris. Hitch those horses to this wagon, go around town course, be the best time back here." She then looks and points at the banner strung across the road, then saying, "Crossing that banner."

"Ah, yes, yes. All right, you have fresh horses, like the other contestants. On my signal, hitch the horses to the wagon, mount the wagon, then, drive the wagon around Cascade, following the course, ending here."

Mr. Glover and the Mayor are standing next to Mother Amadeus, as she shouts, "Go get 'em, Mary." She and everyone looks at Mother Amadeus, who blushes slightly, standing on her tip-toes, trying to look over the crowd at Mary.

Looking back, Mary smiles, and shouts, "Thank ya Mother."

"Alright, are ya ready?" shouts Agent Harris.

The crowd becomes even more anxious. Mary looks at Joseph, and says, "We ready Joseph?"

"Ready as we can be, Mary."

"Thanks, Joseph." She then looks at Agent Harris, and says, "Ready!"

Agent Harris brings out his pocket watch, and looks at it, as everyone else looks at theirs or someone else's watch. Agent Harris studies his watch, then brings his gun out and points it into the air, firing the gun.

Mary runs to the horses Joseph brought out, and unties one of the reins from the hitching rail, backing the horse to the left side of the tongue, into its position. She looks at the horse, taking a piece of apple out of her pocket, and giving it to the animal. The other horse shakes, then, nods his head, making noises. She looks at the horse, and says, "There's more where that came from, ya win this race." She secures the horse in the tongue, and then rushes to the other one, taking another piece of apple out of her pocket, and giving it to him. She unties the horse, and moves it into its position on the right side of the wagon tongue.

Moments later, Mary is finishing securing the second horse to the tongue, tying its reins to the front of the wagon. She then quickly checks the bits in the horses' mouths, pulling on their straps. She steps back and looks at the team, eyeing her rigging, and then quickly walks around the wagon, as Mother Amadeus shouts, "Hurry Mary...hurry!"

Mary quickly checks another strap, then hurries to the front of the wagon, climbs aboard, and sits on the bench seat. Some of the spectators cheer her on, along with Mr. Glover, shouting, "Be quick Mary! Hurry, hurry!"

The Mayor shouts, "Come on Mary!"

Mother Amadeus shouts, "Go Mary go!"

And Joseph is shouting, "Mary...go Mary go!"

Mary takes the reins in her gloved hands. She releases the brake, then whipping the reins, shouting, "Yah...yah, hah, hah, yah!" The wagon takes off down the road, in a cloud of dust towards the center of town. Most of the townspeople are waving and shouting, cheering Mary on, as she flies by them, whipping the reins, shouting, "Hah, hah...yah, yah...hah!"

Some of the spectators, townspeople, ranchers, cowboys, and frontiersmen are cheering Mary on. The wagon rolls quickly down the road headed for the edge of town, and the first turn. When the wagon nears the turn, she pulls on the reins, slowing the wagon, then, pulling on the right reins, leaning to her right, and turning the team of horses. The wagon slides, kicking up more dust, making the turn, as Mary whips the reins shouting, "Hah, yah...yah, yah...hah!" The wagon quickly gains speed again disappearing behind the town buildings. Several townspeople run to look at Mary's dust she is leaving behind.

Moments later, at the Wells Fargo - Cascade stables. Some of the townspeople who were at the other end of town, watching Mary turn the corner, are now running back to the finish line, to join the other spectators looking down the road for any signs of Mary and the wagon, coming from the other direction.

The crowd quiets, when in the distance the sound of Mary shouting, is heard, "Yah, yah, hah, hah," coming from behind the town's buildings several blocks away.

Joseph begins jumping up and down with excitement, shouting, "Come on Mary, come on!" Several spectators at the other end of town, begin running back to the start/finish line, shouting, "Here she comes!"

All of a sudden the wagon comes skidding around the corner at the edge of town, kicking up dust. Mary pulls the reins, straightening the wagon out, then whipping the reins, driving the team of horses, pulling the wagon towards the finish line.

The crowd suddenly erupts with elation, cheering Mary on, as Mr. Glover shouts, "Come on...Mary, come on!" ...and simultaneously, the Mayor shouts, "Come on, Mary!"

Mother Amadeus has a hold of Joseph's arm, squeezing his arm, as Joseph yelps, "Ouch!" Mother Amadeus quickly lets go of his arm. She looks at him embarrassed, and says, "...Oh, I'm so sorry Joseph, I'm just so excited."

"That's alright Mother," says Joseph.

They both quickly turn and look at Mary driving the wagon at full speed across the finish line, with a dust trail following behind her.

Mary slows, and turns the team of horses, stopping the wagon.

The crowd goes wild with cheers, at the tenacity of Mary handling the horses and wagon. They rush to Mary and the wagon, celebrating her gallant ride. She stands in the foot box, pulls the brake handle, holding the reins in her hands, and steading the team of horses, saying, "Whoa...whoa...whoa..." The horses settle.

Mary ties off the reins to the wagon, as Mr. Glover steps up, and puts his hand out to help her step off the foot box. She is breathing hard, while she looks at Mr. Glover smiling, taking his hand, saying, "Why thank ya...Mr. Glover." She takes hold of Mr. Glover's hand and jumps off the wagon, landing both feet on the ground. All the spectators that can reach her, are patting her on the back.

Joseph, Mother Amadeus and the Mayor, are making their way through the crowd towards Mary.

She is talking with Mr. Glover and the townspeople, as Joseph with a big grin reaches Mary first, and quickly hugs her. He says, "Mary, you were fantastic!"

"Why thank ya, Joseph," says Mary.

The Mayor looks at Mary, and says, "Pardon me Mary, I must say, you handled that team of horses like I never seen before!"

"Thank ya, Mayor, nothin' to it."

"Mary, I think you won?" says Mother Amadeus.

A quiet murmur settles in the crowd. Mary, Mother Amadeus and the others look at Agent Harris. He is writing on his tablet, and then looks at his watch quickly, then back to the tablet, scratching his head. He clears his throat and looks at the crowd of spectators, and says, "The winner is, nine minutes..." Then he looks at the tablet again, and then says, "Eleven seconds, Mary Fields."

Much of the crowd erupts with enthusiasm. Some cowboys fire their guns into the air.

The crowd congratulates Mary by patting her on the back, and shaking her hands, as she looks at Mother Amadeus, and smiles. She then quickly walks over to Mother Amadeus, wrapping her arms around her, picking her up with excitement, and shouting, "I did it, I did it, alright...thank ya Mother."

"Yes, you did Mary, thank the Lord..." says Mother Amadeus. Mary spins around once with Mother in her arms. Mother Amadeus holds onto her habit, saying, "...Mary, please put me down."

Mary puts Mother Amadeus back down on the ground. She then turns, and looks at Mr. Glover and kisses him on the cheek. She turns again to the Mayor, and kisses him on the forehead. She then looks at Joseph, she grabs his hand, pulls him to her, and kisses him on the cheek, as he blushes.

Mr. Glover looks at Mary, saying, "Mary, the next drink is on me."

"Thank ya, Mr. Glover, sure thin'," She then looks at Joseph, saying, "Joseph, ya mind takin' Mother to the train station for me. She has to go to Helena."

"No problem Mary...Oh, here's your pistol."

Joseph hands Mary her gun and gun belt. She puts the gun into her holster, and straps the holster belt under her skirt waistband, with the pistol in front of her, under her buckskin coat. She then turns, looks at Mother Amadeus, and says, "Mother, Mr. Glover invited me for a drink. Joseph goin' to take ya to the train station when ya ready."

Mother Amadeus, with concern, looks at Mary, takes her by the hand, leads her away from the crowd of spectators, then looks at her, and says, "Mary, I wish you wouldn't drink whiskey, and...come to church."

"Mother, I already told ya, I'm not goin' to stop drinkin', and my church is in my heart, not man made buildins'..." Then with empathy, she says, "I'm sorry Mother...come, let me walk ya to the wagon."

Mary holds her hand out to Mother Amadeus, who sighs, then looks at her and smiles. She takes her hand, and they both walk to the mission wagon as Joseph follows.

Several hours later, a smoky haze hangs in the festive Silver Dollar saloon. The usual piano music, and saloon girls entertain patrons, while other patrons play poker at the tables.

Harry, the bartender is serving a patron at the bar. Mary is standing next to the patron, downing a shot of whiskey, putting the glass back on the bar. She then puts one of her homemade cigars up to her mouth, gripping it with her lips, puffing till the end turns cherry red. She then picks up a bottle of whiskey in front of her, and pours another round in her glass.

Several of the hardcore contestants from the competition are at the other end of the bar, talking to one another, occasionally looking at Mary. One of the contestants, a stranger in town, is staring at her. He steps back from the bar, and faces her. He then yells at Mary with a disrespectful tone, "Nigger...ya as fast with that gun as ya are with a wagon...cause I think ya cheated!?"

Mary looks down and sees part of her pistol handle is exposed. She pulls her coat over her gun. She knows the stranger is looking for trouble, so she ignores him staring ahead, smoking her cigar, as he shouts, "Hey Nigger! I said, ya as fast with that gun as ya are with a wagon, NIGGER!"

Mary turns, smiles and looks at the stranger, saying, "Mister...I ain't gotta cheat, and I ain't lookin' for no trouble."

"Well...I am, NIGGER! I came all the way here for that job, I still say ya cheated...and no Nigger gonna take a job from me!" He quickly looks left and right at the room, then looking back at Mary, he says, I'm gonna give ya some trouble...NIGGER!"

The piano player has stopped playing. The patrons at the bar and tables, clear away quickly to the walls, leaving Mary leaning sideways against the bar. She stares at the stranger and several of the other hardcore contestants standing behind him. She points to them, then says, "Mister, why don't ya turn back around, and enjoy yourself with..."

"Mary, Mr. Glover said he be back in an hour," a worried Harry, says interrupting.

"That's all right Harry. Mr. Glover can take care of himself...I can take care of me!"

"Bitch Nigger, ya ain't gonna take care of shit...ya gonna die!" says the stranger. Slowly, the stranger pulls back his coat revealing his gun. The hardcore contestants standing behind him, move away quickly.

Mary then looks up to the ceiling, and softly speaking, says, "Oh...here we go again Lord."

Mary takes the cigar out of her mouth laying it on the bar. She slowly backs away from the bar, then, turns to the stranger with a determined look. She now faces the stranger, pulling back her coat, revealing her pistol. Mary, with her hands now poised, says, "Mister...ya can end this here and now, by turnin' back around and enjoyin' yourself with your friends."

"I'm gonna end it all right," says the stranger.

The stranger goes for his gun. However, Mary is much faster, pulling her gun cocking the hammer, aiming her pistol right at the stranger's head with purpose. The stranger, looking at Mary, has just pulled his gun out of its holster.

The entire room gasps.

The stranger, looking at Mary, has a surprised expression on his face, as Mary says, "Do ya wanta' meet your 'maker' now...or later when he's a callin' for ya?"

"That's not fair, ya drew first!" says the stranger.

"I thought that's what it was about!" Says Mary shaking her head. She sees the stranger has an itchy trigger finger, therefore, with a resolved look in her eyes, she says, "Tell ya what mister. ...I'll put my pistol back, ya put yours back...I'll give ya another chance."

Mary keeps an eye on the stranger. She slowly releases the hammer on her thirty-eight, putting her pistol back in her holster. The stranger eagerly re-holsters his gun. He licks his lips, feeling he's bagged a lamb. He settles in his stance, then, looks around the room.

Everyone is shaking their heads, ever so slightly. The stranger questions his eyesight. He wipes his eyes. He then looks back at the patrons in the saloon again, still shaking their heads. He becomes uneasy, and begins to sweat a little. He looks back at Mary with doubt, stuttering, he says, "...She...couldn't...be...that fast?"

"Oh yes she is!" says Harry.

The stranger quickly looks at Harry behind the bar, then at everyone else in the saloon nodding their heads exaggeratedly.

Mary stands ready. The stranger swallows hard, and eases out of his stance. He then turns, and looks at the other hardcore contestants that were with him. They look at him, as if saying, *it's your fight*. The stranger turns away, and quickly walks towards the swinging doors and out of the saloon. The other contestants follow, not looking back.

The saloon patrons go back to their tables and positions at the bar. The piano player begins playing. The swinging doors slow in motion, as Mr. Glover pushes them back open, walking into the saloon, followed by Agent Harris with a rolled-up canvas under his arm.

Mr. Glover looks around the saloon, then, he sees Mary. He walks towards her, and when he approaches, he looks over his shoulder, and says, "Where's part of the party going?" Then he looks back at her.

"They goin' a lookin' for another job," says Mary. She smiles then turns back to the bar, putting the cigar up to her mouth, and grips it with her lips. Mr. Glover looks back at the doors, and says, "Hope they find one."

Agent Harris walks by Mr. Glover, and up to the bar next to Mary. He lays the rolled canvas on top. Mary looks at him, and says, "Hello Agent Harris...is that the route and schedule?"

"Ya Mary..." Then with resolve, Agent Harris says, "Mary, that was some fancy ridin' ya did, never seen nothing like it."

"It was nothin', Agent Harris...I just wanted the job," says Mary.

Mr. Glover walks up to the bar in back of Agent Harris, and says, "Harry, whiskey for Mary and me."

Agent Harris smiles at Mary, and then unfurls the canvas. He removes several documents, then, pointing to the canvas, saying, "This is the route map, Mary. Tomorrow, at six in the mornin' sharp, you'll pick up the mail and parcels from the train station here in Cascade and start your delivery..." He then points to the map, and says, "Your first stop is the new mission post office, here, then all the way up the Mullen Road."

One of the approximate routes of Mary Fields to the mission.

The next day, it's early in the morning, on the Cascade Train Station platform. Mary is tossing several mailbags on the buckboard wagon with her shotgun propped upright, laying against the bench seat.

Seven hours later, Mary is greeting Mother Amadeus at the mission Post Office, and handing the mission's mailbag to Sister Clara. Mary then, jumps off the wagon, onto the ground, and hugs all the children that are there, eagerly waiting to hug her.

St. Peter's Mission – Montana – Post Office – Circa 1896

Several days later, Mary is on the trail driving the mail wagon, on her way to Great Falls. She sees several Blackfoot & Cheyenne Indians, sitting bareback on their ponies, on a hill not far away, watching her roll along. She takes the shotgun by the middle of the barrel, and raises it into the air. The Indians seeing Mary raising her shotgun, also, raise their rifles, in the air by the middle of the barrel, in acknowledgement. Mary smiles, looking at them, then, she puts the shotgun on her lap, as the wagon rolls along.

That coming winter, Mary is in the Cascade General Store buying a buffalo coat. Several evenings later, she's delivering mail to miners, at their shacks in the Badland country of central northern Montana.

The next year in Cascade, townspeople, cowboys, and ranchers, are crowding around the door of the Wells Fargo – Cascade Office. Some are standing on their tiptoes, peering in the office, as a familiar voice, emanates from within, yelling, "...Ya a damn 'lie' Charlie Russell!" yells Mary.

"It's just a picture Mary. I didn't mean anything by the drawing," says Charlie.

"I 'never' sold bad food in my restaurant!" yells Mary.

"I never said you did, Mary," says Charlie.

"Then why ya draw me with baby chicks comin' out of my eggs?!"

"It's just a comical drawing Mary. Nothing is meant by the picture," says Charlie.

MARY FIELDS aka STAGECOACH MARY

"Then change the picture!" says Mary.

"I can't change the picture," says Charlie.

"Damn ya Charlie Russell!" Mary says angrily. She storms out, through the parting crowd, that's standing at the door.

'A Quiet Day In Cascade' – Circa 1897
Artist: Charlie Russell
Charlie, standing in front of railroad tracks, 'R', is sketching himself, sketching, the scene with Mary at bottom center.
Courtesy: Archives and Special Collections, the Town of Cascade, Montana

"A Quiet Day In Cascade"

To get the picture in perspective you must remember that it is a scene of Front Street with the viewer facing east, the buildings mostly facing east. Shepard & Flinn was on the corner of Central Avenue and Front Street, and the H.W. Kraus Sample Room was across the street where what is known as the Cascade Drug Store now stands. The saloon south of this was also on Front Street. The other buildings were not on Front Street but in the background. On Central Avenue the blacksmith shop was on the southeast corner of Central Avenue and First Street where Murrill's Bar & Cafe now stands, and the Church was a block up the street on the southwest corner of Central Avenue and Second Street at the present site of the C.S. Moore home. Russell "squeezed" the town together, picturing mostly the landmarks he could see as he stood (as he pictured himself) across the railroad tracks to the east. None of the buildings pictured remain at this time in 1970.

The pen sketch "A Quiet Day In Cascade" was drawn in 1897 when Russell lived in Cascade, where he married Nancy Cooper in 1896. It was originally owned by Ed Kraus who operated the Sample Room. C.R. Tintinger obtained the sketch when he purchased a one-half interest in the building from John Harvey, a real old timer who owned it. After selling the building Mr. Tintinger kept the picture and hung it in the Cascade Hotel until about 1915 when he sold it to E.L. Dana, one of the area's largest cattle ranchers. Mrs. Dana became owner on Mr. Dana's death and she donated it to the Town of Cascade. It hung in the Stockmens Bank until the summer of 1970 when it was loaned to the Montana Historical Society and (the original) now hangs in its new Russell gallery in Helena.

The picture is said to illustrate actual occurrences that took place at previous times, not all at once. Russell shows himself, sash and all, standing near the railroad tracks drawing the picture.

Russell's inborn humor shows throughout the sketch. Mary Fields (Nigger Mary) is shown being upset by a hog and spilling her groceries. Russell showed one little chick running from a broken egg and Mary always said that was a "damned lie, I don't serve that kind of eggs in my restaurant." Another hog is upsetting young Gorham Roberts from his bicycle. The runaway spring wagon was the St. Peter's Mission stage and Pat Morah is said to be the stage driver but the woman falling out is unknown.

The brand NS on the bucking horse refers to the NS horse ranch of Dan Morris, who is said to have had as many as 7,000 head of horses. The donkey belonged to Ben Roberts and Bill Davis is being bucked from it. Bob Chestnut is pictured in front of the saloon dressed in buckskin and shooting off his gun in the air. Ben Roberts is pushing the go-cart for Shepard & Flinn. The Chinaman operated a laundry in Cascade. Old John Harvey is the one with the heavy beard crossing Central Avenue and Ed Krause is in front of his saloon where someone is being squirted with a water hose.

In front of the other saloon a cowboy is shooting at the feet of a dancing dude and someone is painting "warpaint" on the fellow sleeping against the building. It really takes a lot of study to see all of the action of the over 50 characters and animals in the sketch. It is just too bad that a record was not kept of who each person was and what incident was depicted.

Sam Gilluy, Director of the Montana Historical Society Gallery, said the sketch makes an interesting and graphic addition to the Society's gallery, and Branson Stevenson of Great Falls, Society Trustee, who arranged the loan with the Town of Cascade officials has termed it an outstanding example of the Russell wit and humor.

One year later, it's dusk, as older Mary, wrapped in her buffalo coat with her coon cap pulled tightly over her head, and a scarf wrapped around her face, drives a team of two horses, pulling the mail wagon through the blowing snow. She is on her way to the mission with a full mailbag setting beside her and mission supplies tied down in the back. All of a sudden, a pack of wolves appear several yards ahead of the wagon, just off the beaten path. They start growling and bearing teeth at the team of horses and Mary. Not wasting any time, she yells, "Yah," at the horses, whipping the reins. However, the team of horses stop, and rear-up, overturning the mail wagon, and dumping Mary, the mail and supplies into the snow, with a loud wood cracking sound of the rear axle breaking. Quickly, she regains her composure, looks around for her shotgun. She sees the shotgun laying on top of the snow several feet from her.

The wolves are growling, sensing food, and fresh horsemeat. They begin approaching the wagon supplies strewn about on the snow, and the horses. The team of horses, feeling trapped, start rearing up, causing the wolves to veer off from them, moving more towards the supplies. Mary leaps for the shotgun, picking it up, cocking one hammer, and firing, far over the heads of the wolves. The report causes the wolves to take off with their tails between their legs, leaving Mary, the broken wagon and mission supplies in the snow. Several moments later, the wind blows snow horizontally at her, as she breaks apart pieces of the wagon, and starts a small fire with the pieces. She stands guard, pacing back and forth, keeping warm near the fire, with the shotgun cradled in her arms, and a cigar between her lips.

The next morning, the snow has stopped, and the sky is clearing. It's very cold, as a light chilly wind blows. Mary, with icicles hanging off her cap, scarf, buffalo coat, and cigar, has channeled a path in the snow, by the small fire. She is quickly pacing back and forth, trying to keep warm. The sun has started to crest over the horizon. She looks at the sun coming up, smiles, then she listens to the distance, and hears the sound of a team of horses coming from not far away. She begins trudging through the knee-deep snow towards the sounds and begins to shout, "Help, over here! Help over here!"

Several hours later, in front of the mission, Mother Amadeus, Joseph, several nuns, including Sister Clara, are helping Mary off a freight wagon, as Mother Amadeus says, "What happened Mary."

"Some wolves upset the team, causin' 'em to rear, tippin' over the wagon. The rear axle broke so I was stuck in the snow all night. Couldn't leave the supplies, the wolves would have gotten it so I stood guard all night."

"My dear lord child! It must have been twenty to thirty degrees below zero..." says Sister Clara.

Looking at all around her, Mary says, "Thank God I have my buffalo coat!"

Joseph is untying Mary's team of horses from the back of the freight wagon. The freight hauler that found her is unloading the mission supplies off the wagon. Mother Amadeus looks at her, and says, "Mary, the mission has a buckboard you can use. You aren't hauling the large freight you once were."

"Thank ya Mother. I do believe the old wagon has seen her better days."

Mary steps over to Mother Amadeus, and hugs her, as she hugs Mary back.

Mary Fields aka Stagecoach Mary on buckboard, mailbag setting beside her, with her mule Moses – Circa 1900

A month later, Mary is wearing her buffalo coat, driving the mail buckboard in the blowing snow. The buckboard becomes stuck in the heavy drifts. She reaches in the back, and gathers her snowshoes. She hangs her feet over the side, and puts them on. Mary jumps down to the snow, and unhitches the mule. She then shoulders the mailbag, and begins walking through the snow, with shotgun in one hand, leading the mule with the other, headed to the mission.

Several weeks later, Mary is driving the empty mail buckboard in front of her cabin, pulling up on the reins, saying, "Whoa." The mule stops the buckboard as she pulls the brake handle, and looks at the mule, saying, "Moses, ya a good mule, thank ya."

The next year, Agent Harris is at his desk, writing in a book when the door opens, and a gust of wind blows dust into the room. Mary enters with her shotgun in her gloved hand, wearing her buckskin coat, wool dress, and a scarf wrapped around her face. She pushs the door closed against the strong wind behind her.

Mary walks to an empty chair in the room, and lays her shotgun across the arms of the chair. She then unwraps the scarf from around her face and neck, and then looks at Agent Harris who's looking in a book in front of him, as she says, "Where's the passenger that's goin' to the mission?"

"Went outside...said he be back. Told him to look for your buckboard." He then looks at her, and says, "Mary...ya got a great record goin', ya haven't missed any days assigned in four years since ya started...and ya had no losses. That's a very good record for the mail service, and as far as I know, Wells Fargo for that fact."

"Shoot I'm lucky I made it this long Agent Harris, all that snow, 'em wolves and all kinds of critters chasin' after me." Then she says seriously, "Then some 'em bandits thought I wouldn't shoot...'huh', they found out different...ain't nobody gonna take somethin' from Mary!"

"Ya have made a name for yourself around these parts. Mary, even the Indians gave you a name, White Crow."

"I heard that some time ago," says Mary.

"Ya keep up the good work...you'll have your five years next year, in the new century."

"Ya mean in the new millennium, don't ya Agent Harris?" says Mary.

Agent Harris smiles, and says, "Ya Mary, the new millennium."

Mary looks out the window, and then at Agent Harris, saying, "I'm goin' to take this..." Mary takes her pistol out from the front of her dress, and un-holsters her gun belt, laying both on the stool of the chair with the shotgun. She then begins unbuttoning her skirt, continuing saying, "...skirt off...it blows up in my face in the wind, driving the buckboard." Agent Harris turns away quickly from her, as Mary chuckles, saying, "Don't worry Agent Harris, I've got buckskin pants on underneath."

Agent Harris slowly turns around, and looks back at Mary, unbuttoning her skirt. He then looks outside, and says, "Looks like your passenger is sittin' on the wagon seat."

Mary looks out the window while folding her skirt. She sees a priest sitting on the wagon seat, blocking the wind with his gloved hands, and hat. Mary wearing her buckskin pants, picks up her holster belt, and fastens it around her. She then picks up her pistol and puts it in the holster, and looks at Agent Harris, saying, "Better get goin' before he gets wind blasted out there. See ya in the late mornin' Agent Harris."

"See ya Mary," says Agent Harris.

Mary in full buckskin, picks up her shotgun, then takes her folded skirt and puts it under the same arm. With the other hand, she wraps her scarf around her face and neck, just below her eyes.

Moments later, Mary walks outside, and struggles closing the door behind her against the wind. She finally closes the door, and turns walking around the rear of the buckboard, walking to the bench seat. She reaches the buckboard seat, and over the noise of the wind, she shouts, "Howdy, father." The priest doesn't hear her. She puts her folded skirt next to him, then says, "Those your bags?"

The priest, a little startled, says, "...Oh, howdy...ah yes, those are my bags, you're the driver?"

"Yup." Mary lays the shotgun against the seat, and then pulls herself aboard the buckboard, taking a rope from the foot box, climbs in the back bed, and ties down the priest's bags. She then climbs back onto the buckboard seat, releasing the brake handle, and whips the reins, shouting, "Yah, yah..." The buckboard rolls away from the office into the whirling wind of Montana.

Eight hours later, the wind howls and swirls dust around Mary driving the wagon into the valley, headed to St. Peter's Mission. She looks at the priest, blocking the wind and dust from his face with his hands and hat, as she says, "That's the mission over there."

Mary points to the mission. The priest looks, squinting, then acknowledges with a nod of his head, as he looks at Mary, saying, "This is my first time here."

"Oh. It's very nice here, Father. Mother Amadeus gives the Indian and territory children a good home, and schoolin'."

The wind howls, as the priest leans over to Mary, shouting, "...I'm sorry, I couldn't understand what you just said."

Mary acknowledges with a nod of her head. She drives the buckboard in front of the mission, stopping the wagon, saying, "Whoa...whoa, whoa."

Joseph walks from around the side of the mission, pulling his coat closed. He walks into the wind towards the wagon, blocking the wind from his face with his arms.

Mary is tying the reins to the wagon, as Joseph approaches, and looks at the priest, saying, "Father, I'm Joseph, welcome to St. Peters."

"Thank you Joseph," says the priest.

"Father, let me get you out of this wind," says Joseph.

Mary jumps down from the wagon, as Joseph extends his arm to the priest. The priest grabs his arm, and steps off the buckboard. He then looks at Mary grabbing her shotgun, saying, "Excuse me, 'sir', please bring my bags."

Joseph, looks at Mary, and begins to snicker. She looks up in the sky, shaking her head, as she unties the priest bags. She then reaches in the buckboard bed, and picks up the bags with one hand, then grabbing her shotgun with the other. She turns to the mission, as Joseph escorts the priest, holding his hat on his head, walking up the mission steps with Mary following, carrying the shotgun and bags, giving Joseph the evil eye.

Moments later, Mother Amadeus and Sister Clara are walking down the stairs as Mary closes the door behind them, setting the priest's bags down, and then lays her shotgun against the wall. Mother Amadeus says, "Ah, Father Crow, welcome to St. Peter's."

Father Crow brushing the dust off his clothes, then removing his hat, looks at Mother, descending the stairs, saying, "Mother Amadeus, thank you...quite dusty and windy I must say."

"We do experience rough weather here, from time to time, Father, but praise the 'Lord', we have this new mission, keeping the weather out."

Mother Amadeus and Sister Clara reach the first floor. Father Crow removes his gloves, and looks at Mary, saying, "Sir, thank you very much for bringing me to the mission in this weather...you can put my bags..." Father Crow looks at Mother Amadeus who is chuckling, holding her hand over her mouth, along with Sister Clara, and then he looks at Joseph snickering.

Mary looks at Father Crow, saying, "Excuse me Father." Father Crow looks at Mary, who has removed her scarf from around her face, saying, "My name is Mary...where do ya want your bags father."

Father Crow is astonished, taken aback. He looks at Mary, up and down. He looks back at Mother Amadeus, then back to Mary, saying, "...Ah, ah, I'm ...I'm so sorry...ah, ah I didn't know you were...ah, a woman."

Mary smiles at Father Crow, as she says, "That's alright father."

"Father Crow, Mary has experienced this mistake before," says Mother Amadeus. Then, Mother looks at her, and says, "Mary please take Father's bags upstairs, first room on the right...Mary, will you be able to stay for supper?"

"Yes Mother, but got to eat fast, got to be up early back at the stables in the mornin'." Mary picks up Father Crow's bags, and walks up the stairs.

The next morning, Mary wearing her buckskins, drives the buckboard down the partially deserted town road towards the Wells Fargo – Cascade office. She stops her buckboard short of the stables, saying, "Whoa." Then pulling the brake handle. She sees a stagecoach parked in front of the office with a wood plaque affixed above the door, top center, with the carved words, 'Wells Fargo & Co. Overland Stage'. She grabs her shotgun and jumps off the buckboard, tucking the shotgun under her armpit, and then walks towards the office. As she nears the office, she stops near the stagecoach team of four horses. She takes off a glove, putting her hand in her coat pocket, bringing out an apple, and looking at the horses, saying, "Sorry mister horses, I've only got two, need to give the other one to my mule." She then takes the apple with her two thumbs, splits it in half from the top. She then breaks the other halves, in half, walking around the horses, giving each a treat.

Agent Harris opens the door and looks at Mary with urgency, saying, "Mary, inside quickly."

Mary looks at Agent Harris. She wipes her hands on her legs hurrying towards the front door.

Moments later in the Wells Fargo - Cascade office, Mary walks through the door closing it behind her, looking at Agent Harris. She then turns and looks at a man, leaning against a post in the middle of the office, drinking coffee, who almost chokes on the coffee when he looks at her. He has silvery white curly hair, which protrudes out from his cowboy hat, and a Winchester Rifle that lays against the post near him.

Agent Harris walks over to the potbelly stove, and with one hand, he takes two coffee cups off a wire hanger, hanging off the exhaust pipe. He then picks up the coffee pot from the stove top with the other hand, looking at Mary, saying, "Coffee, Mary?"

"Sure thin' Agent Harris."

"Did you get any sleep?" says Agent Harris?

"Yeah a little. Slept off the road a couple of hours."

Mary sets the shotgun against the wall. Agent Harris hands her a cup, then pours her coffee. She looks at the man, still astonished, while looking at her. She then looks back at Agent Harris, saying, "Somethin' wrong Agent Harris?" as she sips her coffee.

He looks from Mary, to the man. Agent Harris then pours his coffee, then looking back at her, saying, "Mary, this is Gary the stagecoach driver for Wells Fargo, northern line. His partner took sick. He's over at the doc's now."

Mary puts down her coffee cup, turns back to the door, walking, looks back over her shoulder at Agent Harris, saying, "I'll have him back on his feet in no time."

"No, Mary," says Agent Harris stopping Mary in her tracks. She then turns around, and looks at Agent Harris, as he says, "The doc got him restin' comfortably. Thank you Mary for your concern, but that's not why I called you in here."

Mary looks at Gary who's expression has returned to normal, then she looks back at Agent Harris with concern, saying, "Did I do somethin' wrong?"

Gary chuckles, and says, "No, not at all Mary, on the contrary...Agent Harris has told me about you, and your excellent record."

"Mary, Gary needs a shotgun guard for what he's carryin' in this strongbox here." Agent Harris points at the metal clad box positioned on the floor beside Gary, as Mary says, "What's in the box?"

"Can't tell ya..." says Agent Harris.

"Agent Harris," says Gary interrupting, as he then says, "If Mary gonna guard the shipment, she should know." He then looks at her, saying, "Mary, in this strongbox is payroll for Fort Benton. Wells Fargo has taken over the contract for payMaster shipments relating to the army."

"Mary, at this time, 'no one' knows, except Washington, 'Wells Fargo' and us here in this office that the stagecoach is carrying the army's pay."

"What Agent Harris is saying, is that we shouldn't have no problems. However, if we did...Agent Harris said you'll know how to take care of it!"

Mary smiles proudly, and says, "Gentlemen..." Mary walks over and picks up her shotgun, then, saying, "When do we start?"

Agent Harris and Gary put down their coffee cups, and both reach down and pick up the strongbox, as Gary also reaches and grabs his Winchester rifle with his other hand.

Moments later, outside the office, the morning sun, cast shadows on the road, from the town's buildings. Mary opens the door, and steps outside the office, with her shotgun in hand, very calmly, looking in both directions. She sees no one is near the office. She looks back at the men, saying, "Okay, it's clear."

MARY FIELDS aka STAGECOACH MARY

Mary walks across the porch and steps off the platform, walking to the stagecoach. As she reaches the coach, she opens the door with Agent Harris, and Gary following, putting the strongbox on the floor. Gary then pushes it into the coach, under the front bench seat. She closes' the coach door, as Gary puts his rifle into the foot-box, and climbs aboard. She points to her wagon looking at Agent Harris, and says, "Agent Harris, ya mind handin' my bag to me from under the bench seat."

Agent Harris walks over to the wagon and grabs her bag. Mary looks around the town, and then looks at Agent Harris, and says, "Also Agent Harris, please have the stable boy unhitch Mosses from the wagon, and take him into the stables, then store the wagon at my home."

"No problem, Mary, as soon as he gets here, and don't worry about the mail, I'll hold it until you return."

Mary agrees with a nod of her head, then, lays her shotgun against the stagecoach wheel hub. Agent Harris hands Mary her bag. She opens the bag and takes out several hands full of shotgun shells, putting them in her coat pocket. She then sticks the bag through the window opening of the coach, dropping it inside.

Agent Harris looks at Mary, saying, "See ya in five days Mary."

She turns around, and smiles at Agent Harris, and says, "See ya in five days." Mary shakes Agent Harris' hand, and picks up her shotgun, turning back to the stagecoach. She hands the shotgun to Gary up top, then climbing aboard the coach. She sits down on the bench seat. Gary hands her the shotgun. He then releases the brake and whips the reins. The team of horses pulls the stagecoach towards the edge of town with Mary riding shotgun.

Later that day, the stagecoach rolls along a road with the breeze blowing in Mary's face, with her holding her shotgun laying across her lap. Gary's Winchester rifle is setting upright between her and him, as he drives the team of horses on the road through a heavily wooded forest.

Mary scouts the trees in front of her. She then looks at the edge of the wooded forest, to her right many yards away, then to her left, looking up a hill they are approaching, then turning around, looking in back of the stagecoach. Gary looks at Mary, saying, "...We should be in Great Falls tonight, make Fort Benton by tomorrow evening." The stagecoach rolls on a few more yards, as he then says, "...Mary, you said you've been in Montana territory since eighty-five?"

"Yep, was workin' for St. Peter's Mission before I got fired...had a restaurant that failed twice, then I got the job with the postal system through Wells Fargo. What about yourself?"

"Worked for Wells Fargo since the war...nothin' much else to tell...maybe, go to California after I retire." He then looks at Mary, and says, "Why they fire you from the mission?"

Mary sighs, as she says, "...A few problems. Two frontiersmen looking for work, threaten me, one took a swing at me, and then I hit him, knocking him down. He drew on me. I drew faster, and I defended myself...didn't try to kill 'em...just scare him and his friend off." Then she chuckles, and says, "When I was shootin' at his tail end, I hit the Bishops' new silk britches hanging on the clothesline...the Bishop had some other reports against me...that was his last straw."

Gary chuckles, and says, "You hit the Bishops' britches."

"...Yah," says Mary also laughing. Both are having a good laugh. Gary looks at the rifle setting between them, then, he looks at Mary, and says, "You've ever shot one of these before?"

Mary looks at the rifle, then at Gary, saying, "Naw..." She pats her shotgun, saying, "Just Betsey here and her cousin." She pulls back her coat revealing the Smith & Wesson thirty-eight in her holster. He smiles and looks back at the road, whipping the reins, as he then looks at the rifle, and says, "Give her a try Mary...think you'll like it. That's a Winchester ninety-two, repeater, forty-four forty, one of the best they've made...holds fifteen in the belly, and one chambered."

Mary lays her shotgun next to the rifle, and then picks up the weapon. She feels the weight, holding it out with both hands, in front of her, turning it, and admiring the rifle, saying, "Pretty light, got a good feel." She then aims the rifle at a tree in the distance.

Gary says, "Take a couple of shots Mary." She brings the rifle down a little, looking at him, over the top of the rifle, then puts the rifle back up to her shoulder, looks down the barrel, takes aim at a tree in the distance, as he says, "What are you aiming at, Mary?"

"That tree branch, comin' off that lower limb on the left side of that tree up ahead on the right."

Mary fires the rifle, hitting the branch, breaking it off the tree. Gary looks at her, and says, "Pretty good shot" ...He smiles, then kiddingly, he says, "Was that luck?"

Mary looks at Gary. She then stands up in the foot box, braces herself, looks at the tree, cocks the lever action with purpose, and begins rapid firing. She breaks off five of the remaining branches along the limb. She then brings the rifle down, and looks at him, and says, "Luck?"

Gary smiles, and then says, "Mighty good luck."

Mary sits back down on the bench seat, setting the rifle beside the shotgun. Gary looks at a box under his legs, and says, "Mary under my legs, there's more ammunition in that box...careful, it's pretty heavy."

"No problem, I can handle it."

Mary looks, and then reaches down pulling the box up on the seat in-between her and Gary. He looks at Mary with a slight smile, shaking his head, at the ease of her picking up the box. She unlatches the box, opening it, reaches in, brings out several rounds of ammunition and begins reloading the rifle, while keeping an eagle eye on the countryside.

The stagecoach rolls along, as Mary takes one more bullet out of the box, holding it in her hand, and then inserting the bullet through the side trap door of the rifle.

Mary then closes the box, and slides it back down under Gary's legs, as Gary looks at Mary, and says, "Thought you said you didn't fire one of those before?"

"Hadn't," says Mary.

"Then how come you are so good with it?"

Mary smiles, and says, "God given talent."

"Praise the Lord," says Gary. Suddenly, a shot rings out, hitting Gary's hat, causing it to fly off his head in front of him. He shouts, "Shit!" They quickly scoot down low from where they were sitting. He whips the reins, and shouts, "Hah, hah, hah…yah…yah!"

The stagecoach takes off with Mary grabbing the rifle, laying next to the shotgun. She looks in back of the coach, and then to both sides quickly, looking for the shooter. Another shot rings out, hitting the stagecoach in back of Gary. She shouts, "Here they come!"

Gary looks over his shoulder and sees over a half-dozen masked bandits on horseback, riding out of the woods, on both sides, chasing after them through their dust.

Gary turns back quickly, and whips the reins, shouting, "Yah, yah…hah!"

Mary shouts, "I thought ya said no one knows about this!"

Gary shouts, "They ain't suppose too!"

Mary gives a look at Gary, and then lying low, she looks at one of the masked bandits on horseback, riding up fast and getting close. She takes aim and fires, hitting the bandit, knocking him off his horse. The other bandits give chase, firing at the stagecoach, with several shots hitting the coach, causing Mary to lower her head. She cocks the rifle, then raising up a little and firing several shots at the bandits on one side.

Gary quickly glances back to where Mary just shot. While, on the other side, just ahead of the stagecoach, several more masked men on horseback, emerge out of the woods ahead of the coach. The masked men then spur their horses up to speed, just as the coach passes by their location, shooting at them, trying to stop the coach.

Mary is keeping the bandits that are chasing them at a distance. Several more shots hit the stagecoach. She lowers her head again, just as one of the bandits, spurring his horse, reaches the coach at the rear boot. The bandit grabs onto the railing pulling himself off his horse with his body bouncing off the leather cover of the boot. The stagecoach rolls down the road, as the bandit is now pulling himself along the rear railing till he gets to the corner of the coach. He then wraps his leg around the corner and attempts to put his foot on the bouncing rear window ledge. He finally gets his foot on the ledge, keeping low, out of Mary's sight, pulling himself around the corner of the coach.

Mary peers up from the foot box, and looks out. She takes a shot at another bandit, while on her blind side, the bandit on the stagecoach, is now making his way forward along the edge of the base of the coach. He stops, hanging off the side, not far from Mary. She is focusing on another bandit riding up fast towards the back of the stagecoach. She takes aim, the masked bandit that's now perched on the front window ledge, hanging on the side railing, springs up, knocking the rifle out of Mary's hands.

Mary somewhat surprised, looks at the bandit, and with resolve, shouts, "Oh, ya didn't want to do that!"

The determined bandit holding on to the railing with one hand, swings at Mary with the other fist. She catches the bandits' fist in the palm of her hand, in mid-air. Briefly, the Bandit with an astonished expression, looks at her. She swings her fist, hitting the Bandit, square in the face, sending him flying off the stagecoach, hitting the ground, rolling in the coach's dust.

In the meantime, Gary is whipping the reins. Mary looks at her shotgun, bouncing against the bench. She quickly picks up the shotgun, as several more shots hit the stagecoach, then one hitting Gary in the back of the arm. He yells in pain. She quickly looks at him, as he painfully shouts, "I'm alright...keep FIRING, KEEP FIRING!"

Mary, crouching down with a determined look, cocks both hammers of the shotgun. She looks at the remaining bandits giving chase, and fires one barrel knocking a bandit off his horse, then pivoting, firing the second barrel, knocking a second bandit off his horse. She quickly brakes open the shotgun, removes the two spent shells, then reaches in her coat pocket, and brings out two new shells, sliding them into the chambers, and closing the shotgun. She then looks at the last three bandits still giving chase.

Two of the bandits are riding side-by-side, gaining on the stagecoach. Mary cocks both hammers, aims and fires both barrels hitting the two bandits knocking them off their horses.

Mary quickly brakes open the shotgun again, removes the two spent shells, reaches in her other pocket and brings out two more shells, sliding them into the chambers, and closing the shotgun. She then cocks both hammers back, aiming at the last bandit, who quickly pulls up on his reins, slowing and stopping his horse in the coach's remaining dust.

Gary is still driving the stagecoach at a fast rate. Mary looks at him, and says, "They stopped!"

Gary turns and looks at the stagecoach's dust, and doesn't see any bandits. He turns and tries to slow the team of horses, looking at Mary in pain, saying, "…Mary…help me slow the team."

Mary quickly eases the hammers back and sets the shotgun against the bench. She takes the reins from Gary and begins slowing the stagecoach, looking over both of her shoulders. He looks at her, saying, "Don't stop 'em…let's put some distance between us and them."

"No problem with that," says Mary. She slows the team to a trot, looking at Gary's blood soaked shirtsleeve, then at Gary who is in severe pain. She says, "We got to slow that bleedin' before ya bleed to death, and get ya to a doctor fast." She then looks at his shirt, and says, "Gary, I need a piece of your shirt to tie around your arm."

Mary looks behind her, as does Gary, who nods his head at her. She begins slowing the team of horses, saying, "Whoa, whoa…whoa," stopping the stagecoach quickly. Gary pulls one end of his shirt up with his good hand, as Mary hands him the reins. She quickly takes the shirt end and tears' a long piece from it, then, she ties it above the wound on Gary's arm.

Gary smiles at Mary, as he says, "Come, come sit here at the drivers spot, near the brake." He slides left, giving her the reins. She takes the reins. She steps into the driver's spot. She looks back, over her shoulders quickly, and then forward, looking at the team of horses, saying, "Get on, 'good boys', get on, yah." The team of horses, trot off, pulling the stagecoach down the road, towards Great Falls and Fort Benton.

Five days later, in the town of Cascade, the stagecoach comes rolling into town. Mary is driving the team of horses pulling the coach, with her shotgun leaning against the bench, and Gary sitting next to the shotgun, with his arm in a sling.

The townspeople that are outside begin clapping, while the townspeople that were inside buildings, drift out onto the road, looking at Mary driving the stagecoach. They also begin clapping as the coach rolls down the town's road.

The doors open at the Wells Fargo – Cascade Office. Mother Amadeus and Joseph come walking out, followed by Agent Harris. They look at the stagecoach and Mary holding the reins, driving the team of horses, and as the coach approaches, they also begin clapping.

Mary is holding the reins in her hands, as she waves back to the townspeople. The stagecoach rolls through town, nearing the office with the townspeople following. Mary is slowing the coach, when she sees Mother Amadeus standing on the platform with Agent Harris and Joseph, excitedly giving her and Gary big waves.

The team of horses, is pulling the stagecoach near the stables, as Mary pulls on the reins, turning the horses, turning the coach, and then shouting to the team of horses, "Whoa...whoa, whoa." The stagecoach slows in the turn, and comes to a stop. The townspeople gather, as Joseph, Mother Amadeus and Agent Harris rush to the coach, making their way through the crowd.

Mary pulls the brake handle, then, ties the reins to the stagecoach. Gary looks at her, saying, "Good job Mary, thank you and Wells Fargo thanks you too."

"Why thank ya Gary, it was my pleasure...and ya tell Wells Fargo, no problem too."

Joseph is first to reach the stagecoach with Mother Amadeus and Agent Harris following, with the crowd gathering around the coach. Joseph looks up at Mary, and says, "Mary, we got word. Wow...ya saved the army's payroll from the bandits...that sure is something."

"Thanks Joseph, it was nothin'. Just a bunch of misguided boys that wanted to meet their maker, sooner than later."

"Mary!" says Mother Amadeus.

Mary looks at Mother Amadeus, as she says, "Praise the Lord, I'm so glad you are safe...I'm very proud of you, Mary."

"Thank ya Mother." Some of the crowd moves in congratulating Mary, moving Mother Amadeus aside. While on the other side of the stagecoach, the crowd is congratulating Gary.

Agent Harris, standing in front of the coach, looks up at Mary and Gary, then shouts, "Mary...Gary." They both look at him with a happy smile, as he says, "Come in the office."

"Sure thin' Agent Harris," says Mary.

Agent Harris turns and makes his way through the crowd towards the office. Mary climbs down from the stagecoach, with the crowd backing up giving her room. She then turns and looks up at Gary. He hands her the shotgun, he then slides over, turns, and begins climbing down. Mary reaches up and helps him, as Joseph, hurries to assist.

Later in the Wells Fargo – Cascade Office, Joseph is standing by Mother Amadeus, sitting in a chair near Agent Harris' desk. Mary is leaning against the wall in back of Agent Harris' desk, smoking a cigar, near the calendar on the wall, turned to the date, 'September 9, 1899'.

Gary is sitting in a chair across from Agent Harris talking with him, saying, "...and you should of seen the robber's face when Mary caught his fist in midair." He then chuckles, and says, "When Mary hit him...it was like a tree hit him, holding on to the stage."

"That's the one the Army caught in Great Falls in the doc's office...he came in with a broken jaw. He ain't talkin' yet...they'll find out how they knew!" says Agent Harris.

Excited, Joseph says, "Mary...you're a hero!"

"Stop it Joseph," says Mary kiddingly, as she then says, "I'm just doin' my job."

"And a great job you are doing, Mary," says Agent Harris.

Mary looks at Agent Harris, and says, "Thank ya, Agent Harris."

With concern, Mother Amadeus says, "...Mary, you are almost seventy..."

"No I'm not Mother, I'm...sixty seven!" says Mary.

"Mary, what Mother is trying to say is you should think about what are you going to do when you can't work for the postal system?" says Joseph.

Mary thinks for a second, putting the cigar in her mouth. She shrugs her shoulders looking at Joseph, then takes the cigar out of her mouth, looking at Mother Amadeus, saying, "Haven't givin' it much thought..." She then shrugs her shoulders, and says, "Thought I would quit in about...three to four years."

"Mary, Mr. Glover and the Mayor are in Helena for a conference on the growth of the area for the new century," says Mother Amadeus.

"What's that got to do with me?" asks Mary.

"You won't have any income after you stop working..." says Mother Amadeus.

"I've been savin' my money like we've talked Mother."

"That may not be enough Mary...I have an idea how you can make extra money for yourself."

Mary with an interested smile, looks at Mother Amadeus, and says, "...I'm listenin' Mother."

Mother Amadeus smiles, stands and walks over to Mary, saying, "Mary, you can start a laundry service out of your home, and you are very good with children...the people are going to need their laundry done and someone to watch over their children."

Mary smiles, and says, "Ya know Mother, ya got somethin' there!" Mary looks at everyone and smiles, and then puts the cigar in her mouth taking a puff.

The End of Mary's Story

Seven years later, in 1907, light smoke floats in the air, floating by Mary, coming from a burning fire under a pot of boiling water near her. She is moving more slowly, and looking a little older, as she scrubs a shirt on a washboard setting in a washtub, along side of her cabin. Several children are playing on a teeter-totter, and another plays on a swing in the back yard. She finishes scrubbing the shirt, and wrings it out, looking at the children playing. She steps to another tub, and begins thrusting the shirt through the water, then scrubbing the shirt between her two hands. She hears the sound of a wagon approaching. She looks and sees Joseph, and quickly waves at him, as he slows the wagon, saying, "Whoa…" The wagon slows, and then comes to a stop.

Mary wringing the water out of the shirt, looks at Joseph pulling the brake handle, and says, "Hey Joseph, just finishin' the last of the laundry now. Ya can take the mission's laundry from inside…" Then proud, she says, "Already starched and ironed." She then walks over to the clothesline that is nearly full of clothes. She stops at an empty spot, reaching in her apron pocket, and brings out two split-wood clothespins, and hangs the shirt in an open space on the line.

Joseph stops in front of her, looking at the clothesline, and says, "Mary you're busier than ever, you've been in business for about four years now, since the postal service with Wells Fargo…you're doing pretty good for yourself."

Joseph looks at the children, then, he looks at Mary finishing hanging the shirt, and whispers, "The Chinese laundry…the woman, Yvette Fong, she said you, Stagecoach Mary took their business."

Mary, with a side look at Joseph, softly says, "It's not my fault Joseph. The people like my starch better than theirs!"

"They just jealous, Mary," says Joseph.

Mary with resolve, pointedly says, "I know Joseph…instead of bein' mad and jealous…they should learn how to make their starch better!"

They both chuckle, as Joseph looks at Mary, and says, "Who do you think is going to win the championship baseball game tomorrow?"

Mary kiddingly, but, very serious, says, "Joseph don't even start with me…ya know who's goin' to win, Cascade!" She looks towards her house wiping her hands on her apron. She then looks at Joseph, saying, "Come Joseph, I'll help ya load the mission's laundry on the wagon." As they walk towards the house, she looks at Joseph, and says, "Oh, I have some candy for ya to give to the children at the mission, after they have their supper. Joseph…and there's something for ya too."

"Thank you Mary. You know I have a sweet tooth, like the children. They have been askin' about Miss Mary, and when she's going to bring candy…they are really going to love this, Mary."

She stops, and looks at Joseph, somewhat teary eyed, and says, "…I sure miss Mother."

"Yah, I know Mary. Mother has only been gone to Alaska for a year to start that new mission."

Mary sighs, and then says, "Seems longer Joseph." Then with cheer, she says, "Hey Joseph, I'm goin' into town after I drop the children off at their homes, come on over to the Silver Dollar if ya get a chance."

"Got some chores to do before going back to the mission, maybe afterwards Mary." She turns and walks to the porch, steps up, and walks to her open door, reaches in, and brings out a stack of folded laundry, and hands it to Joseph, then she reaches back in for another stack of clothes, handing them to Joseph.

Later that night, in the Silver Dollar Saloon, the usual smoky festive saloon atmosphere is in full swing. The piano player is playing 'The Entertainer', as saloon girls entertain the gentlemen playing poker at the tables, including Mr. Glover playing poker at his usual table in the corner.

The saloon girl at Mr. Glover's table walks away with her tray in hand, walking towards the bar with several gentlemen reaching for her. Some gentlemen are kidding and others are serious in their intent. She dodges each one, and walks up to the bar. She looks at Harry working behind the bar, and says, "Harry, two whiskeys."

Mary is standing several patrons down from the saloon girl, leaning against the bar on her elbows, and smoking her cigar. She stands straight up and finishes her drink, then puts the glass down on the bar, and looks at Harry, and says, "One more Harry."

"Sure thin' Mary," says Harry.

She then puts the cigar up to her mouth, holding it with her lips, and turns, looking out at the saloon patrons enjoying the evening. She sees Joseph walking through the saloon doors, stopping, then looking around the saloon, till he sees Mary at the bar acknowledging him.

Joseph makes his way past saloon patrons and tables, towards Mary. However, Mary suddenly, looks past Joseph, and looks at a gun-toting rancher neatly dressed with crisp starched shirt collars, cuffed sleeves, and vest, walking through the swinging doors.

Mary turns, taking the cigar out of her mouth, putting it on the bar, then, turns back, and looks at the rancher walking to the middle of the room. He stops at a poker table, reaches in his pocket, and brings out several silver dollar coins, holding them in his hand.

Joseph reaches the bar next to Mary, and looking at her, saying, "Sorry I'm kinda late..."

However, Mary is walking away, focused on the rancher standing at a poker table. She makes her way through the saloon patrons. She stops and stands on the other side of the table, staring at the rancher fingering the coins in his hand.

The rancher is concentrating on the poker game at the table and doesn't notice Mary right away, until he looks up, and sees her, staring at him. The rancher quickly looks to his money in his hand, then nervously puts the money back into his pocket, and begins backing away from the table, and from her.

Mary makes her way around the table towards the rancher, who hurries towards the swinging doors. She shouts at him, "Come back here! Where's my money!"

The entire saloon quiets to a murmur. The rancher briefly had stopped at Mary's shout, looking back at her, but now turns, and hurries out the swinging doors of the saloon. She shouts again, "Hey!" She quickly follows him to the doors, and now, so does the entire saloon, following her.

A moment later, outside the Silver Dollar Saloon, a light wind blows, flickering the flames in the hanging lanterns, hanging off the buildings, lighting up the town. The rancher hurries towards the middle of the road, as Mary pushes the saloon swinging doors open, looking at the rancher, looking back over his shoulder at her, as she yells at him, "Where's my money!? Stop!"

The rancher stops in his tracks, and turns looking back at Mary walking towards him, rolling up her sleeves. Mr. Glover, Joseph and the saloon patrons empty out of the saloon looking at the situation.

Other townspeople, who were going about their business, have now stopped, and look at Mary standing in front of the rancher, yelling at him, "I thought ya said today, ya didn't have any money till the first of the month! Where did ya get money to gamble!?"

"None of your business," says the rancher.

"Then your laundry bill is nine months old. Pay-up!"

"I don't use your laundry any more. I ain't payin' ya nothin'!"

The rancher, serious, takes a step backwards, and puts his fist up, standing his ground. His eyes are wide open, looking at Mary, saying, "I've never hit a woman before...ya gonna be the first if ya come any closer."

With resolve, Mary says, "I ain't lookin' for no trouble. I just want what's owed me. I did your laundry, extra starch!"

Mary holds her hand out, and slowly walks towards the rancher, still standing his ground with his fists up, saying, "I said, I ain't payin' ya..."

"I said ya are!" says Mary, walking closer to the rancher. He lunges at her, and swings. She blocks his fist, and swings with a left cross, catching the rancher square on the chin, dropping him like a sack of potatoes. She looks at the rancher asleep on the ground. She then turns, looking at the crowd that has gathered on the saloon platform and other parts of the town. She walks back to the saloon, and as she approaches, the crowd parts open for her. She stops, and looks back at the rancher. Several townsmen, walk over to the rancher, and help the punch-drunk rancher to his feet. Mary looks back at the crowd, and pointedly, says, "His bill is paid!" She steps up on the platform, and walks to the swinging doors, pushing them open, walking into the saloon with the saloon patrons following.

Joseph, walking back to the saloon, looks at Mr. Glover, saying, "Think he'll pay his bill from now on Mr. Glover?"

Mr. Glover smiles, and says, "I believe so Joseph." He and Mr. Glover follow the last of the saloon patrons through the swinging doors. The piano player begins playing, *Take Me Out To The Ball Game*, as Joseph looks at Mr. Glover, saying, "Tomorrow is a big day Mr. Glover...I hope our team wins, I know our mascot is going to help us, huh Mr. Glover."

"She sure is, I just wish we could win the games, as easy as Mary wins the arguments of politics, and the calls on the diamond." Mr. Glover smiles at Joseph as they make their way towards Mary standing at the bar smoking her cigar.

Three years later in the Silver Dollar Saloon, Mr. Glover is sitting at his usual table in the corner, talking with a gentleman, signing papers, saying, "...and as agreed in this lease agreement, Mary Fields will have free meals at the 'The New Cascade Hotel', for the rest of her life, whenever she wants." Mr. Glover looks at the gentleman, and says, "Do you have any questions, Mr. Kirk Huntley?"

"Ah, no Mr. Glover, as agreed, Mary will have free meals," says Mr. Huntley. Mr. Glover stands, and so does Mr. Huntley. They shake hands. Mr. Glover hands Mr. Huntley the papers, and says, "Here's your lease Mr. Huntley, and..." He then reaches into a folder, brings out another piece of paper, and says, "Here's a copy of the 1910 Census of Cascade."

Mr. Huntley takes the census from Mr. Glover, and says, "Thank you, Mr. Glover."

*Thirteenth Census of the United States 1910 Population –
Cascade, Montana
Mary Fields is number 87*

Two years later, Mary is outside her cabin, doing laundry, when smoke begins to waft by her, causing her to look up. She sees smoke and flames coming from her window near the stove exhaust pipe. "Oh my God, oh my God!" she yells. She then shouts, "Fire! Fire! Fire!" She runs to the well, still shouting, "Fire! Fire! Fire!" She grabs the well bucket, and drops it into the well, and watches the crank handle speed up until the bucket hits the water. Once it hits the water, she furiously begins cranking the handle, quickly bringing up the water. The bucket comes to the top, she retrieves the bucket from the well rope hook, and then, runs to her cabin, yelling, "Fire! Fire! Fire!" She stops at the doorway, and looks at the fire within.

Entering the cabin, Mary sees the stove, and the entire wall on the right going up in flames. She tosses the water out of the bucket, onto the fire, then, throwing the bucket down. She hurries to her table, grabs her shotgun, and then grabs the rocking chair, turns, and rushes towards the front door. Next she tosses the rocking chair outside, then grabs her coat rack, with her winter coats and runs out.

Mary quickly hurries to a safe area. She puts down the coat rack, and shotgun, then, she retrieves the rocking chair. The flames are now roaring in her cabin, and now begin coming out from the door and the other windows. She frantically shouts, Fire! Fire! Fire! In the distance, she hears the town's volunteer fire departments' bell, coming from up the road. She watches the fire beginning to consume her cabin, when the fire department arrives, with their two horse drawn, fire plump fighting apparatus. Mr. Glover, the Mayor, townspeople, some ranchers, and cowboys also come running, and riding up to her cabin. The firemen and townspeople, man the apparatus pump handles on both sides, as a feed line is tossed down Mary's well, and they begin manual hand pumping the water through their hose lines, onto the fire.

About an hour later, the firemen have the fire out, but Mary's cabin is a charred smoldering shell, destroyed. The entire town is now at Mary's place. Mr. Glover and the Mayor, are consoling Mary, sitting on a log. She looks up at them, and sadly, she says, "The only thing I got left, is this rocking chair, my winter coats, what's in the buckboard, Betsey and her cousin here." Mary picks the shotgun up from the ground, and pats her belly where the pistol is in her holster.

"Mary, we'll help you take your stuff over to the hotel. I'll take care of any expenses," says Mr. Glover.

"Ya Mary. We'll figure something out for you, but in the meantime, let's get you to the hotel," says the Mayor.

Mary looks up at the Mayor, and Mr. Glover, nodding her head. She rises.

"...and after we get ya settled in, come on over to the saloon," says Mr. Glover.

COLORED MARY'S laundry in Cascade before it was destroyed by fire. Her real name was Mary Field and she became famous in early Montana days by driving a stage between Cascade and nearby points. She first came to St. Peter's mission in 1884. A likeness of her is to be found in one of Charley Russell's pictures. She died in 1914 and is buried at Cascade.

Mary Fields standing in the doorway of her cabin, and laundry

service, before fire. - Circa 1912

Later at the Silver Dollar Saloon, Mary, Mr. Glover and the Mayor, are sitting at Mr. Glover's favorite table in the corner. Several patrons walk over to the table and offer their condolences to Mary, who has a blank stare on her face. After some of the patrons have left, and some, are rubbing her shoulders, and holding her hand, the Mayor looks at her, and says, "Mary, Mr. Glover and I...well, we put our heads together, and came up with a way to get you a new home. We, and the town of Cascade, are going to rebuild your home for you, Mary."

She seems to come out of the blank stare, then, looking at both men, with tears beginning to well up in her eyes, Mary says, "...Ya are goin'...to rebuild my cabin? How am I to pay ya back?"

"Don't worry about that Mary, call it a gift of the Town of Cascade...and yes ma'am, we are going to build you a new home," says the Mayor.

Mary stands, and so do both men. She walks over and hugs Mr. Glover, and then the Mayor, and says, "Thank ya, gentlemen. Please, let me buy ya a drink. Harry owes me a few."

"No Mary...drink is on me," says Mr. Glover. He signals for a saloon girl then looks at Mary, and says, "Mary, remember tomorrow, a photographer is going to take a team picture, first here in town, then out on the field after the game. He said he is going to also take a picture of Cascade. If you don't feel like it, we understand, Mary."

"Oh...that's right," says Mary, looking out in a daze. She then looks at Mr. Glover, and says, "I don't have any flowers to give them if they win...they burnt up in the fire."

"Don't worry about the flowers Mary. Your presence at the game is all the team needs," says the Mayor.

She looks at them with a determined look, and says, "That's my team, and I'm their mascot. I'll be there!"

The next day, the Montana big blue sky is abundant. Mary, Mr. Glover, the umpire and the Cascade baseball team, are gathering for their picture near a town building. The photographer is setting up his camera, and then waves at Mary. She begins collecting the team in their places for the picture, saying, "Okay everyone, take your places." The team gathers against a building, posing for the picture, as Mary says, "Ready everyone?"

Everyone replies, "Yes."

Mary looks at the photographer, and says, "Okay, Mr. Photographer."

Flash, the photographer takes the picture, with a townswoman looking out the building door on the right.

MARY FIELDS aka STAGECOACH MARY

Mary and the Cascade baseball team, in the town of Cascade - Circa 1912

Several hours later, at the Cascade Baseball Field, the stands are full of both team fans. The scoreboard boy sits in a chair, by the hand printed wooden plaque scoreboard numbers, and the scoreboard that displays the score. Cascade '5', Helena '4', bottom of the '9th', '1' out. The Cascade team, with the letter 'C' on the left side of their uniforms, is in the field, and Helena's team is at bat, with one man on second base.

The pitcher studies the batter, then looks over his shoulder, eyeing the runner on second base taking his lead, as Mary shouts, "Watch him Jimmy!"

Mary is holding in one hand her homemade team pennant on a stick with red, white and blue color streamers. In the other hand, she is holding her cigar between her fingers.

Mary is sitting next to Mr. Glover on the lower bleachers. Joseph and the Mayor are sitting on the next tier, above them, with other townspeople, ranchers, cowboys sitting around them watching the game, cheering their team on.

Mr. Glover looks at the third baseman, several feet from the base. He cups his hands over his mouth, and shouts, "Get ready A. P.!" A. P. hits his glove with his fist, and then looks at the runner in his stance, several yards from second base.

Jimmy looks back at the batter. He then turns fast, throwing the ball to the second baseman.

The runner retreats back, sliding, head first. He touches second base with his hand, just as the ball arrives in the second baseman's glove.

"Safe!" shouts the umpire, standing halfway between the pitcher's mound and home plate.

The second baseman throws the ball back to Jimmy, as Mary shouts, "That's alright Jimmy...u'll get him next time!"

Mr. Glover motions with his hand to the outfield to move in a little. Jimmy looks around at his teammates, then back to the batter and catcher.

The catcher gives his signs.

Jimmy acknowledges, and takes his ready position, looking at the runner, cautiously taking his lead again. He then looks back to the batter. He winds-up, looks at the runner, then to home plate, throwing the ball.

The ball crosses the plate, and the catcher, catches the ball.

"Strike two!" shouts the umpire, as he then says, "Two and two."

"One more strike, Jimmy!" shouts Mary.

The catcher throws the ball back to Jimmy. He looks at the batter stepping back into the batters' box. Then, he looks at the runner at second base again, cautiously taking his lead. He looks back at the catcher, giving his signals.

Jimmy acknowledges a sign, then takes his ready position, and again, he looks at the runner in his stance near second, then back to the batter, as Mary shouts, "Come on Jimmy...one more!"

Jimmy winds-up, and throws the ball to the catcher, and at the same time, the runner takes off for third base.

The catcher, catches the ball.

The umpire yells, "Ball!" While at the same time, the catcher throws the ball to A. P., as the runner nears third base. A. P. misses the ball. It goes by him.

The runner steps on third plate, running to home plate. However, the shortstop has run behind A. P., retrieving the ball. He throws it off balance on one foot, to the catcher at home plate.

The catcher readies himself for the ball, and the runner, running at him full speed. The ball flies by the runner. The catcher, catches the ball and tags the runner's foot sliding by him towards home plate.

"You're out!" shouts the umpire, throwing his thumb up in the air.

The Cascade crowd cheers. The scoreboard boy changes the number on the 'out column', from '1' to, '2'.

Mr. Glover looks at the catcher, and shouts, "That's the way to go Smith!"

"One more strike, one more out Jimmy!" shouts Mary.

The umpire brushes off home plate.

The batter returns to the batter's box.

Jimmy looks at Smith the catcher, giving his sign, and as Jimmy acknowledges, he takes his ready position. He then winds-up, and throws the ball hard as he can to Smith, and as the ball flies by the batter, Smith catches the ball.

"Strike 'three...you're out!" shouts the umpire.

All the Cascade team yells with joy, throwing their hats into the air, and then rushes out towards Jimmy. At the same time, the Cascade fans burst into cheers.

Mary hugs Mr. Glover, picking him up and turning him around in a circle, then putting him back down. She looks at him, saying, "We did it, Mr. Glover."

"Yes, we did, Mary," replies Mr. Glover.

She hurries out on the field, as the Helena team is congratulating the Cascade team, while all the fans congratulate each other.

The Mayor steps down on the ground from the bleachers, with Joseph following. The Mayor shakes Mr. Glover's hand, saying, "Good job R. B."

Joseph looking at Mr. Glover, says, "Good game, Mr. Glover."

"Thank you, Joseph, thank you, Mayor," says Mr. Glover.

"R. B., the photographer wants to take a picture of you and the team."

"Sure thing, Mayor," says Mr. Glover. He looks at Joseph, and says, "Joseph, go out on the field and tell Mary we're going to take a picture, get the team ready."

"Okay, Mr. Glover," says Joseph. He maneuvers through the crowd and hurries out onto the field towards Mary.

Moments later, on the baseball field, the photographer sets up his camera, as Mary, with cigar in hand, and team pennant under her arm, assembles the baseball team. Joseph lays out the baseball equipment, four bats, two facemasks, and the catcher's chest pad in front of the players for the group picture.

Mr. Glover and the umpire approach, looking at the nine Cascade baseball players, positioned in two rows. In the first row, five players are sitting with their legs crossed, except for the player on the left, who squats with his left foot forward.

In the second row, four players are standing.

Mr. Glover and the umpire walk up to Mary, and ask, "Where do you want us, Mary?"

"Mr. Glover, ya and the umpire are in the middle, in the back." Mr. Glover and the umpire walk to the back of the team, positioning themselves in the middle of the four players, with Mr. Glover standing next to A. P. on the left, and the umpire standing next to Jimmy on the right.

Mary is standing in front of the team, looking at the group, and says, "Okay, everyone ready?"

"Ready, Mary. We love you Mary," says Mr. Glover.

At the same time, the umpire and the team, shout, "We love you Mary."

She smiles, and says, "Thank ya all." Mary then walks to the left side of the players, to the back row, standing to the left of Smith. She then holds her pennant streamers in her right hand, holding it in front of her at an angle pointing downward. In her left hand, she is holding a cigar in between her fingers. She looks at the photographer with Joseph and the Mayor standing next to him, and says, "Okay, mister photographer, we're ready."

The photographer shouts, "Ready," as he flashes his strobe.

Mary and The Cascade Baseball Team on the Cascade Baseball Field – Circa 1912

The team looks at each other smiling, and then breaking up, with some of the players gathering in groups talking. Mary, Mr. Glover and the Mayor are talking in their group.

Joseph begins picking up the equipment, as Mary looks at him, and says, "Joseph, put Smith's chest pad in my wagon...got to do some mendin' on the front-side."

"Okay Mary, we'll speak later," says Joseph.

"Love ya Joseph," says Mary. She then looks back at Mr. Glover finishing his conversation with the Mayor, saying, "...I'm sorry Mr. Glover, what were ya sayin'?"

"...As I was just telling the Mayor...this is nineteen twelve, in a few more years, the town should..."

"Mr. Glover," says Mary interrupting, as she then says, "I hope to be alive in a few years!"

"Mary, you're gonna live forever. You have the vitality of a forty year old woman, plus you are very smart and strong."

"Mayor, I'm about eighty years old, and my house just burned down. I'm tired. I'm not foolin' no one, the good Lord is goin' to be callin' 'all' of us one day." Everyone looks at each other with agreement.

South Cascade, Montana – Circa 1912. Missouri River in background

Several years later, late fall, its cold. Two young boys dressed in heavy coats, are playing on one of several teeter-totters, next to several empty swings. Older Mary, wearing her wool coat, is looking a little ill, sitting in a chair on the porch of her new cabin, watching the children play in the yard.

As Mary sits on the porch, she looks out in the distance and sees three young teenage boys walking along the road towards her house. She slowly stands and walks to the edge of the porch looking at the teens approaching. They stop. Mary then slowly raises her hand, and waves at them.

The teens begin running towards Mary standing on the porch. The boys on the teeter-totter stop rocking, and look at the teens racing each other. The boys then begin cheering the teens on.

One of the teens, a handsome young man, out distances himself from the other two. The handsome teenager is the first one to reach the porch, as the other two follow.

The handsome teenager turns around and looks at the other teenagers, running alongside one another, as both reach the porch together. The handsome teen looks at them, and says, "I won again!"

The teenager out of breath, says, "...Ya got a head start Frank!"

"No I didn't..." says Frank.

"Lester...even if Frank did get a head start...he beat ya, and your friend here by a lot," says Mary.

"Yes Miss Stagecoach Mary," says Lester.

Mary then looks at the two boys on the teeter-totter playing. She then turns back, and looks at Lester, saying, "Your two brothers are surely sproutin' up Lester."

"My mom said it's the vegetables from your garden."

Mary Fields in her garden. Circa 1914

"My mother said the same thing before I went to Europe, Stagecoach...I didn't like vegetables that much until I ate yours," says Frank.

"Thank ya Frank...tell your mothers I said thanks..." says Mary. She turns and looks at their friend, saying, "Who's your friend?"

The friend has been staring at Mary, astonished the whole time they have been there, as he says, "...My name is...Bill, I...I just moved here from, ah...Chicago. Frank and Lester told me..."

"Told ya what Bill?" says, Mary interrupting.

Bill stutters a little more, as he says, "...How...how big...you are...I've...never seen a woman as...big as you before."

Frank and Bill are shying away a little.

Mary smiles at Bill, saying, "...I eat my vegetables."

Frank and Bill, stop shying away. They all look at one another, smiling, and then look at Mary and laugh, as Bill looks at Mary, and says, "Why they call you Stagecoach Mary?"

She smiles, and says, "Well, people started callin' me that name over ten years ago when I worked for the United States Postal System, out of the Wells Fargo - Cascade Office."

Bill excited, his eyes, wide open, says, "You worked for Wells Fargo!? You, you, you drove stagecoaches?"

"Rode shotgun, one time on the stage, really never drove one...how I got my name...for eight years I never missed an assignment, always got the mail through on my wagons and buckboard, even though bandits shot at me, and the weather tried to stop me..." Then theatrically, she says, "...Along with 'all 'em 'critters''tryin' to get at me!"

"If I eat vegetables, 'I' can be like you?!" says Bill.

"Maybe Bill, maybe even bigger?"

Mary smiles, and winks at Bill. Lester looks at Mary, and says, "What are ya going to plant this spring, Mary?"

She sighs, and then with resolve, Mary says, "...I think...I'm not goin' to be plantin' this sprin'...Stagecoach Mary is gettin' a little tired boys."

"Are you okay, Stagecoach?" says Frank with concern.

"Yes Frank, I'm okay, I'm just a little tired," says Mary.

Mary walks back to her chair and sits down.

The teenagers follow. Lester and the teens stop in front of Mary, as Lester looks at her, saying, "Stagecoach Mary, Frank, Bill and I...we'll help you turn the soil."

"That's mighty nice of ya boys, thank ya...your help won't be needed..." says Mary. She quickly looks at Frank to change the subject, saying, "Frank, ya been back two weeks now, been to my home at least four times, and ya still haven't told me everythin' about Europe, and your school."

"I told you Stagecoach...glad I don't have to go back...I'm a cowboy...no grit and dirt like here in Montana, all you do is study."

"Frank James Cooper, ya get your schoolin'...school is very important, readin', writin', and arithmetic...ya gonna be famous one day...ya handsome and a smart boy."

Frank thinks for a second, then reaches in his back pocket and brings out a folded newspaper, and says, "Oh, here's the day's newspaper from the store, Mary."

Frank hands the newspaper to Mary, as she says, "Thank ya Frank, I'm tired...I'll read it tomorrow."

The next day, in Mary's cabin, the sound of creaking wood is heard. Mary is rocking in her chair, looking ill, as she says, "Well...that's the end of my story."

Mary continues rocking, then slowly stops and sits for several minutes in deep thought. She then puts a cigar in her mouth and takes a quick puff, blowing a little of the smoke out. She stands up with the cigar in her mouth, and unfastens her gun belt, taking it off, with her pistol, from around her waist, and then lays the belt on the rocker.

Mary bends down and hikes up her dress, revealing her buckskin pant leg. She then slides her pant leg up above her boot top, and removes the knife from her boot that George gave her from the Warner plantation during the Civil War. She looks at the knife, cherishing it, then, placing it on the chair next to the gun belt.

Mary slowly walks over to the table, to the properly set eating area, along with her Bible and shotgun. She then takes the cigar out of her mouth, laying it on the table edge. She picks up the newspaper, and unfolding it the rest of the way, looking at the headlines, 'Montana Cascade Courier – Sports Section – Tuesday, December 1, 1914 – Cascade Baseball team expected to go all the way next year'. She says to herself, "We are champions."

She puts the newspaper back on the table, and looks around her house in deep thought. She walks towards a shelf, briefly stopping, looking at baseball pictures of her and the team, hanging on the wall. She then retrieves several blankets from the shelf. She then walks towards the front door, stops at the coat rack she saved from the fire. Mary puts the blankets between her legs, as she takes the buckskin coat off the coat rack.

Moments later, Mary opens the door, and walks out with her buckskin coat on, carrying her blankets under one arm. She closes the door with the other hand. She turns slowly and walks to the edge of the porch and looks around. She steps off the porch, and begins walking down the road away from her cabin.

Mary continues walking until she reaches an area of tall grass, just off the road. She walks into the grass, several yards, looking around, stopping near a tree. She looks at one area, and lays her blanket down covering the grass.

A golden eagle squawks as it flies overhead, then glides to the tree above Mary, and lands on a limb high above. She looks up to the eagle, and smiles. She then kneels on the blanket and lays down, curling up into a fetal position, then covering herself with the other blanket, looking up at the eagle, saying, "Birds fly free. I am free."

Mary slowly bunches up one end of the blanket with her hand, and then, lays her head down, as the eagle flies off.

Two days later, Frank is driving a team of horses, pulling a large flatbed wagon with Lester sitting next to him. Bill sitting in the back of the wagon bed, is bouncing on his rear end, holding on to a rope that's tied from side to side of the wagon seat.

As the wagon nears Mary's cabin, Frank looks at Lester, saying, "Stagecoach is going to be surprised when we tell her Lester."

"She sure is Frank," says Lester.

Frank drives the wagon in front of Mary's cabin pulling the reins, stopping the horses. He looks at Lester, saying, "Lester, go get Stagecoach."

Lester jumps off the wagon, and runs up on the porch and knocks on the door. They look at the door. Lester waits a few moments, and knocks again, then waiting a few moments more. He looks at Frank, saying, "She's not here."

"She's got to be...look inside," says Frank.

Lester opens the door slowly, and he shouts out, "Stagecoach Mary? Stagecoach Mary?" Lester peers in, then slowly walks inside. A few moments pass, and he walks back outside, and looks at Frank, and says, "She's not here. Her pistol and shotgun are inside...Stagecoach Mary don't go far without them...I'll look around back."

"Okay," says Frank.

Lester hurries around one side of the cabin, and quickly appears on the other side. He looks at Frank and shrugs his shoulders, saying, "She's nowhere in sight."

Frank looks around the property. He then looks at Lester, saying, "Maybe she went for a walk?"

"Not without her guns!" says Lester. The teenagers look around the property. Lester sees a baseball lying on top of a wood barrel on the porch. He looks at Frank and Bill, saying, "Let's play catch until she returns."

"Okay," says Frank.

Bill jumps off the back of the wagon. Lester runs up on the porch, picks up the baseball and throws the ball to Bill backing up. Bill catches the ball, and then throws the ball to Frank. He catches the ball, and then throws the ball to Bill. However, the ball goes over Bill's head, landing in the tall grass.

Bill runs to the area where the ball landed, and looks around, finding the ball, and picks it up and throws the ball to Lester. Lester catches the ball, and then throws the ball to Frank. Frank in turns catches the ball, and then looks at Bill, saying, "Bill, I'm going to throw it high."

Bill acknowledges with his hand.

Frank throws the ball high into the air.

Bill looks up and sees the eagle circling high above, and then quickly focuses back on the ball. He begins to position himself under the ball, as the ball comes down towards him. Bill moves sideways, when he falls down disappearing into the tall grass. Frank and Lester begin laughing, as Bill cry's out, "Hey guys...guys, come here, quick!"

Frank looks at Lester, both stop laughing and look at the area where Bill disappeared into the grass. They both run towards Bill, as fast as they can. Bill stands up quickly, looking into the tall grass in front of him.

As Frank and Lester near Bill, he puts his hand out for them to slow down. Frank and Lester slow down. When they get close, they begin walking on their toes, peering into the tall grass, where Bill is looking.

Frank is slightly ahead of Lester. He stops in his tracks, looking at the grass where Bill is looking. Lester runs into the back of Frank looking at Mary unconscious, laying on her blanket, partially covered by the other blanket. Lester looks at his friends with urgency, saying, "Is she ok...is she 'alive'? We just saw her two days ago. Wonder how long she's been laying here?"

The teenagers all look at one another. Frank drops to his knees, removes the blanket and feels her wrist. Lester looks at Frank, saying, "What are ya doing?"

"I'm feeling for her..." He looks at his friends heartfelt, sad, and says, "...her heart beat." Frank quickly looks at her, then at his friends with urgency. Mary barely conscious, begins to move around and moan, as Frank says, "She's alive! Lester, something is wrong with her. We got to get her to the doc fast!" Frank then looks at Lester, and says, "Lester, get the wagon, hurry!"

Lester takes off running towards the wagon.

Five days later, at the Cascade cemetery, all the town of Cascade, ranchers, cowboys, from surrounding communities, along with several nuns, and priest, are standing solemn, standing with Mr. Glover, the Mayor and Joseph, looking at a casket covered with floral arrangements.

Reverend Father John J. Casey, is reading from the Bible. He closes the Good book, saying, "The Lord giveth and the Lord taketh away. In the name of the Father, the Son, and the Holy Ghost, Amen."

The golden eagle squawks from high above, circling overhead.

A week later, there is no music coming out of the Silver Dollar Saloon. Patrons entertain themselves, as a saloon girl places a drink in front of Mr. Glover, and walks away, leaving him seated at the table in the corner, by himself.

Joseph walks in through the swinging doors, looking around until he sees Mr. Glover at the table. He then hurries past the saloon patrons walking to Mr. Glover. Joseph reaches the table, handing Mr. Glover the Cascade Courier newspaper dated December 11, 1914, while pointing to the article, *Great crowd at Fields funeral – The funeral was one of the largest ever held in Cascade.*

Mr. Glover picks up his drink, and looks up to the ceiling, as does Joseph.

The End

Mary Field, aka, Stagecoach Mary, died at the approximate age of eighty-two, from liver failure on December 5, 1914, at Columbus Hospital, in Great Falls, Montana.

While Annie Oakley and Martha Canary (Calamity Jane) were creating their history with Buffalo Bill, Stagecoach Mary was making her epic journey.

ERICH MARTIN HICKS

WEDSWORTH MEMORIAL LIBRARY
CASCADE, MONTANA

from the CASCADE COURIER, Friday December 11, 1914

OLD TIMER PASSES AWAY

The funeral services of Mary Fields were held in the Pastime Theatre Tuesday afternoon at 3:15. Rev. John J. Casey of St. Peter's Mission conducted the services. Miss Mamie McDonald and Mrs. Arthur McCollim rendered several vocal selections. There was a large attendance of friends and acquaintances of the deceased, many of them having known her for over twenty-five years, who left nothing undone to make the services complete in every respect for one of the oldest land marks in Cascade. The floral contributions were especially in evidence.

The pallbearers were R. B. Glover, F. N. Askew, Walter McKay, J. H. Jones, D. W. Munroe and James Travis. Interment was made in Hillside cemetery.

Mary Fields, who was taken to Great Falls last week, died in the Columbus Hospital Saturday evening, December 5, at 6 o'clock. For several months Mary had been in failing health and about four weeks ago she was compelled to forsake her usual activities for the sick bed. When it was thought best to care for her in the hospital, it was no easy matter to gain her consent to the change, for no doubt she realized that she would never see her friends in Cascade again.

The following article from the files of the COURIER in 1910 is interesting and as accurate as can be ascertained.

Seventy-eight years ago last Tuesday, March 15, Mary Fields was born in old Hickman County, Tennessee. Mary was born a slave and received her freedom by the passing of the 14th amendment.

An interesting phase in her life is that she was employed as second chambermaid on the great Mississippi river steamboat, Robert E. Lee, the best and fastest boat at the time it had its world famous race with the steamer Natches and won the race. It was during this race that barrels of resin, sacks and boxes of hams and bacon were thrown into the furnaces of the Robert E. Lee in order to make quick steam, as is related in Bill Bludso, "men sat on the safety valves of the Lee to keep every ounce of steam in her boilers."

Mary Fields was right there, and says, "It was so hot up in the cabins that the passengers were forced to take to the decks. It was expected that the boilers would burst."

Mary Fields is quite a character, and is known over a large portion of Montana by the early settler. She was the second woman in the United States to regularly drive a mail stage. This she did from a point which is now known as Cascade to St. Peter's Mission. It was not all smooth sailing in those early pioneer days, and Mary soon became known to be a crack shot with a revolver. She has lived in the state for 30 years, 17 of which she has resided in this immediate neighborhood and for 10 years she lived at the Mission.

She is well and hearty today and is able to do much hard labor. She is a familiar figure on the streets of the town, walking along smoking her cigar which she thoroughly enjoys.

This information is 50% correct

MARY FIELDS aka STAGECOACH MARY

Mary Fields Death Certificate – Circa, December 8, 1914

Epilogue

HISTORY of PASCO COUNTY, 'FLORIDA' and Judge Edmund Francis Dunne

"Judge EDMUND F. DUNNE (1835-1904) was born in Little Falls, New York. He went to California in 1852 where he was elected to the California legislature in 1862. In 1864 he served on the constitutional convention for the new state of Nevada and later served eight terms as a member of the Nevada judiciary. In 1874 President Grant appointed him chief justice of the Arizona Territory. Dunne's legal position that Catholics and other religious groups should receive tax funding for their schools caused President Grant to force his resignation. According to a biography in Great Floridians 2000, after his removal, Dunne was hired by Hamilton Disston, a wealthy Philadelphia saw manufacturer, to select lands in a four million-acre purchase Disston had made in Florida, and in 1881, Dunne was given 50,000 acres of land to begin the Catholic colony of San Antonio. However, according to an account in Dunne People and Places by Joe Dunne, in 1882 Edmund Dunne purchased 50,000 acres of land in through the assistance of his brother John, who was the attorney for the Disston Company and controlled large tracts of land in Florida. Eddie Herrmann suggests that Dunne may have had rights to the land but did not own it. Dunne explained the procedure to a reporter for the Baltimore Catholic Mirror in 1885:

I was selected by Mr. Disston as his attorney to go to Florida and assist in the selection and to supervise the taking out of the title deeds. I obtained, as part of this arrangement, the right to have the first selection, out of the purchase, 50,000 acres of land for a Catholic colony, with the privilege that when I had sold a certain amount I should have the further privilege of taking another 50,000 acres for the same purpose. This contract was made August 10, 1881. On August 19 I was in Florida and began the work of this selection.

On February 15, 1882, he selected the colony's site in Pasco County. In 1889, Judge Dunne conveyed his own lands to the order of St. Benedict and a small party of monks led by Father Charles Mohr, O. S. B., arrived to establish a monastery and Catholic school and to found the town of St. Leo. On Aug. 17, 1899, the San Antonio Herald reported, "Hon. E. F. Dunne, the eminent jurist and founder of San Antonio, has left Jacksonville and taken up his residence in Baltimore."

MARY FIELDS aka STAGECOACH MARY

The information in this paragraph was taken from Dunne people and Places by Joe Dunne. Details of Dunn's early education are not available, but as an adult he could speak several languages and had an expert knowledge of history and theology. In 1874 Dunne visited his friends and relatives in Uí Riagáin on his way back to America from a law case he was dealing with in London. He is said to have verified that his father was "the legitimate legal heir of Iregan and chief of the tribe" during this visit. The Genealogical Office in Dublin do not have a record of this pedigree so Judge Dunne may have only received verbal agreement from Irish historians of the day. Pope Pius IX created him a knight of the Order of St. Gregory the Great in 1876 an in 1879 he received a brief from Pope Leo XIII raising him to the rank of Commander of that Order. At the St. Patrick's day celebration at Fort Wayne, Indiana, Dunne 1881 he delivered a famous Land League Lecture which was later adopted and published by the State Land League of Illinois. He established the Catholic colony at San Antonio in pursuance of a project he had previously submitted to Pope Pius IX. The Pope had studied the project in detail as presented by Cardinal Berardi and declared that "I bless this plan and the author of it and will pray for his success." He remained in the colony until 1889 establishing there four Catholic churches, several schools, a convent boarding school for girls and St. Leo' Military College for young men. In recognition of his work for the Catholic Education system, in January 1884 Pope Leo XIII granted him and his descendants in the male line in primogeniture the title Papal Count. In memory of his roots he took the title Count d'Oriagan. He was one of the most noted Catholic laymen in the U.S.A. and was also one of the finest orators of his day. Dunne married Josephine Warner, daughter of Col. Francis Warner of Vicksburg, Mississippi, in Paris in October 1872. Their children were Maria del Carmen, Eugene Antonio, Hilda, Brian Baru, and Mary Eithne."

Source: History of Pasco County, Florida

Author's Opinion

The Dunne children of Mr. John & Mrs. Eleanor O'Dunne are in order of birth: Edmund Francis Dunne-born July 30, 1835, Sarah Dunne, John Joseph Dunne, Mary Ellen Dunne and Sarah 'Theresa' Dunne – later becoming Mother Amadeus. The second born, Sarah Dunne died, June 5, 1838 when she was 2, and Mary Ellen died, 1882.

As you have read in the epilogue, "History of Pasco County, Florida", Judge Edmund Francis Dunne, brother of Mother Amadeus, later mentioned, 'did not' own a plantation in Hickman County, Tennessee. His only holdings and interest were, California, Arizona, Nevada, and Florida.

When Mary Warner – Sister Annunciation's sister, Josephine Cecelia Warner married Judge Edmund Dunne in Europe, this caused these two names to become intermingled.

Mary Fields was apparently the slave of the Warner family, under Colonel Frances Warner, and not the Dunne family. Mary could read and write. Therefore, one would conclude, she was part of the slaves in the great house. In the later part the United States slavery, an African-American/Colored/Negro, knowing how to read and write, would be a torture or death sentence, virtually. The actual location of the plantation, is still somewhat, unknown, however; continual investigation will go on…

Mother Amadeus – Theresa Sarah Dunne was born in Akron, Ohio, July 2, 1846. She went to the Ursuline Convent in Toledo, Ohio, in 1856, at the age of 10, and begun her journey. This is where she met, Mary and Josephine Warner, the later, leaving the 'order'. As the folklore has been written, "Mary Fields was allowed to be friends with Theresa Dunne, thus, this gave her the privilege to read and write, being the playmate of Theresa". However, the Dunne's didn't live in Tennessee, therefore; Mary couldn't have been her playmate, furthermore; Mary was at least 13 years older than Theresa Dunne – Mother Amadeus.

From the many stories written on Mary Fields, the first known book where Mary is included, P.95, 2nd paragraph. "The Reverend Mother Amadeus of the Heart of Jesus" – 1923, by the 'New York - THE PAULIST PRESS'.

MARY FIELDS aka STAGECOACH MARY

Then, the EBONY Magazine's article, October 1959, from the 2 time Academy Award Oscar Winning actor, Gary Cooper, sent the folklore off and running, with "born in Hickman, Tennessee", driving a 'stagecoach' and etc.

The Bird Tail, by Sister Genevieve McBride, O.S.U., published 1974, gave some reality to Mary's story, but no light to her beginning.

The Story of Stagecoach Mary Fields, by Robert Henry Miller, published 1996, added the fuel to the beginning of the, out of control story of, Mary Fields, especially with a picture of a African-American/Black woman, in action, whirling a whip, driving a stagecoach.

Then comes, "Mary Fields – The Story of Black Mary", by James Franks, published 2000, that fed off the other stories before him, and the many that have proceeded James Franks.

This information by no means, is meant to take away the attributes of Mary Fields. Mary had no relatives, no sisters, or brothers. Her mother died early, father apparently beaten and sold off to another plantation in the slave states, according to current written documents. The Ursuline Nuns, would have written something regarding any relatives in the numerous books and documents they and others have written of that time period with respects to Mary Fields aka Stagecoach Mary.

How are a people kept down? 'Never know' their history.

"If a race has no history, it has no worthwhile tradition, it becomes a negligible factor in the thought of the world, and it stands in danger of being exterminated."
Dr. Carter G. Woodson 1875 – 1950

"A people without the knowledge of their past history, origin and culture is like a tree without roots."
Marcus Garvey 1887 - 1940

"A tree without roots can bear no fruit, it will die."
Erich Martin Hicks 1952 - Present

Keep telling that history.

DISCLAMER:

1. Mary did not work for 'Wells Fargo', or drive a stagecoach, nor was a shotgun rider. There are no official written documents supporting her being a shotgun rider, or driving a stagecoach. In this story, it was added as an entertainment pleasure.

2. Mary did not have any relatives, 98.9% sure. If any person feels that they are kin to Mary Fields, a simple blood test can be done, at the requesters' expense. Contact the Town of Cascade, Montana to start the procedures.

A second hypothesis to Mary's early life. Still being a slave of Colonel Frances Warner, after the emancipation, she went to work on the Robert E. Lee. During her tenure on the Lee, Edmund Dunne married Josephine Warner, in Europe, 1872. They had several children, however, Josephine died 10 years later, in 1882. Because Mary was most likely on the Warner plantation farm, as a slave, Josephine would have known Mary, therefore, I say this because there are several reports, that Mary was asked to take the children, from the family home in Florida, to Judge Dunne's sister, Mother Amadeus at the convent in Toledo, Ohio, after Josephine's death. Mary wouldn't have been asked to care for, and transport the children of Edmund and Josephine Dunne, from Florida, to Toledo, if they didn't have confidence, or know her, moreover, this is where Mary became part of the Urseline convent, and her later journey begins, where Mary's later life is well documented.

Additional Historical and Validation Photos

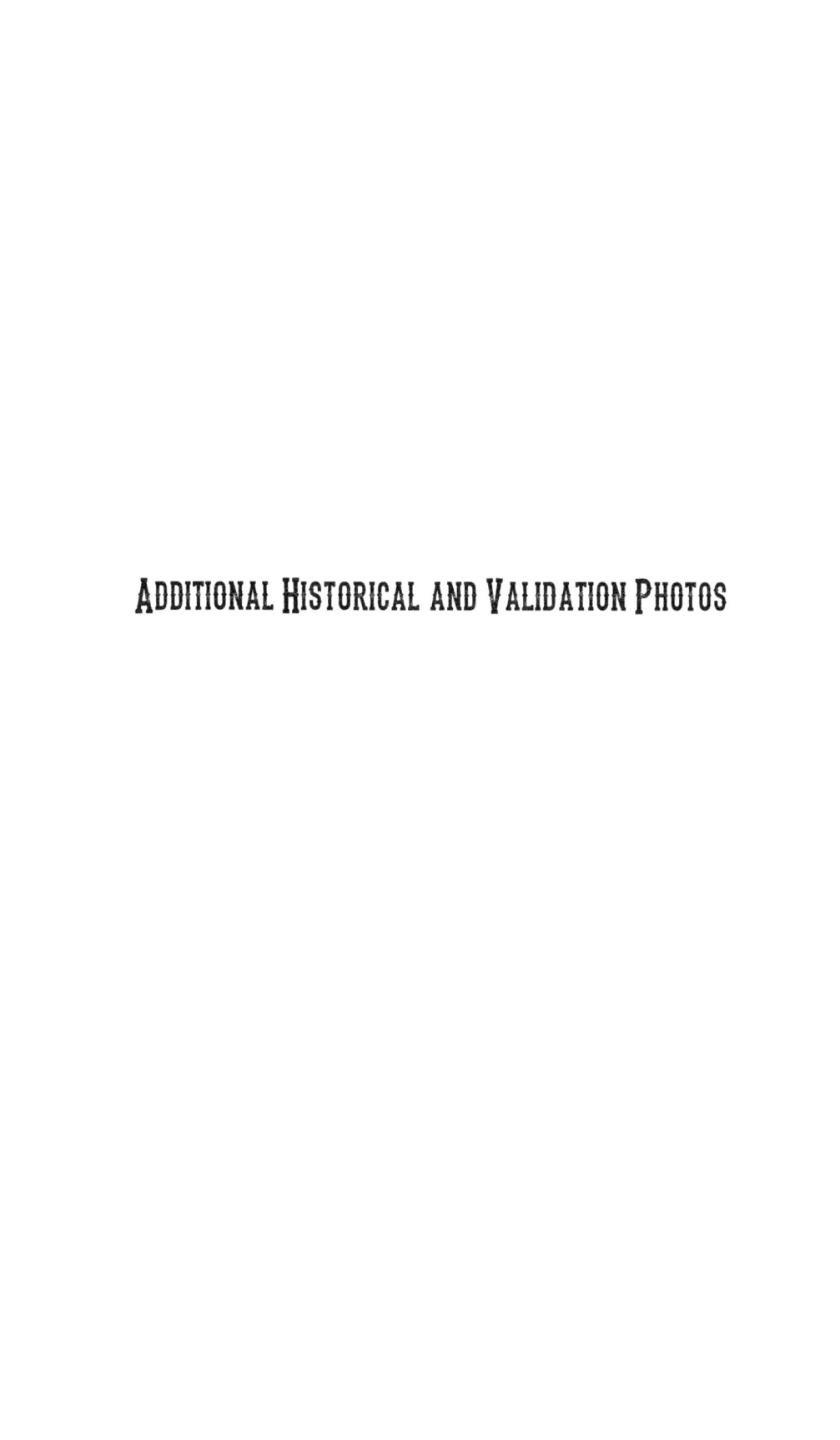

ERICH MARTIN HICKS

(A.) Mary's claim to fame, attracted some of the most notables of the twentieth century, like two time Academy Award Winner, Gary Cooper, who exaggerated most of his story in EBONY, based upon folklore.

STAGE COACH MARY
Gun-toting Montanan delivered U. S. mail

BY GARY COOPER
As Told To Marc Crawford

THEY SAY "Black Mary" could whip any two men in the territory. She wore a 38 Smith & Wesson strapped under her apron and they swear she couldn't miss a thing within 50 paces. She was tall, weighing well over 200 pounds, and, except for an apron and skirt, wore men's clothes.

"Black Mary" was what they called her, but her real name was Mary Fields, one of the most picturesque characters in the history of Montana. She was a stage coach driver, the second female ever to drive a U. S. Mail route. Maybe because she was a Negro, she was never bothered by Indians. I remember seeing her in Cascade when I was just a little shaver of nine or so. She smoked cigars until the day she died in 1914. She must have been about 81 as near as any one could figure. She celebrated two birthdays a year because she didn't know the exact date of her birth, but they would close Cascade schools in her honor whenever she felt like having one.

They say Mary had a fondness for hard liquor that was matched only by her capacity to put it away and it's historical fact that one of Cascade's early mayors, D. W. Monroe gave special permission to let Mary drink in the saloons with men, a privilege, if you want to call it one, given to no other woman.

Born a slave somewhere in Tennessee, some say in 1832, Mary lived to become one of the freest souls ever to draw a breath or a .38, and she was celebrated in a pen and ink drawing that hangs in the Cascade Bank even now. It was done by the late Charlie Russell, a cowboy artist and the greatest one to come out of the West. Mary lived in Mississippi for a time and was a passenger on board the Robert E. Lee when it participated in the race on the Mississippi with Steamboat Bill's Natchez, as famed in story and song, and she took great pride in telling how the hams and sides of bacon were fed into the firebox to keep up steam that June 30, 1870. Mary later moved to Ohio, where she worked at the Ursulines Convent in Toledo. Here she met Mother Amadeus, a Catholic nun, whom she revered and loved, though one account has it that Mary was a slave and confidential servant in the household of Judge Dunne, the nun's oldest brother. Others say Mary had been the nun's personal maid before her mistress took the vows.

Picture of intrepid Mary Fields, armed with shotgun, was believed taken sometime in late 1880s. Mary's grave in Hillside Cemetery (below) is unmarked except for cross. Her old stage coach and mail route ran between the mountains and cemetery.

Montana-born Gary Cooper, ex-cowboy and two-times Academy Award winning actor, says he does not know why Negroes are not used in Western movies. A Helena native, Cooper as a boy often visited relatives in Cascade, where his mother now lives.

Continued on Next Page 97

Article in-part Ebony Magazine – Circa 1959

MARY FIELDS aka STAGECOACH MARY

(B.) As Mary's story spread during the twentieth century, it attracted some of the most notables, such as, Esther Rolle, from the situation comedy, "Good Times".

'South by Northwest' article in the Great Falls Tribune – Circa 1975

(C.) Esther Rolle portraying Mary Fields in a trailer, 'South by Northwest'

Produced by Washington State University – Circa 1975

(D.) Metal sign on approach to St. Peter's Mission

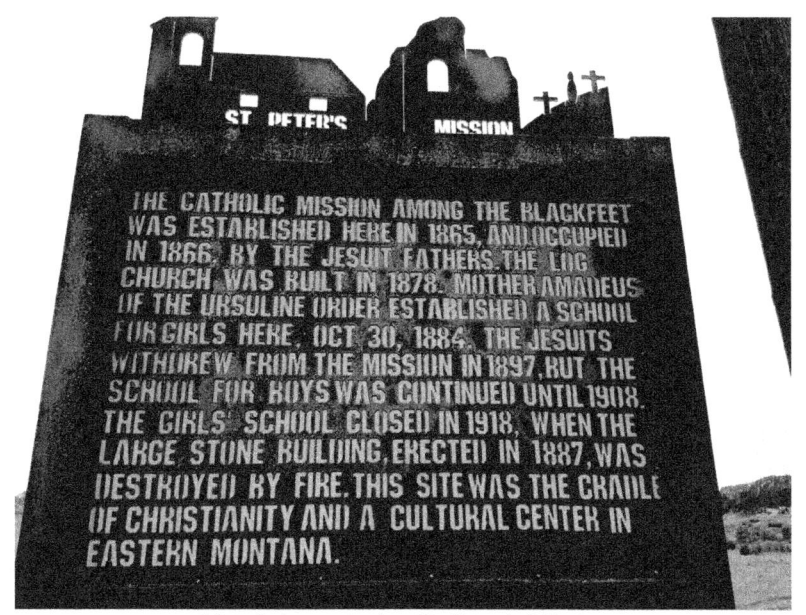

> THE CATHOLIC MISSION AMONG THE BLACKFEET WAS ESTABLISHED HERE IN 1865, AND OCCUPIED IN 1866, BY THE JESUIT FATHERS. THE LOG CHURCH WAS BUILT IN 1878. MOTHER AMADEUS OF THE URSULINE ORDER ESTABLISHED A SCHOOL FOR GIRLS HERE, OCT 30, 1884. THE JESUITS WITHDREW FROM THE MISSION IN 1897, BUT THE SCHOOL FOR BOYS WAS CONTINUED UNTIL 1908. THE GIRLS' SCHOOL CLOSED IN 1918, WHEN THE LARGE STONE BUILDING, ERECTED IN 1887, WAS DESTROYED BY FIRE. THIS SITE WAS THE CRADLE OF CHRISTIANITY AND A CULTURAL CENTER IN EASTERN MONTANA.

Metal sign entering St. Peter's Mission

(E.) A 'Birds Tail' view of St. Peter's Mission, and buildings

Photo of St. Peter's Mission from 'Bird Tail' – Circa 1908
St. Peter's Missions' Buildings from left to right, upper right, Opera House; Girls School; Boys School; and original mission, lower right, with bell tower.

(F.) St. Peter's Mission Girl's School

St. Peter's Mission Girls' School – Circa 1998
Note the bent exhaust pipe on the chimney center, and the missing one on the right side. Those exhaust pipes were for the Bolton Heaters, which were needed to keep out the forty below zero temperatures in the winter, at the base of the Great Rocky Mountains.

(G.) St. Peter's Missions nuns, enjoying a day at the mission pond. The Mission Opera House is left in background, Girls School, is right foreground.

St. Peter's Mission Pond – Circa 1898

(H.) St. Peter's Mission's steam heating plant

St. Peter's Mission's hot water & steam plant, where hot water was produced, piping the water into the mission, of both girls' and boys' schools – Circa 1900

(I.) St. Peter's Mission Girls' School

St. Peter's Mission Girls' School after fire – Circa 1918

(J.) Fort Shaw Metal Post Sign

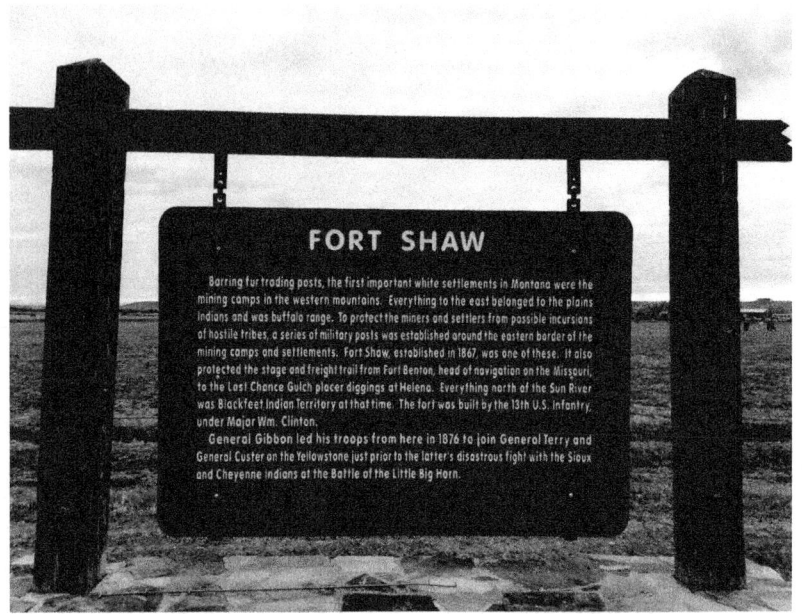

Fort Shaw was renamed from Camp Reynolds in 1867
Mary visited Fort Shaw on several occasions

(K.) Fort Shaw Post Plaque

Fort Shaw Plaque showing the 25th U.S. Infantry
commanding the post 1888 - 1891

MARY FIELDS aka STAGECOACH MARY

(L.) St. Peter's Opera House

Panoramic view of St. Peter's Opera House

(M.) The Great Falls Tribune Newspaper

The Great Fall Newspaper with all names of the Cascade baseball team – Circa 1914

(N.) St. Peter's Mission Church

St. Peter's Mission Church with Bird Tail in background

(O.) St. Peter's Mission Plaque

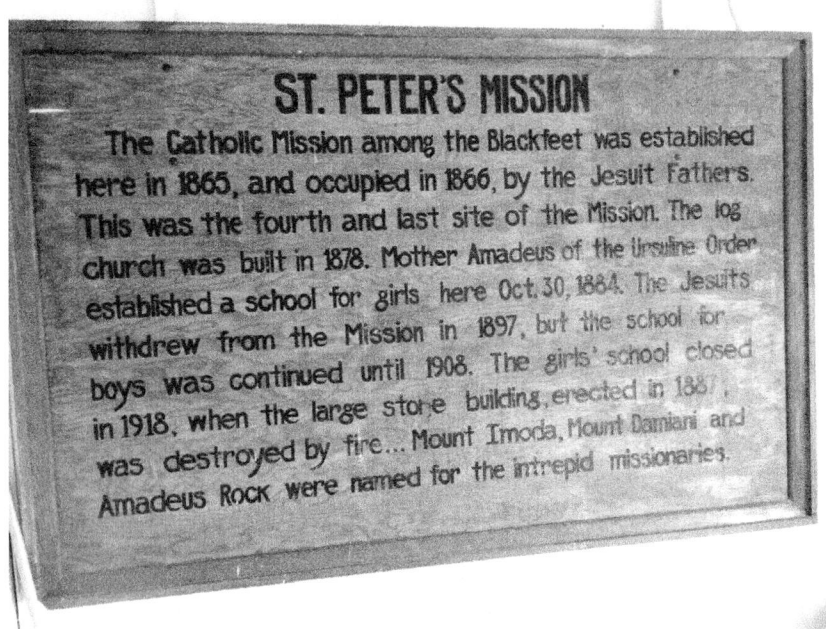

Plaque within St. Peter's Church

(P.) St. Peter's Church

Erich standing next to the entrance of St. Peter's Church

(Q.)

"At least 18 women reportedly carried mail on contract routes in the 1890s, including the legendary "Stagecoach" Mary Fields and Sarah M. Burks. Fields, a former slave, is the earliest African-American woman known to have carried mail. Fields drove the mail wagon from Cascade to St. Peter's Mission, Montana, from 1895 to 1903. She was well known in the town of Cascade for being a cigar-smoking "crack shot" with a heart of gold; the news of her death in December 1914 was carried on the front pages of both local newspapers."

From
'Women Mail Carriers'

(R.) Receipt Letter

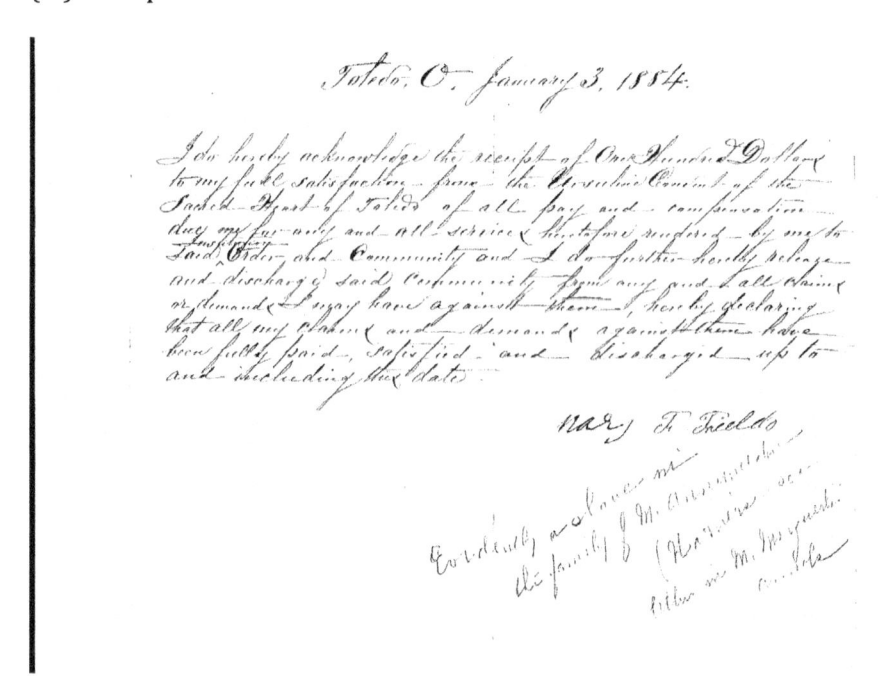

Receipt letter made out for Mary, with Mary's signature; note middle initial 'F'

See following page for retyped receipt letter

Toledo O. January 3, 1884

"I do hereby acknowledge the receipt of One Hundred Dollars
To my full satisfaction from the Ursuline Convent of the

Sacred Heart of Toledo of all pay and compensation

due me for any and all services heretofore rendered by me to

said (indiscernible word) Order and community and I do further hereby release

and discharge said community from any and all claims

or demands I may have against them, hereby declaring

that all my claims and demands against them have

been fully paid satisfied and discharge up to and including this date."

Mary F. Fields

The main document was apparently prepared by another party, being that Mary's apparent signature is different from the embodiment of the letter.

The writing below the main embodiment, was apparently added later, by someone…"Evidently a slave in this family of Mother Annunciation …"

(S.) Account Receipt

Receipt for Mary Fields – note the middle initial 'E' top

MARY FIELDS aka STAGECOACH MARY

(T.)

Erich at Mary Fields' Grave with her favorite flower – The Pansy

References

- The Reverend Mother Amadeus of the Heart of Jesus; Published 1923
  By: The Paulist Press

- Gary Cooper's article on Mary Fields; Published October 1959
  By: EBONY Magazine

- The Bird Tail; Published 1974
  By: Sister Genevieve McBride, O.S.U.

- The Black West; Published February 7, 1996
  By: William Loren Katz

- The Story of Stagecoach Mary Fields; Published 1996
  By: Robert Henry Miller

- The Story of Black Mary; Published 2000
  By: James Franks

- Ursuline Convent, Toledo, Ohio

- Ursuline Convent, Great Falls, Montana

- Wedsworth Memorial Library, Cascade, Montana

- The History Museum, Great Falls, Montana

- Stockmens Bank, Cascade, Montana

- Cascade Courier, Cascade, Montana

- The Great Falls Tribune, Great Falls, Montana

- St. Peter's Mission Annals

Current News of Mary Fields

Mary Fields was inducted into the Montana Cowboy Hall of Fame, on Feb. 6, 2016.

MARY FIELDS aka STAGECOACH MARY

MT Cowboy Hall of Fame

Continued from front page

Miller Brothers Land and Livestock, Chinook (tie).
- District 5 (Cascade, Glacier, Pondera, Teton, & Toole Counties): Living Award – Jay Joseph Contway, Great Falls. Legacy Award – Alfred Bertram "Bud" Guthrie, Jr., Choteau and Mary "Stagecoach Mary" Fields, Cascade (tie) and Doctor Ernest Bigalow Maynard, Choteau (tie).
- District 6 (Fergus, Golden Valley, Judith Basin, Musselshell, Petroleum, & Wheatland Counties): Living Award – Eldon H. Snyder, Lewistown. Legacy Award – Montana Cowboy Poetry Gathering and Western Music Rendezvous, Lewistown and Merle J. Boyce, Winifred.
- District 7 (Big Horn, Carbon, Stillwater, Sweet Grass, & Yellowstone Counties): Living Award – Henry Albert "Hank" Scobee, Hardin. Legacy Award – Malcolm S. Mackay, Roscoe and Charlotte "Rusty" Linderman Spaulding, Belfry.
- District 8 (Broadwater, Jefferson, & Lewis and Clark Counties): Living Award – Joseph W. "Joe" Enger, Helena. Legacy Award – Auchard Creek School, Augusta.
- District 9 (Gallatin, Meagher, & Park Counties): Legacy Award – Robert "Bob" Shiplet, Clyde Park and Thomas R. "Tom" Hunter, Clyde Park (tie) and Robert Anderson "Bob" Haugland, Belgrade (tie).
- District 10 (Flathead, Lake, Lincoln, & Sanders Counties): Living Award – Richard B. "Dick" & Patricia B. "Tricia" Vinson, Thompson Falls. Legacy Award – C.R. Williams, Kalispell.
- District 11 (Mineral, Missoula, & Ravalli Counties): Living Award – Frank R. Mason, Jr., Corvallis. Legacy Award – Vernon Woolsey, Stevensville and Clarence Barron "C.B." Rich, Seeley Lake.
- District 12 (Deer Lodge, Beaverhead, Silver Bow, Granite, Madison, & Powell Counties): Living Award (three-way tie) Edward Francis "Butch" O'Connell, Butte, "Gunner" Gun Again, Dillon, and John W. "Jack" Briggs, Dell. Legacy Award – Melvin R. Icenoggle, Ennis and Scottish Chieftain, Hamilton.

Since the initial round of inductions to the Montana Cowboy Hall of Fame in 2008, including this year's inductions, 240 inductees have been honored. Full biographies for past inductees are available on the MCHF & WHC's website, http://www.montanacowboyfame.org.

In July, the MCHF & WHC commenced its first phase of construction in the central location of Big Timber, Mont., with modifications to the Hall of Fame headquarters and the creation of a world-class outdoor arena. The arena's programming will allow the MCHF & WHC to highlight and celebrate the many traditions of our western heritage and cowboy way of life through quality western sporting events.

For more information about the MCHF & WHC, or for more details on the Montana Cowboy Hall of Fame inductees, please contact Christy Stensland by calling (406) 653-3800, emailing Christy@montanacowboyfame.org, or visiting http://www.montanacowboyfame.org.

The mission of the Montana Cowboy Hall of Fame & Western Heritage Center is to "honor our cowboy way of life, American Indian cultures and collective Montana Western heritage." We exist to serve as a resource to all who wish to see this way of life passed forward to the next generation. Our vision is "to be the state's premier destination attraction that celebrates and passes forward Montana's unique western culture and heritage."

Above, Mary Fields in a buggy; date unknown.

became the forewoman of St. Peter's Mission. The Native Americans called her "White Crow" because they felt "she acts like a white woman but has black skin." A schoolgirl's essay about Mary said: "she drinks whiskey, and she swears, and she is a republican, which makes her a low, foul creature."

In 1894, Mary received several complaints against her. These were followed by an incident where a white man hit her because he refused to "take orders from a nigger woman." As she fell to the ground, the man went for his gun. Mary drew her pistol and shot him, fast as any gunslinger. She was then relieved of her duties at the Mission.

At about the age of sixty-years-old, Mary applied for the position of mail carrier in the Cascade region. She was rewarded the position by hitching a 6-up team faster than anyone else. Despite the thieves and wolves, Mary loved the job. She drove the route with horses and a mule named Moses. On many winter occasions she had to leave her team on the drifted road and deliver mail on foot using snowshoes. She would throw the sacks over her shoulder, and sometimes walk ten miles back to the Depot. Mary never missed a day – rain, hail, sleet or snow! It was during this time that Mary received the nickname Stagecoach Mary.

Stagecoach Mary eventually slowed down by opening a laundry, keeping her garden, and supporting the local baseball team by selling flowers. When Montana prohibited women from entering bars, Cascade's Mayor granted an exception for this particular gal. The town so loved and respected Mary that on her birthday they closed the schools to celebrate. The Cascade townspeople laid her to rest below the mountain trail leading to St Peter's Mission in 1914, after over 80 years of life.

Gary Cooper wrote an article for Ebony magazine saying, "born a slave somewhere in Tennessee, Mary lived to become one of the freest souls ever to draw a breath."

Several movies portray Mary Fields as a true to life character. In the 1976 TV documentary *South by Northwest: Homesteaders*, Fields was played by Esther Rolle. In the 1996 TV movie *The Cherokee Kid*, Fields was played by Dawn Lewis, and in the 2012 TV movie *Hannah's Law* she was played by Kimberly Elise.

Stagecoach Mary Fields broke all boundaries of race, gender and age. She left a legacy by being the second woman, and first African-American woman, to deliver mail in the United States. Her job and her involvement with the community and its people places Stagecoach Mary Fields as a true pioneer of Montana and especially the Cascade area.

Article date: August 13, 2015

MARY FIELDS aka STAGECOACH MARY

Other news of "Mary Fields aka Stagecoach Mary". She has been featured in television movies, such as, 'Cherokee Kid'; 'Hannah's Law'; and now has appeared on several episodes of, 'Hell on Wheels'.

This story was written as a feature film, that I transformed into this novel. Keep watching the news, and airways for the feature film of,

"Mary Fields aka Stagecoach Mary".

This photo is dedicated to all re-enactment groups, keeping history alive and well.

The Buffalo Soldiers Mounted Cavalry Unit – Los Angeles, California

This group, the "Buffalo Soldiers Mounted Cavalry Unit" (re-enactors) represents, brotherhood, and unity, of what the Buffalo Soldiers represented during their eras.

Names from left to right:

1. Jonathan Collins
2. Joe Lawrence
3. Erich Hicks – Author
4. Arthur Dyson III
5. Arthur Dyson II
6. Jay Collins
7. Justin Collins
8. Clyde Phillips